PRAISE FOR THE CRUIS_ _
DAUGHTER BY MORGAN MAYER

"Mayer presents a novel that's half cozy mystery and half
travel fiction...nicely balances these two genres against each
other...gives Sheila and Shane the calm repartee of a couple
who've known each other for a long time, which makes them
a compelling detective duo."

— KIRKUS REVIEWS

"fun twists and turns...readers will fall in love with the
eccentric (and aptly-named) couple at the focus of the book.
There's humor and wit to each of them and they light up the
pages."

— THE BOOKLIFE PRIZE

THE CRUISE SHIP LOST MY DAUGHTER

Sandy,

THE CRUISE SHIP LOST MY DAUGHTER

Best wishes to you!

MORGAN MAYER

Morgan Mayer

(AKA Carrie Trad')

INDIGO
DOT
PRESS

Indigo Dot Press
indigodotpress@gmail.com

First edition, 2020

Library of Congress Control Number: 2020903333

FIC022070 FICTION / Mystery & Detective / Cozy / General
FIC022100 FICTION / Mystery & Detective / Amateur Sleuth

ISBN 978-1-7328541-3-0 (trade paperback)
ISBN 978-1-7328541-2-3 (ebook)

Cover design by Lance Buckley Design

For Mel
We miss you

THE FOXY GLOSSY MUST GO

SIX WEEKS after Sheila McShane's daughter went missing, the TSA agent took her Foxy Glossy hairspray away.

"Oh no, sugarplum," Sheila said. "I need to keep that. It's from my daughter."

Whether it was the provocative nature of Sheila's voice, unusual for such a slight woman of eighty, or the urgency within it, the bald agent seemed momentarily disarmed. Sheila seized the opportunity to reach across the security belt and snatch the pink canister back. With gnarled hands that moaned on a good day and wailed on a bad, she pressed the cool metal against her neck.

"But ma'am, you're not allowed any liquids over three ounces."

"Oh dear, does that include my bladder?" She looked around for her husband, Shane. As the one most affected by her bathroom frequency, he would appreciate the joke. Unable to spot him, she returned her attention to the agent.

The man scratched his shiny pate and went back to rummaging through her tote bag. "See, you've got all sorts of loose toiletries in here. You can't—"

"You can't get Foxy Glossy just anywhere, you know. My daughter found this one for me. At a garage sale, of all places. Back home in Sherry, New Hampshire." She dabbed at her eyes with a tissue and patted her wispy, shoulder-length hair, its color that of the overcast sky beyond Boston's airport. Though aware she was babbling, her discomfort over the upcoming flight combined with the purpose of their trip had turned her into a tangle of nerves. "She's missing, you see."

The security official's mouth opened and then closed. His doleful expression suggested he had no idea what to say. Still, he held out his meaty palm. Sheila sniffled, straightened her shoulders, and returned the Foxy Glossy canister. After a moment's hesitation, the agent placed it in a bin behind him, where it joined a hodge-podge collection of shampoo, water bottles, and what appeared to be pepper spray.

Determined to keep negative energy at bay, Sheila forced a smile. "We're going to look for her. On the same cruise she disappeared from."

"I'm sorry?"

"We're going on a British Isles cruise to find our daughter. We fly to Amsterdam today and board the ship tomorrow."

"Right, well, um, good luck with that." The agent rubbed his fleshy chin. The growing passenger line behind them rumbled with impatience. "I'm not sure when you flew last, but—"

"It's been ages."

"Yes…well…nowadays you're supposed to place large toiletry items in your checked luggage. And you're technically only allowed one of these." He dangled an empty, resealable bag between his thumb and index finger.

"Those are for sandwiches."

"Those are for toiletries." He placed her smaller toiletries inside it.

"They lost her, you know."

"Uh, who lost what now?"

"The cruise ship. At least we think they did."

Filling a second plastic bag, the agent paused. "Who's 'we'?"

In the queue behind them, a female voice grumbled, "Oh for the love of God, take a train instead."

"My husband and me, of course, Agent..." Sheila reached for the man's name badge and tapped it with a ruby fingernail. "Agent Dickman. Goodness, that's an unfortunate name. No wonder your color is cloudy."

"My color?"

"Years of torment, I imagine. I'm very good at reading people's auras. Well, Shane insists it's body language and facial expressions I'm reading, not actual colors, but tomato, tomahto. Your color is quite sad."

Agent Dickman's jaw sagged, and his shoulders slouched. "Well, I did have some rough times. I..." He cleared his throat and started filling a third plastic bag. "Ma'am, normally you're not allowed to take all these products on the flight. These should've been sorted before you came through security."

"I know what you're thinking. What can two old people do, right?" She stuffed the three plastic bags into her tote. "But someone has to do something. The authorities won't help us. The FBI won't help us." Her voice shook, and her cheeks grew hot. "It's Amsterdam's problem, says the cruise ship. It's the cruise ship's problem, says Amsterdam."

"Do you need me to call someone?"

"To help me find my daughter?" Her eyes widened in hope.

Behind her, a male voice snarled. "Hey, some of us have planes to catch."

Agent Dickman flashed a stern look and held up a hand to silence the man. When he turned back to Sheila, his expression softened. "No, ma'am. I wish I could. I meant do you need help getting to your gate?"

"That's very kind of you, but my husband and I are quite capable. Shane doesn't like being catered to." Sheila scanned the security area for her husband of sixty years. "Shane?" It dawned on her she hadn't seen him for several minutes now. "Where did he go? Shane?" She twisted and kneaded her faux-pearl necklace, anxiety deepening her already muddled state. Beyond the security gate, she saw only a hustling throng of passengers.

Just as she was about to take Agent Dickman up on his offer of help, she spotted the spiky coif of her eighty-four-year-old husband next to the full-body scanner one aisle over. A trio of TSA agents, along with the machine's metal siding, had shielded his trim physique from view. With one hand stroking his chin and the other moving through the air as if taking measurements, he studied the scanner as travelers passed through it, their feet planted wide and their arms forming a diamond above their heads.

Sheila called out to him. He raised his head, blinked, and strolled toward her, his moves as fluid as a man half his age. Other than an occasional twinge from a twelve-year-old hip injury he suffered while skiing, he was in great shape.

"Agent Dickman, this is my husband, Shane McShane."

Never stellar at eye contact, Shane nodded and focused on the security machine nearest them, the one they had already passed through before the TSA agent had discovered Sheila's toiletry arsenal. Inside, a woman with a walking cast struggled to plant her feet on the painted imprint. "These machines are millimeter-wave scanners," Shane said. "Unlike backscatter machines, they use electromagnetic radiation, not x-rays." He crossed his arms. "I would estimate the power density to be very low. Our DNA will be safe."

"That's nice." To Agent Dickman, Sheila said, "When you're our age, you cling to any DNA you have left." She grabbed the agent's hand. "But I think we've taken enough of your time."

"Ya think?" said a traveler behind them.

"I'm sorry I didn't understand these new flying rules. You've been most helpful." Sheila removed her tote bag from the belt and joined Shane, who was reassuring the woman with the walking cast that her DNA would be fine. Over her shoulder, Sheila gave one final glance of longing at her glittering can of Foxy Glossy in the bin behind the counter. In it she saw her forty-six-year-old daughter, and her heart beat a rhythm of sorrow. She turned and walked away.

"Wait." Agent Dickman hustled around the security belt toward her, a sparkly pink can in his hand. He slipped it into her cardigan pocket.

Sheila's throat thickened, and she found it difficult to speak. "Oh, thank you. It's the last thing my daughter gave me."

He tugged at his collar. "Ah, it's nothing. Just don't tell anyone." An airport employee driving an empty shuttle cart approached. Agent Dickman flagged him down. When the young man stopped the vehicle, the TSA agent said, "Please escort Mr. and Mrs. McShane to their gate. They don't have much time before they board."

Sheila thanked the agent one last time. Surely his kindness was a sign they were off to a great start in their journey.

As Agent Dickman helped Sheila and Shane into the cart, a ginger-haired man outside the men's bathroom locked eyes with her. His clenched fists and mottled face suggested anger. Had she held him up in line?

"Oh, and ma'am?" Agent Dickman stole her attention back.

"Yes?" she said, looking over at him as they drove away.

"I sure hope you find your daughter."

2

A WORLD AWAY

To Sheila, entering the *Celestial of the Seas* cruise ship was like entering a nautical palace. Decadent, extravagant, and breathtaking, the three-thousand-passenger vessel was nothing short of a sixteen-deck crystal and marble wonder.

In the grand foyer, silky music flowed from hidden speakers, glass elevators lifted and lowered, and glossy floor tiles reflected the guests who bustled over them. Suspended above it all was a massive chandelier, spanning no less than ten stories, its glittering, concentric circles of light rotating around lavender, phosphorescent cores. Like an electric galaxy, tiny crystal orbs hovered around the entire contraption.

Standing next to Shane, Sheila tipped her head back as far as her arthritic neck would allow. "Just look at that chandelier. Can you imagine something like that in our home?"

"We have nine-foot ceilings."

"A replica, dear."

"Even a reduced model would be more cubic centimeters than—"

"Let's explore." Sheila grabbed Shane's arm. "They said it would be three hours before our stateroom is ready, and I don't think we should ask Guest Relations about Shanna until we've actually set sail."

Judging by Shane's silence and roving index finger, chandelier dimensions still occupied his mind.

"Shaney."

He lowered his head. "Yes. Yes, of course. Better to wait to ask about our daughter until it's too late to disembark." He wiggled an eyebrow. "Assuming they don't make us walk the plank once we start pestering them."

That gesture, combined with the boyish look that accompanied it, sent Sheila back in time to when she was a nineteen-year-old girl determined to survive a first date with a young civil engineer who could barely make eye contact. Luckily, she agreed to date number two. It was then that Shane's gentle nature and dry wit poked through. On date number three, she knew he was the man for her. Even back then he emanated the yellow aura of logic and precision. Within that analytical hue, however, the green of peace and calm also shimmered, a green that balanced the energetic and sometimes demanding nature of her own pink and turquoise.

He must have seen the reminiscing in her eyes, because under that giant chandelier, with passengers of all shapes, sizes, and countries of origin whirring around them, he brought her close and pressed his nose against her hair. "Where would I be without my Sheila anchor?"

She kissed his cheek. "Funny, I was just thinking the same about you." They remained rooted in the splendorous foyer for a few moments longer. Sheila sighed. "What a special trip this would be if we weren't here for such a somber reason."

WITH TIME TO burn before their stateroom was ready, Sheila and Shane explored the ship's offerings, starting first with the busy lunch buffet up on deck fourteen. A mouthwatering assortment of salads, soups, sandwiches, hot dishes, and desserts left Sheila dizzy with indecision.

Forty minutes later, with full bellies and jet-lagged bodies, they wandered the corridors from deck to deck. It wasn't long before Sheila's troublesome foot bones required a respite. The library offered the perfect place. As avid readers they were pleased to discover it on deck ten, the same deck as their still-inaccessible stateroom. Equally pleasing was how well-suited its high-back chairs were for a post-lunch nap.

After an hour of slumber, unread books in their laps, Sheila's energy returned and her feet simmered down to a tolerable ache. A few moments of spine stretching and shoulder rolling got her body to follow suit.

Back to exploring, she and Shane weaved from one cocktail lounge to the next, each unique in its swanky decor and each with far more alcohol choices than she or her husband would need. They then moved on to the solarium on deck twelve, where floor-to-ceiling windows showcased the city of Amsterdam on one side and the swaying sea on the other.

After seeing most of what the upper decks had to offer, they returned to deck ten by way of the elevator to see if their stateroom was ready. Their arms had grown weary from lugging their carry-on bags, and they hoped to finally be free of them. Fortunately, the room was available, and their suitcases were outside the door. The two went to work hunting down their key cards.

"Now where did I put it?" Shane patted the side and breast pockets of his blazer and then shifted to his slacks.

Sheila rummaged around in her tote bag, her purse and raincoat stuffed inside. "I can't seem to find mine either. They said not to lose them."

"They're our 'keys to everything,' including our ship charges." Shane's words parroted the clerk at check-in.

"No credit cards needed, no cash. Imagine that. Think how easy it'll be to rack up charges."

"I imagine that's their plan."

"How do we expect to find our daughter when we can't even find our cards?"

Together they searched pockets and bags for their "keys to everything."

"I still don't understand why room eleven sixty-four is on deck ten." Sheila plucked a partially eaten peanut bar from her tote bag. She stuffed it next to the one in her cardigan pocket. Dr. Hassan Shakir, the family practice physician for whom she had worked as a receptionist for thirty-seven years, told her to always carry a snack for glucose dips. Chewy peanut bars were her blood-sugar rescue of choice, and she had brought plenty of them on the cruise. "It seems like it should be on deck eleven."

Shane fished his wallet from his back pocket and flipped it open. "Architecturally, it makes sense, but I agree, coordination of floor number and stateroom number would be in the best interest of passengers."

"At least we were able to get a room near the one Shanna had. I want to retrace her steps as closely as we can."

"Ah, here it is." Shane plucked his key card from in between a stack of pound and euro notes. He unlocked the door, and they stepped inside.

"Well, isn't this lovely?" Sheila took in the king bed, the wheat-colored woodwork of the shelving and counter tops, and the closet with a sliding door.

"It's roomier than I thought it would be," Shane said.

Sheila entered the bathroom. "Hold that thought." She glanced at the tiny shower enclosed in frosted glass. "At least if we slip, we'll stay upright."

Still, she had no complaints. Even without a veranda, the room was far more elegant than anything she had ever known on vacation. Who needs a balcony, anyway? she thought. With the wind and rain that had whipped and spattered them when they crossed the pool deck, it was abundantly clear that a mid-August British Isles cruise was no Caribbean one.

After unpacking their belongings, their rhythm so in sync after decades of marriage they needed no discussion on where items should go, they headed to deck five for the mandatory safety drill.

Judging by the captain's booming announcements that came from somewhere in their stateroom, there was no escaping it.

After the drill, Sheila tilted Shane's wrist. Her husband loved gadgets, and his complex watch was no exception. At least its large digital display didn't require her reading glasses.

"It's almost five," she said. "We'll set sail soon. Let's sit in the bar across from Guest Relations to wait."

Descending two flights to deck three, Sheila realized they hadn't yet visited the casino or boutiques on decks four and five. *This ship is huge!*

As if reading her thoughts, Shane said, "The casino and shops are closed when the ship's in port. They'll open once we set sail."

Her Shaney. No scrap of information went unread. No map went unstudied.

The Shipmate Bar was located across from Guest Relations. She had noticed it earlier from the grand foyer. With its glossy mahogany bar, leather chairs, and large windows for scenic viewing, she felt as though she had just gained admission to an exclusive, members-only club.

Taking a seat at a dark-wood table topped with a marble inlay, she surveyed the empty bar. "I suppose everyone is up on the top decks for cast off."

"Do you want to join them?"

"No. As exciting as this ship is, we're not here for a pleasure cruise. We have work to do." The tall chair swallowed her petite frame. With her feet barely touching the ground, she swiveled it toward Shane.

A bartender approached. "Hello. Welcome to the *Celestial of the Seas*. Can I offer you something to drink?" His accent sounded Eastern European.

"Perhaps a glass of Pinot Grigio?" Sheila smoothed the seam of her slacks. In the posh and unfamiliar setting, she felt like Dorothy in Oz. Over the years they had traveled to engineering conferences and taken family vacations, but they had never been on a cruise ship. Its grandeur far exceeded the usual Holiday Inn or Best Western hotel.

"Of course, madam. And for you, sir?"

"Red wine would be nice. But nothing too expensive." Shane wasn't a cheap man, but one does not live to be eighty-four years old without experiencing lean times. Sheila knew his frugality had been difficult to shake. Hers too.

Moments later they clicked glasses and sipped wine. "Remind me again of our itinerary?" Sheila said. "Since we don't know exactly when Shanna went missing, we need to assume she was on the ship until the end. And maybe she was. Maybe she did go missing in Amsterdam like the security team says." She rested her head against the leather upholstery. "But my gut tells me otherwise. How likely is it to disappear in a cab ride from ship to airport?"

Shane pulled a notebook out of his blazer pocket. Whether at a grocery store or gas station, it never left his side. Inside was a sheet of paper. He unfolded it and began his recitation. "Tomorrow, day two, we're at sea." He glanced at her. "In the morning, we have the behind-the-scenes ship excursion that Shanna took." She nodded and he continued. "Day three is Inverness, days four and five are Edinburgh, day six is at sea, day seven is Liverpool."

"The Beatles," Sheila murmured, hardly believing she would be visiting any of these locations.

"Yes, The Beatles. Also the home to the first electric elevated railway."

She would have to take his word on that.

"Day eight we visit Belfast," he went on. "Day nine is Dublin, day ten is Cork."

"Cork is in Ireland too, right?"

"Yes. Day eleven is another day at sea. I should think we'll need a good rest by then. Day twelve is Brussels, but remember, we'll be traveling to Ghent."

"Yes, Shanna was particularly excited about that excursion. How lucky she went through her trip schedule with us."

"It's not luck. She's organized and likes a well-planned schedule. I asked for a copy of it. She crosses her t's and dots her i's. Always."

"Like someone else I know."

Shane peered up at Sheila. "Are you mocking me or is that a compliment?"

"Of course, honey."

Shane refolded the itinerary and replaced it in his pocket. "On day thirteen we disembark in Amsterdam again."

"Hopefully with our daughter."

"Hopefully with our daughter."

They sipped in silence, Sheila's wine trickling past the lump in her throat. Once she trusted her voice not to shake, she said, "If only she'd never been sent those brochures. Why did Dreamline Cruises have to market her so doggedly? Without those incessant fliers, she'd never have known about this cruise and she'd still be with us." She tightened her jaw and squeezed her eyes together.

Shane reached across the table for her hand. "I know, I know, Beetle Bug." Pain was evident on his face too.

She lowered her glass. "Did you feel that?"

"We're moving."

Normally, something as monumental as a mammoth ship heading out to sea would have Shane quick-stepping his feet and pumping his arms in that strange boogie he performed whenever he was overly excited. Even their son Paul, who wasn't the laughing sort, tittered at the sight. But the events of the last two months had diminished Shane's sparkle. Sheila's too.

Still, he had enough excitement in him to pontificate on the amount of fuel a ship this size would demand. While he talked of nautical physics and seafaring dynamics, Sheila wondered about her daughter. Had Shanna sat in this bar? Had she sipped a Belgian lager at this very table? Had she watched the lights of Amsterdam slip away as they were doing now?

If so, where was she at this moment?

3

SECURITY SETBACK

ONCE THE SHIP was surrounded by enough water to ensure Sheila and Shane could no longer be escorted off without drowning, they made their way to Guest Relations on the port side. By now the excitement of leaving shore had worn off for the passengers, and clusters of them flooded the third deck. Many strolled into the bar the McShanes had just vacated.

Unfortunately, the Guest Relations counter was similarly crowded. Sheila supposed there was never a shortage of complaints, though what people could find to complain about on such a beautiful vessel, she couldn't imagine.

All six staff members were busy helping passengers, but the lines moved quickly, and within minutes Sheila and Shane reached the counter. A young woman with glossy, black hair greeted them with a smile. Her name badge identified her as Sinta from Indonesia, and her highly spiritual aura of royal blue told Sheila she would certainly understand their plight.

"Good evening. Welcome to Dreamline Cruises, where we put the Snooze in Cruise. What can we help you with?"

"Oh dear," Sheila said, caught off guard. "Perhaps it's your marketing team who could use the help."

"I am sorry?"

Shane leaned on the counter, his blazer buttons clicking against the smooth surface. "We'd like to speak to security, please."

Sinta's color flickered, and her smile faded. Maybe Sheila had overestimated her spiritual essence. "Why don't you tell me what the problem is. I am sure together we can solve it."

"We need to see your security footage," Shane said. "Your ship may have lost our daughter. She never made it home from Amsterdam after she disembarked."

The Indonesian woman's scarlet lips parted. No sound followed.

"More than two hundred people have gone missing from cruise ships in the last two decades, maybe up to three hundred. Statistically, that—"

"What my husband is trying to say is that we were hoping to discuss our concerns with your security team. We simply have a few questions." Sheila placed her liver-spotted hand over Shane's. The tremble of fear and frustration in it matched her own.

"I...well, I..." Sinta's fingers fumbled for the handset of her phone. "I will call my supervisor." She pressed a number on speed dial. An unsettled brown seeped into her aura. "Ms. Donahue, could you come to the counter, please?"

Sheila's flesh grew hot. Lightheadedness and a fine tremor followed. Though she recognized the signs of low blood sugar, the strain of what lay ahead was also culpable. She pulled the half-eaten peanut bar from her cardigan pocket and started nibbling. By the time the statuesque supervisor arrived, the worst of Sheila's hypoglycemic symptoms had passed.

A rather unpleasant back-and-forth ensued, during which Ms. Donahue, an auburn-haired Canadian woman whose uniform showed nary a wrinkle, questioned Sheila and Shane's involvement in what was "clearly a matter for the authorities." Eventually, she relented and placed a call to the security department, as Sheila and Shane had requested. Twenty-five minutes later the two of them sat at a round table in a bland room inside the security suite on deck two. Three uniformed officers surrounded them.

"No. We cannot show you our footage." The head of security

was a man in his fifties with a trim and fit build, closely cropped salt-and-pepper hair, and an irritable red essence. In accented English, he had identified himself as Officer Ivan Hryhorenko. Given the difficult pronunciation of his last name, along with his can't-do atti-tude, Sheila was already referring to him as Officer Sourpuss in her mind. "If you come all this way for that, it is waste of time." He paced around the small room, twirling the arm of his rimless glasses between his thumb and index finger.

Shane's hands fidgeted with his notebook. He cleared his throat but said nothing, his jaw muscles perhaps too tight for speech.

"Ivan," Sheila said, dropping her voice to its most provocative range. "What a strong name for such a strong man. Where are you from, sir?"

Ivan puffed out his chest and put his glasses back on. "Ukraine."

"Oh, that's a beautiful country. Such hard-working and intelli-gent people. My great grandmother hailed from there." Sheila had no idea if her great grandmother had hailed from there or not, but men with hot-tempered auras enjoyed a little coddling. Over the years she had dealt with many of them in Dr. Shakir's clinic. She turned to a younger officer standing to her left, a dark-haired, dark-eyed man who appeared to be in his mid- to late-thirties and made from the mold of a god. "And you, sir? Niko, did you say your name was? I don't think I can pronounce your last name either." She studied his name badge. "Knež...ev...ić. Ooh, that's a tough one. You're from Croatia, is that right?"

Niko pulled out a chair and sat, his smile reassuring. "I am."

"Oh my, you Croatian men are always so handsome." She chuckled and feigned a swoon. "You're like that actor who played an ER doctor on TV." To Sheila, Niko's orange emanations suggested warmth and social confidence. Kindness and honesty too, though she had to consider the possibility that his added ring of golden attractiveness was clouding her judgment. Good looks could do that to a spiritual reader.

Finally, she turned to the third man, Officer Tad Davies, whose jutting jaw, floppy earlobes, and untamed cowlick suggested he had not played an ER doctor from Croatia on TV. Tall and lanky, he looked at least a decade younger than Niko, possibly even more. He stood to the right of Shane, who, if Sheila had guessed correctly, was estimating the square footage of the tiny room and the volume of oxygen left in it.

"Tad is an unusual name. I see from your badge you're from the UK." Sheila smiled warmly and was pleased when the young man did the same. Maybe it was just their superior who was a grumpy Gus. Tad's purple coloring indicated gentleness, but he radiated a subtle yellowish-green hue as well, which suggested discomfort, as if he wanted to prove himself to be more experienced than he appeared.

"Yes, I am British. My name means 'a gift given by God'."

"Well, your mother must be very proud of you. Being a security officer on a cruise ship, and at such a young age."

Tad beamed. He started to tell her about his lovely mother in Brighton, when Ivan cut him off.

"Enough chit chat," the Ukrainian said, his accent thick and rough. "You tell us you want to see security footage from your daughter's cruise eight weeks ago, but it is not for public eyes."

"Why not?" Shane asked quietly.

"Because it is not. It violates other passengers' privacy. It is security risk." His glasses were back in his hands, twirling wildly. "Besides, as we told the authorities many times—both your federal agents from U.S. embassy in Amsterdam and Amsterdam police themselves—she did not disappear from our ship. They investigated ship with us and found nothing."

Sheila started to interrupt, but Ivan cut her off.

"This, your country's agents have told you many times. This, Amsterdam authorities have told you many times. This, we have told you many times." His coloring flushed, and not just his invisible one. "Our call logs from you are longer than the silly novels my wife reads."

"I understand that, but we would appreciate seeing the footage." Sheila struggled to maintain her composure. "We want answers. We need to find our daughter, even if it means having to do it ourselves."

Ivan cleared his throat, the way a man does just before he spits. "You need to be questioning the Amsterdam authorities, not us."

Sheila's calm crumbled. Exhausted from jet lag and unnerved by foreign travel, she felt helpless and vulnerable. She had no idea what she was doing. She only knew she had to find her daughter. "Do you have any children?" she asked Ivan. Gone was the flirtatious tone she had used earlier. In its place, a shaky anger and fear. She looked around the room. "Do any of you have children?" Shane reached for her hand.

Niko interjected before Officer Sourpuss could respond. "I know this is a painful time for you, but what my superior officer means is, as you know, we have already been through the security footage. Many times with many different authorities. Officer Hryhorenko's frustration comes from being unable to locate your daughter, that's all." Niko leaned forward, his bare elbows resting on the table. The lapels of his starched, white uniform displayed two gold officer stripes on a black badge, one stripe less than Ivan's and one more than Tad's.

"Our customer relations staff has addressed your questions too, right?" Tad asked hopefully.

"Yes," Shane said, seemingly knowing, as always, that Sheila was at her limit and that it was time for him to take over. "But no one has any useful answers."

"That is because no one knows what happened to her." Ivan once again paced the small room. "From our footage she is seen getting on and off ship at each port, including final location of Amsterdam. This is proof, yes?"

Sheila couldn't bring herself to look at the man. Intuitively, she understood his gruffness stemmed from defensiveness over having his skills as the head of security questioned, but his powerful red coloring threatened what little control she had left.

Tad scratched one floppy earlobe and sank his tall frame onto the remaining chair. "We understand how frustrating this must be for you."

"Do you?" Shane said, his hand warm and trembling over Sheila's. "Do you also know the fear of not knowing where your daughter is? The terror over what might have happened to her? Not knowing if she's dead or alive? Not knowing if she's floating in the sea or buried ten leagues beneath it?"

Silence enveloped the room. Sheila imagined it might be the only quiet place on the ship. When she finally dared speak again, it was no more than a frail whisper. "We just want to see the footage. We want to see our daughter one more time."

Niko crossed his arms and looked up at Ivan. Tad studied a callus on his hand. Ivan growled like the crimson lion he was. He flicked at his graying temple and smashed his glasses back onto his face. "I am sorry. It is not for me to allow. Only captain can decide." Although his tone was still defensive, his voice was softer. "You should enjoy trip. You should not have come to play amateur detectives. It cannot be good for people your age."

"Will you ask the captain?" Sheila's strength was now fully spent, and she could barely form the words. "Or should we go see him ourselves?"

Ivan's knuckles rapped the table three times. "You cannot bother the captain. Do you think he entertains visitors when it pleases them?"

"Boss, maybe—"

Ivan cut Niko off with a snap of his fingers. "*Achhh,* I will ask, but do not get hopes up. Captain will not allow citizen investigation. He will not want news of missing American woman spreading around. Passengers will not feel safe. If you act foolishly, you will have to leave ship."

Sheila and Shane exchanged mournful glances. In Shane's eyes she saw a mirror image of her own thoughts: Was this trip for naught? Would they never have answers? Would they never see their daughter again?

Sheila slumped down in her chair. Though Niko and Tad seemed ready to assist, Shane was the one who helped her up.

With heavy limbs and heavier hearts, the two of them exited the security suite.

"I won't give up, Shaney, I won't."

"I won't either."

They headed to the elevator. They would dine. They would rest. They would restore their energy. They were not youngsters, after all.

But after?

After, they would ask anyone who would listen about Shanna. Somewhere, somehow, someone on this ship knew something about their daughter.

4

A DINING ROOM DISCOVERY

Sheila and Shane rested on a Victorian bench outside the Dreamscape Dining Room of the *Celestial of the Seas*. Not only were they waiting to be seated, they were waiting to question the staff about their daughter. To heck with Officer Sourpuss.

A cacophony of murmured conversations, bursts of laughter, clinking glasses, and harried waiting staff drifted out from the restaurant's entrance. So too did the aroma of prime rib and garlic-infused side dishes. With each passing minute, Sheila's hunger grew, her pocketed peanut bar long since eaten.

After their disappointing encounter with the security team, they had decided to go directly to the dining room on deck four. They feared if they stopped in their stateroom before dinner, they would collapse on the bed and sleep until morning. Not only did they need their nourishment, they were reluctant to miss out on the included meals, especially given the cost of the cruise. The tickets and airfare had left a noticeable dent in their retirement fund. Even the expedite fee for the passports was expensive. Aside from social security and Shane's pension, their only income was Sheila's part-time work in Dr. Shakir's clinic, and who knew how long she could keep that up? As it was, she suspected the kind doctor kept her on out of loyalty. That and the fact she could soothe even the most disgruntled of patients.

Asking their son for money was not an option. The forty-year-old man wasn't even aware his sister was missing. Paul wasn't like other people, and with his adoration of Shanna, who was truly the only person with whom he had bonded, including Sheila, he wouldn't react well. Given his work as a geologist in Iceland, the secret was easily kept. Best to keep him in the dark until they knew more.

"Goodness, I'm hungry." She placed a hand on her stomach, hoping to quiet the rumblings. Back home in Sherry, dinner was five thirty. Six o'clock at the latest. A glance at Shane's watch indicated it was going on seven now.

"Do you think we're dressed well enough?" he asked.

Sheila glanced at his dark blazer and button-down shirt. "You look marvelous. You always do." Her gaze shifted to her own cotton slacks, ruffled blouse, and cardigan. She had been wearing them all day, but other than a few wrinkles, she felt presentable enough. She had packed lightly, choosing complimentary clothes and cardigan sweaters that would match everything. Plus, her makeup was only as far as her purse, and she had already freshened up in the bathroom near the dining hall.

A few moments later, the hostess with a burgundy suit and immaculate hair left her podium and approached them. Her name badge indicated she was from the Philippines. Sheila had noted it earlier when they had first asked her about seating. At that time, Sheila had also asked if the woman remembered Shanna. She had not.

"Are you sure you do not wish to be seated? With open seating, you may dine anytime between six and ten p.m. I have several tables available."

"You're a doll, thank you, but we'll wait for table seven eighty-seven."

"I understand. I wish I could tell you more about your daughter, but I don't remember her from the picture you showed me. I see so many guests."

Sheila nodded. "Of course you do, dear."

Shane's eyes shifted in calculation. "The *Celestial of the Seas* holds nearly three thousand passengers. It's had four sailings since my daughter's trip, including this one. Statistically, the odds of you recognizing her are slim."

"A numbers man, I see. But you are positive your daughter sat at table seven eighty-seven?"

"Oh yes." Sheila straightened on the plush velvet seat. "You see, she texted us the first night of her voyage. She had just received her shrimp cocktail, and it was so pretty she sent us a picture. A little stand with the table number printed on it was in the corner. She also texted a photo of her waiter, along with the assistant waiter. She gushed about them both. She's rarely giddy like that, so I know she was really excited." Sheila paused, tempted to pull out her phone to reread Shanna's last text. No need. She knew every word of it. "Then she sent us pictures of her stateroom and told us it would be her last text until getting home. She didn't want to pay for the internet."

"The ship's internet cost is ridiculous," Shane said.

"Yes, it's pricey, but that's not the only reason Shanna put her phone into airplane mode. She wanted to disconnect from the digital world." To the hostess, Sheila said, "Her career can be stressful. She's an art restorer. It's very precise and tedious work. While the museum in Boston treats her well, some of her private clients are quite demanding, always calling and emailing her. She wanted to check out completely."

"Her text came in at eight-seventeen p.m. her time, two-seventeen p.m. ours. Then she told us she—" Shane's voice caught.

Sheila caressed his arm and finished the sentence for him. "She told us she loved us and would see us when she returned. She's not normally a demonstrative person, mind you, but her excitement over visiting the UK was obvious." Sheila paused. "That was the last time we ever heard from her."

"At eight-seventeen her time, two-seventeen ours." Shane blinked at his oversized watch.

The hostess sniffled. She tugged the bottom of her suit jacket.

"Just a moment." She stepped back to the podium and snapped her fingers. Within seconds a young member of the dining staff appeared. She whispered something in his ear. He nodded, and she looked back at the McShanes. "We will have table seven eighty-seven cleared for you in just a few minutes."

Concern knitted Sheila's brow. "But what about the people dining at it? We don't want to impose."

"You needn't worry. We will give them a wonderful incentive." When the hostess smiled, a halo of pink shimmered from her lithe frame, a halo that only the most loving and sensitive possessed.

Ten minutes later Sheila and Shane were seated near the window in a dining room that was every bit as exquisite as the ship's grand foyer. Not to be outdone in the lighting department, the restaurant had its own jaw-dropping chandelier, with long cylinders of radiant glass surrounded by a galaxy of electric stars. Shane had already commented on the watt-hours of energy such a fixture would require.

Table 787 had the good fortune of overlooking the water and the burnt-orange sunset reflecting off the waves. It was also in close proximity to one of the small waiters' stations that were strategically placed throughout the enormous, two-story room. Each table was elegantly draped in white linen and adorned with china and crystal place settings. Celtic music with flutes and bagpipes enlivened the atmosphere. The waiting staff, dressed in black pants, black vests, and crisp, white shirts, seemed almost to rush to its beat. Some carried as many as three silver platters on one arm.

The grandeur of it all made Sheila feel like a queen, and the ecru chair with its silky contours was her throne. She stared at her gold-rimmed plate and the arsenal of cutlery surrounding it. "Heavens, what does one do with all this silverware?"

The assistant waiter approached their table and poured ice water into their crystal tumblers. His other arm hugged two menus to his chest. A badge on his vest read *Renny* and below that *Pakistan*. He introduced himself and welcomed them to the *Celestial of the Seas*. "Is this your first time sailing with us?"

"It's our first time sailing with anyone." Sheila recognized the young man from the photos Shanna had sent of the dining room staff. "It's absolutely beautiful."

"I'm glad you are enjoying it." He handed them the menus, which were so heavy Sheila almost dropped hers.

"You are very young," she said.

"Oh, not so young as you might think."

"And you're such a cutie pie. Isn't he a cutie pie, Shane?"

The assistant waiter laughed and thanked her. Sheila was pleased to see it was a genuine laugh, not a courtesy laugh to appease the customer. Then again, she expected nothing less from a man bathed in such gold radiance. She half expected him to be lifted off to heaven right then and there, though she certainly hoped he wouldn't be.

"You are a man of gold, I can tell."

Renny held the pitcher of water against his chest, condensation dripping down its stainless-steel side. He winked. "If only."

"Not in richness, perhaps, but in admiration and affection from others."

His smile faltered, and his cheeks blushed.

"Sheila, leave the poor man be." Shane realigned one of his knives to parallel the other. "She's a good reader of people, whether they want to be read or not."

Another waiter, older in appearance, maybe mid-thirties, hustled over to the table. Renny slipped away to other guests, his water pitcher at the ready.

"Welcome, welcome." The new waiter's accented voice was smoother than a public radio host's. He adjusted his black-framed glasses. "My name is Victor. I will be your waiter tonight, and every night should you reserve this table."

As with Renny, Sheila recognized him from Shanna's photos. Sheila had learned from Dr. Shakir's nurse, Gloria, who was an avid cruiser, that crew members worked several months in a row before getting time off. Though Sheila imagined the challenge that must be, she was grateful for their continuity now. "Lovely to meet you, Victor." She squinted at his name badge. "I see you're from India.

How wonderful. It's like we're taking a trip around the world without ever leaving the ship."

"Indeed, madam. Over seventy countries are represented by our ship's staff." Victor stood at full posture, hands behind his back. A hue of kindness and sensitivity shimmered around him. "Tonight we will be having a superb prime rib au jus for our main entrée recommendation. May I also be recommending to you the Alaskan salmon as a starter or the *crema di funghi selvatica*."

Sheila had no idea what crema di foo foo was, but she murmured in approval as if she did.

"I will give you a moment to look over the menu. Tina will help you with your wine order."

As Victor jetted off, a young woman with a tight bun and impeccable makeup marched up to the table and introduced herself in such a commanding manner that a salute seemed in order. Her name was Tina, and like Sinta at the Guest Relations desk, her country of origin was Indonesia. Unlike Sinta, Tina lacked any spiritual yellowness. Instead, the sommelier was a blue blur of efficiency. Sheila and Shane had barely uttered their wine preferences before the woman darted off to a room in the back, just beyond the massive chandelier.

"Oh dear." Sheila sank into the inviting chair, the menu weighting her lap like one of her daughter's dumbbells. "They're all so busy. How will we ask them about Shanna?"

Shane thumped his own menu on the table. When it flipped over his fork, he righted the utensil to its original place. "They can spare two minutes to look at her picture and hear what we have to say."

He pulled his pen from an inside pocket of his blazer. Silver and plump, with even more features than his watch, it was more than a mere writing tool. At the flick of a button, the small digital screen displayed the time, temperature, or direction. Another button activated either a laser pointer or flashlight. A gift from Shanna two Christmases ago, it had quickly become his most prized possession. In the past six weeks since their daughter went missing, Sheila had caught Shane in his favorite chair in the living room, staring off into space, holding the pen. Not using it, just rolling it back and forth between his palms, a doleful look on his face. Now, however, he used the flashlight feature to better read the menu. Unlike Sheila, who needed reading glasses most of the time, Shane could get by without them if the lighting was strong enough.

She plucked her glasses from her purse and put them on. She also retrieved her mobile phone and opened the photos app. Save for an emergency text-and-calling plan in case there was word of Shanna, she had no intention of using her phone overseas. She only wanted to show her daughter's picture.

And there Shanna was, staring directly at the camera, her straight, red-brown hair tucked behind her ears. Despite the early hint of a smile, her fern-colored eyes were raised in question. Sheila had snapped it while Shanna and Shane were discussing the electoral college system. Her daughter hadn't yet finished the debate when Sheila had ordered her to smile.

Being lost in thought was Shanna's natural state. If interrupted, she usually required a few moments of stammering before shifting her mental wheels. Because of that, some people found her inarticulate or scatterbrained. Shanna was neither of those things. She was rational, focused, and intense. She was also quiet, at least until someone roused a topic that impassioned her. Then the dear girl would never shut up. Emanating the same analytical yellow as her father, she shared his logic and intelligence. She also shared his desire for solitude. That loner status, combined with Shanna's workaholic tendencies, had made her unlucky in love. Her longest relationship was her last one. It ended when her accountant boyfriend went to jail for fraud.

Despite all that yellow, there was pinkness too. The same pinkness of sensitivity and sixth-sense intuition that Sheila herself possessed. Shanna, of course, rolled her eyes at any such assertion, but Sheila saw it. A little something extra passed on from mother to daughter. Sheila smiled at the thought, some of her angst lifting.

Shane's voice broke her reverie. "You still have the prettiest smile of anyone I know. You always have."

"You're such a dear, thank you." She put the phone on the table,

Shanna's image still gazing up at her. "I was just thinking about our baby."

"We'll find her, Beetle Bug." Despite his assurance, his eyes conveyed uncertainty.

"Remember that old car?"

"You should have listened to me."

Indeed she should have. Back in 1958, at the age of twenty-one, Sheila got her first car: a used, pale blue Volkswagen Beetle from Stan's Used Car Emporium outside Manchester, New Hampshire. Shane had warned her it wasn't practical for New England weather. "You'll never make it up the driveway in the snow." But she had insisted on it.

Turned out he was right.

He had been calling her *Beetle Bug* ever since.

Tina, the brisk sommelier, returned to their table with a bottle of wine in each hand, one red, one white. She poured a splash of white into Sheila's glass and waited.

"Heavens, is that all I get?"

"You must taste it, madam. Make sure it is adequate for you."

Sheila felt her face flush in embarrassment. "Oops, of course. My brain is failing me." She scanned the opulent surroundings. "I'm sure any wine you serve us will be more than adequate."

Tina emitted a strange yip of a laugh that would frighten a child. Shane waved off his own wine tasting, and into his glass flowed a burgundy blend that matched the capillaries on his cheeks.

Victor returned to the table with Renny behind him.

"Have you made your dinner selections?" the waiter asked.

With all three servers at the table, Sheila seized the opportunity. She entered the passcode into her phone and brought up the image. "This is our daughter, Shanna. She was on your June sailing and she went missing and we're looking for her." Her words rushed out in a husky torrent. "Do you remember anything about her? Anything at all?"

A beat or two of blinking from the crew members followed. Tina leaned forward and peered at Shanna's image. "She is a wine drinker?"

"No, she prefers beer, but—"

"Then I do not remember her. Sorry. I wish you well in finding her." The sommelier hurried off, her departure probably more economic than rude. Empty wine glasses were everywhere.

"May I?" Renny pulled Sheila's phone closer. "Hmm, she looks familiar." While he was contemplating, an important looking man barked his name and pointed to a table several feet away. Renny tapped the back of Sheila's chair. "I'm sorry. I must go. But I will think about it."

Victor stood pensively, tablet and pen pressed against his waist with one hand, chin resting in the other. His index finger tapped his lip. "Yes, maybe. Let me think about it while I work. Sometimes thoughts fall into our heads when we don't try so hard, you know?"

Sheila did know. She thanked him, but when he asked what they wanted for dinner, she realized she hadn't even checked the menu. It was still upright in her lap, its weight pressing into her thighs. She scanned it but couldn't focus, her mind still on her daughter.

Shane rescued her. "We'll both have the shrimp cocktail and the prime rib, medium rare." As always, his gift of preparation left her grateful.

Thirty minutes later, after an appetizer of artfully presented shrimp cocktail, Sheila and Shane cut into meat so tender it was like cutting into flan. When her mouth was full of the succulent beef, Victor returned to check on them. He seemed excited.

"I do remember your daughter. I do indeed. We talked about her beaver."

Sheila's fork clattered to the china plate. Shane looked as shocked as she did.

"I think I misunderstood you, sweetie," she sputtered.

"I told her I collect beavers, and she told me about hers."

Things were going from bad to worse. Sheila pulled her cardigan together and cinched the fabric at her neck. Shane's ongoing eye contact with the waiter entered record-breaking territory.

Victor seemed puzzled by their discomfort. "Not real beavers of course, but similes of the animal."

"I see," Sheila said. She didn't see, but at least she was breathing better now. She eased up on her cardigan.

"Oh yes." Victor adjusted his eyeglasses. "I have crystal ones, wood ones, ceramic ones, even ones made of chocolate, if you can believe that."

"Chocolate beavers. Sounds delightful." Sheila took a large gulp of wine. "But what does that have to do with my Shanna?"

"Don't you see? I remember your daughter because she told me she was restoring an old painting of a beaver."

"Ahhhh." Sheila and Shane's understanding was simultaneous.

Shane spoke first. "Yes, that's our daughter. She works at the Boston art museum."

Victor's excitement matched Shane's. "Then yes, that is the woman I remember."

Sheila pressed a hand against her heart to steady its thumping. *Just because he remembers Shanna doesn't mean he knows what happened to her.* Still, his news gave her hope, especially after being dismissed by the security team.

Victor's elation broke. "I'm sorry to hear she is missing though. That is sad news indeed." He pushed his glasses up and stared out at the sea.

"Can you tell us anything about her? Anything that might help us?" Sheila tried to keep the desperation out of her plea.

"I'm not sure I can. She dined at this table, you are correct about that. I remember her being prompt."

"That's my Shanna," Shane said. He removed his notebook from his blazer pocket and flipped it open, ready to take notes. "Did she eat here every night?"

Victor folded his arms and chewed his lower lip. Sheila knew he had work to do, and she didn't want to get him in trouble, but she craved something to go on, something to reassure them this trip hadn't been in vain.

"I don't think every night," he finally said. "Maybe not so much near the end, in fact, but I can't remember the last time I served her." Victor closed his eyes behind his thick lenses. From the waiters' station behind them, someone called out his name. His eyelids fluttered open. "I know she was by herself the first night or two. That was when we talked about her beaver painting."

Sheila prodded him on with a waggle of her fingers. She had heard enough about beavers.

"Then she started coming in with a man."

"A man?" Again, Sheila and Shane spoke in unison.

"Yes, he was a handsome man. Dark hair, slightly crooked nose, Australian accent, rugged and muscular one might even say." A dreamy look came over Victor. He gave his head a shake and added, "But he did not—"

"Victor." The tone was sharper than before.

Sheila's shoulders tensed. "You better go. We don't want to get you in trouble. But you were saying the man 'did not'... did not what?"

At that moment Renny came by to refill their water glasses. Victor turned to him. "Renny, please take the meals out to table seven ninety-two. Tell Sanjay I will be right there, but this is very important." When Renny darted off to comply, Victor leaned closer to the McShanes. "The man was handsome, but he didn't smell right. Do you know what I mean?"

Shane frowned. "He had body odor?"

"No, not that kind of smelly. He just didn't smell right to me." Victor shook his head in obvious frustration. "That sounds foolish. I'm not explaining myself well."

"It doesn't sound foolish at all." Sheila understood perfectly. The pink and purple shades of intuitiveness were all over Victor now, and she trusted his instinct. Of course, she herself saw colors rather than smelled them, but who was she to argue with Victor's gift?

"Let me think." Victor went back to his hand-to-chin posture. "Your daughter ate alone through the Inverness stop on day three. After that, we sailed to Edinburgh." His face lit up. "Yes, Edinburgh, that was it. That was when she first came in with the spiritually smelly man. I remember because they were laughing about the terrible tenders we use to transport people from the ship to the shore. We can't bring the ship there directly, you understand."

She didn't, though she was sure Shane did. She scooted to the edge of her seat, her tender prime rib long since forgotten. "And then what?"

"I'm not sure whether it was the first night or the second night in Edinburgh, but I know it was that stop, because the man used the talk of the transport tenders as an opportunity to join your daughter at her table."

"Did you hear them discuss anything else?" Shane's pen was poised at the ready.

"I heard them chat about her work at the art museum, and then they talked about the ship's art auction. But that is all I remember, I'm sorry."

Renewed hope energized Sheila. She felt like she could run four times around the ship's exterior jogging track, troublesome foot bones and all. "Thank you, you've been most helpful. This is a start for sure. Did they eat together every night after that?"

"Maybe, but as I said, I can't remember when I last saw her come in. They might have eaten in the specialty restaurants after that."

"What are those?" Sheila asked.

"They are our themed restaurants. They are not inclusive like this dining room. You must pay an extra fee to eat in them. We have four on the ship: a steak grill, an Italian restaurant, a Japanese hibachi, and a French bistro."

"I don't think our daughter would have paid extra for meals when there's perfectly delicious food in here, but please, if you do remember, let us know."

Victor promised he would. Sheila stood and gave him a hug, and then waved him off with another apology for keeping him from his work. She knew how much the crew members relied on their jobs. Dr. Shakir's nurse had told her the tiniest infraction could get them fired, with a long line of men and women eager to take their places. She made a note to praise Victor to Guest Relations.

She sat back down. Her hands trembled slightly, and she felt the heat in her face. "Our first lead."

Though Shane's own excitement was obvious, he cautioned

Sheila not to get overeager. "This man could simply have been a dinner companion for Shanna."

Sheila shrugged her thin shoulders. "Maybe. But if Victor says the man didn't smell right, that's good enough for me." She stabbed a piece of meat, popped it in her mouth, and chewed.

5

THE CRUISE, THE WHOLE CRUISE,
AND NOTHING BUT THE CRUISE

AFTER DINNER, Sheila followed Shane down the narrow corridor of deck ten to stateroom number 1164. Though countless activities were taking place all over the ship, from theater shows to dancing to karaoke, the McShanes were ready for bed.

Before retiring, Sheila hoped to meet their stateroom attendant. She was excited about their discovery of the man who didn't smell right—at least to their waiter—and she was eager to learn if their steward had anything to add. Hopefully, he or she was the same crew member who had cleaned Shanna's stateroom.

The hallway stretched on forever, one cabin door after another on either side of them. Though carpet cushioned their steps, the padding was no match for Sheila's aching feet, which had endured a full day of ship exploration. Even in her dependable, orthotic Mary Janes, each footfall stabbed like jagged rock. Thanks to an impoverished childhood filled with ill-fitting shoes, she had more spurs than a cowboy.

Despite all their wandering, the boat's layout was still confusing to her. She couldn't remember whether their cabin was aft or forward, port or starboard. To Shane it was doubtless as clear as the crystal glasses in the dining room. She could tell she was not alone in her physical discomfort though. Shane's slight limp suggested his hip was bothering him. They were both in need of a long night's sleep, and judging by the ship's gentle rocking motion, they would have no trouble finding it.

When they finally reached their stateroom, they stared at each other, each hoping the other would produce a key card.

"Isn't yours still in your wallet?" Sheila's tone carried a touch of irritation.

"Isn't yours still in your purse?" Shane's tone carried a touch of his own.

They sighed and began the process of checking pockets, wallets, and purses for their keys to everything.

"Do you think this Mr. Smelly is involved in Shanna's disappearance?" Sheila pulled a wad of tissues out of her handbag and shook it. No key card. She stuffed the mass back in.

"Mr. Smelly?"

"If the shoe fits." She opened her pocketbook. No key card.

Two teenage girls, their noses buried in phones, wandered down the hallway. They looked up, but upon seeing nothing but old people, returned to their screens and squeezed past them.

"It's at least a start." Shane rummaged around the inside pocket of his blazer. He pulled out his notebook and flipped it open. Out popped his key card. He scratched his spiky hair and stared at it on the floor. "Well, how in the world did it get in there?"

Being the nimbler of the two, he bent down and picked it up. He had just unlocked the door when a stocky man, maybe in his early thirties, hurried over to them.

"Hello, hello, very happy to meet you." The man's doughy cheeks topped a wide jaw, and his chin showed a hard day's stubble. "My name is Raoul. I will be your stateroom attendant. I will clean your room twice a day. I just completed your turndown service, but please, you must let me know if anything is not to your liking."

The McShanes introduced themselves and assured him they would. Sheila squinted at his name badge. "You're from Venezuela. How lovely. Do you have a family there?"

"Yes, I have a wife and four children." Despite Raoul's amiable smile and likable essence, Sheila sensed a disturbance within him. Shane would say such a deduction was obvious given the man's wringing hands and shifting eyes, but Sheila saw something deeper. She saw the green aura of a hard-working perfectionist overshadowed by a gray cloud of anxiety. Regardless, she was eager to ask him about Shanna.

She pulled out her phone. "Do you remember our daughter? She was in a stateroom just two doors down from this one back in June. We're looking for her." She held Shanna's image out to Raoul.

He scrunched his face and studied the picture. His bushy eyebrows lifted. "Oh yes, I remember your daughter. She was very neat and quiet. I did not see much of her."

Sheila's skin tingled in excitement, her energy renewed. "That's definitely our Shanna." She exchanged a hopeful look with Shane, whose hand dropped from the door handle. He reached for his notebook and pen.

Raoul's face saddened. "This must mean you have not found her yet."

"You know she's missing?" Sheila pressed a palm against her chest. "How? When? Do you know what happened?"

"Oh, no, madam. I'm sorry to mislead you. The reason I recognize her so easily is because security questioned me when she was reported missing."

Sheila exhaled. That made sense, though she wondered why the security staff hadn't similarly questioned the dining crew. Her blue calm flamed to a fiery red at the thought of a shoddy investigation. Then again, if Officer Sourpuss was convinced Shanna left the boat in Amsterdam on the last day of the cruise, he probably figured there was little reason to question the entire crew.

"Yes," Raoul continued. "The security officers said an American woman never returned home from the cruise. They wanted to know if I had any information to share."

"And did you?" Sheila held her breath. A child raced down the corridor, and a father trotted after him. For more privacy, she invited Raoul into their stateroom. Sensing his hesitancy, she said, "I know you're very busy, but please, we would just like to ask you a few more questions."

He stepped into the room. "I'm sorry. I have nothing else to tell you. I said the same to security."

"Did you see her every day?" Shane asked. He took Sheila's purse and placed it on the small desk next to a flat-screen TV. "Sit down, Beetle Bug. Your feet must be killing you."

Sheila sank down on the king-sized mattress, which was really two twin beds pushed together. Next to her, a collection of bathroom towels had been cleverly twisted and folded into the shape of an elephant. Were she in a different state of mind, she would have delighted over Raoul's creation.

"Not every day, no. She was often gone by the time I got to her room, though sometimes I spotted her in the hallway."

"Do you think she went missing before the end of the cruise? My gut tells me she did." Sheila asked the question, but it was Shane who was poised to scribble the answer in his notebook.

"Her bed had been slept in every night, and her belongings were there until the last day, just like everyone else's."

Shane sat down next to Sheila. In the tiny space, the bathroom was only two feet away. He said, "That implies the ship's security team is correct, that she vanished in Amsterdam. But the odds of her disappearing between ship disembarkation and arrival at the airport are very low. That's a small window, and according to the authorities, no cab drivers remembered her." He lowered his notebook and seemed to shrink an inch, the puzzle too vexing.

Sheila nodded. "I agree. It's a pocket-sized window. That's why I'm convinced she went missing from the ship." Another thought came to her. "What if someone only made it *look* like she was on the ship the whole time?"

Raoul crinkled his forehead. "Why would someone do that?"

"Our waiter, Victor, said Shanna met a man. A man who didn't—" Sheila was about to say *smell right*, but she caught herself and switched to a less odd description. "A man who didn't seem right."

Raoul shrugged his broad shoulders. "I'm sorry, but I do not remember any man." His cheeks rouged. "As far as I can tell, only one person slept in this room while your daughter sailed with us."

Though Sheila would have been the first to applaud if her introverted daughter had indulged in a fling, she was relieved at Raoul's words. Even without seeing Victor's man, she knew he was smelly. She felt it in her heart.

"When do you remember last seeing her? The final day of the cruise? Halfway through? Sometime in between?" Shane's pen hovered over a fresh page in his notebook.

"I'm truly sorry, but I don't remember. We get so many guests, you know?"

A sudden thought came to Sheila, and she shifted to Shane in hope. "What about a tip? If Shanna didn't leave Raoul one, wouldn't that prove she left the ship early? She always tips well."

"She pre-paid her gratuities, remember?" Shane said.

Sheila's face deflated. "Yes, that's right." She rocked forward a few times to propel her exhausted body off the bed and escort Raoul out of the stateroom. "Thank you for your time. We'll let you get back to work. I'm sure you have many rooms left to turndown."

"Oh yes, I'm very busy, this is true." The steward's hand-wringing returned.

Shane was back on his feet as well. "You won't have much to do for us. My Sheila is the neatest traveler around. She doesn't like people picking up after her."

Raoul seemed distressed by this. "But that is my job, sir. I assure you, I'm very good at it." His wide eyes and worried brow reminded Sheila once again of her colleague's words about how hard crew members worked to keep their jobs. "You will tell me if something is not good, yes? Please tell me first. No need to go to my supervisor before me." His speech quickened, and the gray aura of anxiety practically consumed him.

Sheila wrapped her gnarled hands around his, temporarily stilling his wringing. "Oh my dear man, is someone already making your life miserable? On the first day of the cruise?"

Raoul said nothing, but the flash of affirmation in his brown eyes gave Sheila her answer. He quickly resumed his professionalism, however, and opened the door. "Everything is fine, madam. Please, enjoy your cruise." As if remembering that was not what they were there for, he added, "I mean to say, good luck in finding your daughter. If I remember anything I will tell you."

Sheila watched him walk away. Four rooms down on the left, he paused. Given the extra space between the doors, the cabin appeared wider than the McShanes' inside stateroom. Its peripheral location likely afforded it a balcony too. Raoul glanced at the closed door, his hands back to a skin-bruising chafing. When he finally hurried off, Sheila wondered who was inside that had him so worried.

6

DON'T EAT THE MOUSSE

A FULL NIGHT's sleep followed by fifteen minutes of gentle yoga in the narrow space between the bed and the desk rendered Sheila mobile and functional enough to step into the shower. Five minutes of warm water and cherry-almond body wash rinsed the rest of her jet lag away. Fortunately, she hadn't dropped any of the complimentary spa products. Retrieving their slippery bottles from the floor of the compact shower would require no less than a contortionist act.

Holding onto the shower's swinging door, she carefully stepped out. Bathroom falls were common in the elderly, and she was not about to become one of Shane's statistics. She toweled off and began applying her makeup, mindful not to drop anything into the unforgiving toilet. Never in her life had she heard such a frightful, sucking flush. *Thwuuuuuuup.* Any object inhaled into its vacuum would never be seen again. Except maybe by fish.

At least the toilet was clean. Raoul had made sure of that. In fact, the entire stateroom was immaculate. Not an unwanted hair or stain or crumb in sight.

A knock on the bathroom door made her jump. Her hand jerked, and the mascara wand within it streaked her cheek like war paint.

"We have to go, Beetle Bug. The behind-the-scenes tour starts at eight. It's now seven forty-three."

"And sixteen seconds?" Sheila grumbled. "Your continuous countdown isn't helping me move faster." She plucked a tissue from a porcelain box and rubbed the black mark off her face.

"Fifty-two seconds, actually. Well, now fifty-three. And now fifty-four…" Shane's voice trailed off. As Sheila sprayed Foxy Glossy in her silvery hair, she imagined him moving to the cabin door, his hand on the knob, his feet tapping in impatience.

Despite her annoyance at his stringency, she didn't want to be late either. They were about to get an inside view of the ship, not because they were dying to discover its inner workings, though that would indeed be fascinating, but because Shanna had taken the same tour. Their goal was to follow their daughter's footsteps as closely as possible and to query anyone who might have crossed paths with her.

"It's now seven forty-five."

"Read the daily planner while you wait."

"I've already read it three times." Shane's voice was back outside the bathroom door. After a curt knock, he opened it. "We need to— What in the world are you doing?"

Sheila was bent over, her back to him. When she finished her task, she stood to full height, a little woozy from the sudden ascent. "Imagine the time Raoul loses by shaping the ends of everyone's toilet paper into a V. I'm simply helping the poor man out."

Her husband stared at her. After several wordless blinks, he said, "Shall we go?"

They exited the stateroom, Shane dressed in jeans and a button-down shirt sans blazer, notebook and pen already in hand, and Sheila in capri pants and a magenta sweater set that matched her lips. As always, a peanut bar filled one cardigan pocket and a mass of tissues the other. Wanting to be unencumbered by a purse, she had locked it in the room safe earlier, but not before retrieving her phone, which she now slipped into her back pants pocket. She would need it to show Shanna's picture.

Before they got on the elevator to descend to the tour's meeting point, they stopped in the library just beyond it. They knew from their first visit it contained a hot beverage station. Though they had ordered room service for breakfast, both decided additional caffeine was in order. "After all, it's free." Sheila grabbed a paper cup and fitted it with a sleeve.

"Free?" Shane's eyebrows lifted, the wayward salt-and-pepper hairs in need of a visit to the ship's salon. "With the price tag of this cruise, nothing is free."

He was right, Sheila supposed. Still, it felt free, as did grabbing a cookie from The Sweet Spot on deck five or a plump orange from The Juice Bar by the pool.

While Shane poured his coffee, Sheila glanced around the small library. In the corner near the entrance sat a cherry wood desk with a brass name plate announcing *Concierge*. The chair behind the desk was currently empty, just as it had been the day before when they had paused their ship exploration for a nap in the library. Two round tables filled the center of the room, and scattered around the rest of the library were wingback chairs and semicircular pods that looked more like the Pac-Man characters in her son's old arcade game than seats. Though their deep centers and navy cushions made for perfect reading seclusion, Sheila worried if she climbed into one, she would never be able to climb back out.

Seated at one of the tables was a boy of about twelve, along with an older couple. The boy was performing sleight-of-hand movements with coins. He glanced up and caught Sheila watching. "Wanna see a trick?" His grin was full of preadolescent teeth and framed with dimples.

Sheila peeked at Shane's watch. The big digital numbers announced they had less than six minutes before their ship tour started. "I'm sorry, dear, we don't have time. Maybe later."

"Sure. No problem." The kid shifted a Minnesota Twins baseball cap over his thick curls. "Name's Carson. Carson Quick. My stage name, anyway. Look for me. I'll be around."

Sheila cocked her head, but it was Shane who asked the question she was thinking. "Do you work here?"

The scrawny boy laughed. "Nah. I'm here with my family. But I accept tips." He whipped off his hat, held it upside down as if collecting money, and winked. "I'm saving for a trunk for my magic gear."

"Later it is then." Sheila waved goodbye to Carson Quick. Then she and her husband boarded the elevator for a glass-encased descent to the Shipmate Bar, the meeting point for the behind-the-scenes ship tour.

THEIR EXCURSION GUIDE was a bull of a man named Pedro, who said he came from "a Chilean town so small you could spit across it."

With humor and efficiency, he ushered the McShanes and fourteen other guests, mostly middle-aged couples and a few lone males, through long corridors and numerous departments within the *Celestial of the Seas*.

Their first stop was the bridge on deck ten. Officers in spotless uniforms milled around a control desk that was loaded with so many navigational screens and knobs it sent Shane into a nautical tizzy. The same thing happened in the Engine Control Room on deck two, its panels and gauges more enticing to Shane than any woman or fine wine could be. Unfortunately, her husband's childlike fascination kept him from the task at hand: inquiring about their daughter.

Every time Sheila showed Shanna's picture to a crew member, trying to be as unobtrusive as possible to avoid annoying the other tourists, Shane veered off into discussions of engine maintenance (there were four engines and three generators) or water processing (thousands of gallons of seawater per hour were processed into safe drinking water while not in port). By the time the group trailed Pedro to the Environmental Department in the bowels of the ship, Sheila worried Shane had lost complete sight of their mission.

Still, he deserved this cerebral intermission. To her civil-engineer husband, learning about the ship's inner workings was nothing short of nirvana. Besides, so far, none of the crew members had recognized Shanna from her own behind-the-scenes tour back in

June. Why would they? Unlike Shane, their quiet daughter wouldn't have peppered the staff with questions about propulsion systems and fuel consumption, and therefore wouldn't have stood out.

In the Environmental Department, an officer with four gold stripes lined with blue on his epaulets explained the waste management process, using words like *black water*, *gray water*, *solid waste*, and *effluent*, which to Sheila seemed self-explanatory and better off left undefined. When the officer discussed the recycling process, however, and how each crew member was responsible for sorting his or her own garbage and how stateroom attendants did the same for the guests, she listened more closely. She vowed to better separate her trash for Raoul. It was bad enough the man had to fold her toilet paper. He shouldn't have to sort her refuse as well.

When the tour group moved on to the laundry department, a spacious room packed with massive tubs of laundry and machines so big that two would fill Sheila's entire kitchen, they learned that the crew members washed five thousand kilograms of laundry each day, sorting through soiled sheets, dirty towels, and guest clothing hour after hour. As she tried to process those numbers, a crew member rolled another giant tub of towels past her. She wondered if some of them were hers and Shane's, and she had to fight the urge to step forward and assist the young man.

Finally, they made their way to the galley on deck three. Narrow corridors with gray floors painted with red directional arrows took them past bulletin board after bulletin board of safety and procedural posters. A quick peek down the hall of the crew's sleeping quarters revealed cabin doors so closely spaced Sheila was reminded of an institution.

"Most of the crew members sleep on deck zero or deck two," Pedro explained. "Usually four per cabin. But some of the officers are on deck three. And…" he held up a finger, "the luckiest among us have a window." He paused for effect. "I am not one of them."

Many in the group laughed, but Sheila found the joke sad. She supposed the lowest-level rooms were for the lowest-ranked staff. Did that include Raoul? What about their waiters, Renny and Victor? Or even Tina, in all her sommelier perfection? The thought of those dedicated people sleeping in tiny rooms with three other crew members left Sheila feeling guilty. Embarrassed, even. She was privileged and pampered in comparison.

Shane would tell her she was overreacting. "Jobs in the cruise-ship industry are highly sought," he would say. "Their sleeping arrangements are no different than a college dorm." He would then spout a mouthful of statistics, pulling numbers from who knew where. Still, working long hours for months at a time until their contracts ran out had to be difficult. And then, a few weeks later, they started all over again. How heartbreaking to leave one's children, one's spouse, one's home. Frugal or not, Sheila would insist to Shane that they tip them well.

When they finally reached the enormous kitchen galley, Sheila's musings gave way to wonderment, and her mouth dropped open. Never had she seen so much chrome. Chrome counter tops, chrome cabinets, chrome dishwashers, chrome ovens, chrome coolers. Everywhere was a sea of silver. Attached to the upper cabinets and mounted at eye level were dozens of computer screens. According to Pedro, the monitors would display the meal orders of thousands of guests each day.

All around the tour group, kitchen crew darted into coolers or pantries, or whipped up ingredients in giant bowls. Some nodded at the excursion guests. Others went about their work as if they hadn't even noticed them. Dressed in white, the only flash of color they wore was a scarf draped low across their necks. Hierarchy and skill, Pedro explained, determined the scarf's color, from the low-rank yellow scarf of third cook, all the way up to the top-rank black scarf of executive chef.

Despite Sheila's fascination with the kitchen logistics, she worried asking any of these busy workers about her daughter would be impossible. Who among them would have time to chat? Who among them would even remember Shanna?

Before she knew it, they were moving again, this time to the back of the galley, where a counter full of cakes, cookies, and vats of chocolate mousse drew a synchronized chorus of *oohs* and *ahhs*.

Pedro lifted an eyebrow. "Heh heh, looks tasty, si?" He patted his slight paunch. "You can tell how good I am at resisting."

While the group chuckled and made comments about being similarly tempted, Sheila watched a kitchen worker scoop chocolate mousse into dessert glasses and place them on a tray to his left. Farther away on his right, near a door, was another tray off by itself. It was loaded with similar mousse goblets, but unlike the ones on the left, these mousse cups were topped with whipped cream, suggesting they were ready to go. Sheila's mouth watered. Whipped cream was her kryptonite. Though she might not possess Pedro's paunch, she most certainly shared his desire.

He caught her ogling the tantalizing treat. "You like? Surely the kitchen can spare one or two. Or..." He counted the members in the group. "Sixteen."

When Pedro strolled over and picked up a mousse cup from the tray on the right, the prep worker's eyes widened, and he snatched it away. "Oh no, do not take, sir." His English was halting. "Maybe contamination. We discard immediately."

Pedro whistled and lowered the dessert to the tray. "Phew, that was a close one. Pedro has no time for the traveler's trots."

The group laughed, and Pedro told them they would now head to the dining room, where breakfast service would be winding down and the behind-the-scenes tour would be concluded. "There I will tell you how our food service operates. Do you know we can serve up to thirteen hundred guests an hour?"

A murmur went through the small group.

"Plus, we have more than twelve hundred crew members. Do we not need to eat too?" He padded his belly again, which, compared to American standards, was not all that impressive.

"Do you guys eat in the dining room?" a man in the tour group asked.

"No, we have our own space. We're served buffet style and it's very good. It's on deck two near the provisions area, and—" Pedro thumped his head. "Pedro, Pedro, Pedro, what are you doing? I forgot to show you the provisions area on deck two, where we store so much food you will faint at the sight. Come. Come." Pedro clapped his hands. Like good little ducklings, the tour group followed him. When Shane took up the tail end, Sheila pulled him back.

"Maybe we should stay behind," she said. "Ask the kitchen workers if any of them remember seeing Shanna. We won't get another chance back here."

Shane surveyed the commotion around them, skepticism in his face.

"I know it's a long shot, but we have to at least try." Sheila shifted her weight to her left foot. After three hours of behind-the-scenes touring, both of her feet were hollering for a comfy chair, but as usual the right one wailed the most.

By this time, the rest of the group had already rounded a corner and left the main galley. Shane bit the side of his lip. "I don't think we're supposed to be in here on our own."

Moments after he said the words, Tina, the sommelier who had been so swift and efficient with them the night before, entered from the door near the dessert counter, only a dozen feet from where the McShanes now stood. Not wanting to be seen by the woman, Sheila yanked Shane's sleeve and pulled him behind a tall, chrome cart, the kind used to stack dinner trays. Through its metal slats, they watched Tina steal furtive glances around the vicinity, including at the dessert cook who was busy slicing a cake and seemed not to notice her. With the reflexes of a cat burglar, she swiped one of the chocolate mousse goblets from the tray that was meant to be discarded.

Sheila inhaled. To her left, Shane grimaced. Torn between wanting to warn the sommelier the mousse had gone bad and not wanting to be discovered, Sheila wasn't sure what to do. She and Shane hadn't yet had a chance to inquire about Shanna, and if Tina discovered them there alone, she would make them leave.

Sheila's Good Samaritan struggle soon became a moot point. Tina grabbed a spoon from beneath the counter and began shoveling mousse into her mouth as if she hadn't eaten in days. When she walked to a counter a few feet away and dumped the empty glass into a tub of dirty dishes, she glanced in the McShanes' direction behind the cart. For a moment Sheila worried the sommelier had spotted them, but when the woman exited the galley, they felt safe to step out.

"That was close." Sheila's hand covered her drumming heart. "But that poor dear, what if she gets sick?" She plucked her phone from the back pocket of her capri pants and pulled up Shanna's image on the screen. "We better hurry before they kick us out."

For the next fifteen minutes they went from kitchen staff to kitchen staff, asking crew members of both genders from all over the world if anyone had seen their daughter. Every time galley workers shook their heads or said no, Sheila's heart sank deeper. Most seemed puzzled by their presence, and several said, "You should not be here." Whenever they offered to help escort the couple out, Sheila and Shane rushed off, using the excuse that they were just leaving to join the rest of the behind-the-scenes tour group. Once they were in a different part of the galley, they would find a new crew member to query. When they started to see the same faces, they knew they were running out of people to ask.

"I think we better call it a day." Shane's cheeks sagged, and his neck and shoulders carried an uncharacteristic slouch.

Sheila's fatigue was just as pronounced. "Let's try that man over there and then go to lunch. After we eat, we can nap."

Together they approached a man chopping vegetables on a massive cutting board. Piles of carrots, zucchini, and bell peppers formed mounds all around his work area. He turned toward them, and from his name badge Sheila saw he was Michael from Uganda. His aura suggested helpfulness but also a mischievous nature.

"Hi, Michael. We're Sheila and Shane McShane." Sheila held up her phone. "This will sound strange, but do you recognize our daughter? Her name is Shanna, and—"

Michael bellowed a hearty laugh, and both McShanes stepped back in surprise. When he saw their expressions, he said, "Forgive me. I am sorry. But your names." He chuckled again, and in doing so, his knife knocked over a pile of chopped red peppers.

"Our names?" Sheila lowered her phone.

"Sheila, Shane, and Shanna McShane? That does not seem funny to you?"

"Well, perhaps it's—"

"Do you have a son? Is his name Sean?" The man grabbed a large carrot and chortled while he chopped."

"Why, no, his name is Paul."

Michael stopped chopping. He frowned at her. "Well, that one is not funny at all. Why did you not give him the *sh* sound?"

"Because he looked like a Paul."

Confusion clouded Michael's face. "Wait, why are you here? Where did you come from?"

"We're from Sherry, New Hampshire."

Once again, and just as unexpectedly, the cook burst out laughing. "That is not what I meant, but oohwee, that is funny too." He slapped his thigh, fortunately with the hand not brandishing a knife. "Sheila, Shane, and Shanna McShane from Sherry, New Hampshire. You Americans, you are funny, no?"

Sheila fluffed the bottom of her hair. She was starting to reassess Michael's helpfulness. She refreshed her phone's screen and raised it once again. "Our daughter. Have you seen her? She took this same tour about eight weeks ago, but she never returned home from your ship. That means she's been missing for at least six weeks, longer if she disappeared before the two-week cruise was over." No matter how many times she spoke the words *missing* and *disappeared*, they always pierced her tongue like glass.

Michael's good humor vanished. "Oh, I am very sorry." He lowered the knife and examined the picture of Shanna on Sheila's phone. He shook his head. "I do not recognize her. I do not interact with the guests so much."

Sheila sighed. "I understand. Thank you. If you—"

"There they are."

A woman's voice cut Sheila off. She and Shane pivoted around and found Tina in front of them. Standing at her side was Officer Tad, the security guard with the floppy earlobes.

"I *thought* I saw them in the galley." The sommelier crossed her arms and tapped a foot, her blue cloud of efficiency on full display.

"You didn't believe me, but see? I was right." She softened her tone and addressed the McShanes as if they were children. "You cannot be wandering around here on your own. There are safety issues. You could get hurt."

"She's right, you know." The security guard's British accent made him sound smarter than he looked. "What are you doing in here?" Though not said unkindly, Sheila could tell the young man was annoyed.

She hid her phone in her cardigan pocket, its heft weighing down the fabric. "I'm sorry. We were just..." A better schmoozer than liar, Sheila struggled for an explanation.

Shane took over. "We were with the behind-the-scenes tour, but we got separated. Our guide said something about going to the provisions area, but we can't seem to find it." Shane looked around the kitchen, as if still searching.

Tina uncrossed her arms and straightened her tailored blazer. "The provisions area is on deck two. You are on deck three." This time, she enunciated each word as if Sheila and Shane were senile dolts. Michael, on the other hand, leaned against the counter next to his piles of chopped vegetables, seemingly amused by the exchange.

Shane made a dopey face and turned his palms upward. "I guess we got lost."

If Officer Tad and Tina knew anything about Shane, they would know he never got lost. Ever. He was the king of maps. But fortunately, they didn't know Shane. As a result, Tad gave him a sympathetic nod of understanding. To further sell the lie, Sheila put the back of her hand against her forehead. "I'm feeling a bit confused."

Tad gently grabbed Sheila's arm and guided her away, Shane at their side. "I'm going to take your word for it." He opened the main galley door and ushered them down a hallway toward the dining room, where the rest of the tour group was probably long gone. "But no more poking around in places you're not supposed to be, okay?" He paused for a moment and stared at them. Though Sheila could tell he was going for stern, all she could see was somebody's floppy-eared grandson. She bit back a smile. "This ship could be a dangerous place for an elderly couple. Understood?"

She refrained from rolling her eyes. "Understood."

As if to make sure they did, Officer Floppy Ears escorted them all the way up to deck ten, not leaving their side until they were halfway down the corridor to their stateroom.

Over her shoulder, Sheila watched him disappear around the corner back toward the stairwell. "Well, that seemed unnecessary. It's not as if we're children."

Shane yawned, which in turn made Sheila yawn, which in turn made Shane yawn again. "Maybe we better take a nap before lunch instead of after it," he said.

Sheila agreed, but as they neared their stateroom, raised voices broke out of a cabin four rooms down from their own on the other side of the hallway. It was the same room she had seen Raoul pause outside of the evening before.

When they reached it, she hesitated. The door was cracked open an inch, and despite the arguing (or maybe because of it), she couldn't resist peeking inside. What she saw shocked her. Tossed clothes, discarded food wrappers, soda and beer cans on the floor, contents spilling onto the carpet. And that was only a one-inch view. She hated to think what the rest of the room looked like.

Also in her line of sight was Raoul's shoulder, or at least she assumed it was Raoul's, because she recognized his voice and the maroon uniform. With an anxious tone, he repeated "yes, madam" and "yes, sir" over and over again.

"Do you know why we were upgraded to a veranda room?" a woman yipped.

"I do not." Raoul's voice trembled.

"We got it because on the last Dreamline Cruise we took, someone stole stuff from our suitcases when the bags were outside the door." Though Sheila couldn't see what the woman looked like, given her biting tone pointy incisors and claws seemed a reasonable guess.

She threw Shane a chagrined look. He too seemed bothered by

the dispute, but when she made to open the door and storm inside, he held her back.

"But Raoul needs our help."

Shane shook his head in warning. She fisted her gnarled hands and peered into the crack again.

A whiny male voice was now speaking, but Sheila couldn't see its source. "You guys shouldn't make people put their suitcases out the night before departure. We lost valuable stuff." Like the woman's, his accent was American, which made Sheila's face heat in shame.

"I'm very sorry to hear that." Raoul sounded desperate to escape. Sheila imagined him wringing his hands raw. "Please, tell me what I can do to make your stay a pleasant one."

"Just do your job and—" The woman's voice, which seemed frighteningly close to the door now, suddenly cut off. An eyeball, accompanied by a penciled-in eyebrow, half a pale forehead, and a mess of blond curls, stared back at Sheila.

"Oh." Sheila gasped and jumped back.

The eye beyond the door narrowed, and an unseen hand slammed the cabin door shut.

With an energy Sheila hadn't known their old bones possessed, she and her husband scurried four doors down to their own room. Shane fumbled and patted his pockets, looking for his key card.

"Hurry, hurry." Sheila fished around in her own pockets. Tissues went flying. At first she was tense. Then her face relaxed. Then she smiled and started giggling. She couldn't help it. The situation had been so bizarre.

Soon Shane was laughing alongside her, and when he finally found his card and opened the stateroom door, they practically tripped into the room. They plopped down onto the bed together. The action was so swift Sheila nearly bounced back off. Shane grabbed her, and their laughing fit escalated. Sheila held her sides from the ache, but it was a good ache. An ache both of them needed. She hadn't laughed this hard since Dr. Shakir had let a pediatric patient play with his stethoscope, only to find boogers all over it later.

When their laughter finally died down, they sank fully onto the mattress.

She kicked off her shoes. "That tour wore me out."

Shane yawned. "Me too. When Dreamline Cruises says they put the Snooze in Cruise, they really mean it."

Another small giggle from them both.

"I feel sorry for Raoul though," Sheila said. "Those people were awful. He doesn't deserve to be spoken to with such vitriol. He's a good man."

"You've only met him once." Shane's words were swallowed by another yawn.

"I still know he's a good man." Her eyelids grew heavy. "No wonder he was so anxious last night. And to think it's only day two of the cruise." She closed her eyes. "He has eleven more days with those terrible people."

She heard Shane yawn again, but if he said anything else, she didn't catch it. She slipped closer to sleep, thinking first of poor Raoul and then of her daughter. They had learned nothing new from the morning tour that would help them find her. All traces of earlier levity disappeared. In its place came sadness, a sadness Sheila had been cloaked in for weeks.

Her last thought before sleep was a question.

Where are you, my dear daughter?

7

CLUES COME TO THOSE WHO WAIT

DAY three on the *Celestial of the Seas* began much the same way as day two: with yoga and toilet paper folding by Sheila, followed by a tasty breakfast for both the McShanes, albeit this one up on deck fourteen where a buffet served from eight bountiful food stations offered everything from sizzling slices of bacon to spicy international cuisine.

"Do you smell those heavenly waffles? They're calling my name." Sheila followed her nose in their direction, Shane on her heels. Hordes of people darted around them. "If only it wasn't so crowded."

Shane seemed oblivious to the masses, focused only on his first meal of the day. As always, Sheila envied his ability to tune out everything but the task at hand. Shanna, on the other hand, would have abhorred the throngs of guests. She did better one-on-one, or at most in a small group.

In front of the waffle station, Sheila watched a man plop three pancakes onto a plate piled so high with ham, scrambled eggs, and hash browns that food tumbled over the side and onto the floor. He trampled right over it, his sneakers leaving smeared trails of egg behind.

"How crass the crew must find us tourists," she murmured. Still, despite the poor behavior of some of her fellow passengers, she was in good spirits. Before breakfast, she had attended the Rise and Shine Yoga class in the fitness center on deck twelve. Eighty years old or not, she could still move her body. It might comply less and creak more than it used to, but it still functioned, and by God she meant to keep it that way. Shane had his gardening. She had her yoga.

Stretching her limbs hadn't been the only reason for the early-morning visit to the gym. She wanted to ask the staff about Shanna. Her daughter was a fitness enthusiast who worked out every day. She would have visited the facilities often. Unfortunately, the three gym employees Sheila queried hadn't sailed on Shanna's voyage and therefore knew nothing about her.

After breakfast, Sheila and Shane headed to the meeting point for their first excursion off the ship, Shane with his backpack, Sheila with her purse, and both with their raincoats and umbrellas. Shane had decided to use the umbrella hanging in the stateroom closet rather than his own. With its heft and pointy tip, he said it made for a good walking stick, not that he needed one.

When the tourist group lined up to exit at the gangway, their key cards ready to be scanned for proof they had left the ship (and by some miracle, Sheila and Shane found theirs on the first try), she asked the two agents manning the podiums if they recognized Shanna. "We see so many passengers, madam," a polite junior officer from Turkey said. "I do not remember her."

By nine forty-five they were seated in the second row of the coach that would drive them through the Scottish countryside to Inverness, and then on to the Urquhart Castle ruins near the famous Loch Ness. Despite the somber purpose of their cruise, Sheila was excited for the day ahead. She and her husband were about to visit locales they had only dreamed of in the past.

Her spirits dampened, however, when neither their bubbly tour guide nor the taciturn coach driver recognized Shanna from her picture. Though highly sympathetic, the guide had been on vacation the week Shanna visited the castle ruins. As for the coach driver, he only started working with the tour agency the month before. The double strikeout worried Sheila. What if the entire trip passed without any new information about Shanna, beyond Victor's mention of Mr. Smelly?

Still, the beautiful terrain of Scotland was not lost on her. With Shane by her side, jotting away in his notebook, she stared out the bus window. Hills studded with evergreens gave way to golden fields of crops and then to emerald pastures. On both sides of the highway, sheep grazed contentedly on grasses and wildflowers, seemingly unfazed by the overcast sky and drizzle.

All the while, their lyrical tour guide cited facts about the Black Isles, Scottish agriculture, and whiskey distilleries. "There are more than a hundred distilleries in Scotland," she said. "How marvelous for us, don't you think?" Laughter filtered up the aisles, and even Shane seemed to enjoy the ensuing tales of soothsayers, witches, and the Loch Ness monster, though he would, of course, believe none of it.

"Right then. Let's be on the lookout for Nessie when we get to the lake this afternoon," the guide chirped into her microphone. "You never know when you'll spot her long neck or big humps sticking out of the lake."

Three hours later, after touring and lunching in the charming city of Inverness, whose buildings bore the pink-red sandstone of the Black Isles's Tarradale Quarry, Sheila and Shane stood shivering along the shore of Loch Ness. The remains of the thirteenth-century Urquhart Castle towered on hilly land behind them. Wind whipped their raincoats, and rain spattered any exposed skin. As they strolled the pebbly shore, water lapped at their shoes.

Sheila cinched both her hood and umbrella more tightly and gazed out over the picturesque lake to the rolling hills beyond. She did not look for Nessie. She did not wonder about the castle ruins around her. Instead, she thought about her daughter.

Had Shanna stood in this very spot two months ago, the weather perhaps more forgiving? Had she swept her gaze over the water to look for the monster's flesh? (Skeptically, of course. After all, she was her father's daughter.) Had she connected with any of her fellow tourists or had she walked the shore alone?

Sheila absorbed the quiet beauty around her, still not quite believing she was in Scotland, the home of Shane's paternal ancestors. But she saw no sign of the monster. Or Shanna.

What a fanciful idea she and her husband had hatched, she thought. Taking the same cruise as their daughter in hopes of stumbling upon her path. How silly it sounded to her now. Even the wind seemed to mock her, whistling words in her ears: "You're a foolish old woman." Their odds at finding Nessie were probably better.

When they boarded the coach to return to the ship, tired and damp and chilled to the bone, Sheila decided day three of the cruise was a bust. Though a lovely, once-in-a-lifetime experience, the excursion had yielded nothing useful. No new information with which to plan their next move in finding Shanna.

Furthermore, during dinner, neither of their waiters, Victor nor Renny, had anything new to add. Both were too busy to even chat. When Tina approached with their wine, she said nothing about finding them in the galley the day before. In turn, they said nothing about her devouring spoiled chocolate mousse like a starving dog. After dinner, they turned in early, taking no advantage of the theater shows, the bands, the trivia games, the noisy casino.

Neither one felt up to it.

Day four of their cruise was the first of two days in Edinburgh. Given Shanna had not planned to purchase any of the ship's tours for Edinburgh but instead wanted to visit the city on her own via the hop-on/hop-off buses, they would do the same. For the thousandth time, Sheila gave thanks for both Shane and Shanna's attention to detail. It was that need to plan everything out to the minute, combined with Shane's interest in Shanna's trip, that had afforded them her exact itinerary. Of course, nothing said Shanna stuck to it, but for now, it was the only thing they had to go on.

Unfortunately, their bad luck from the day before continued.

After a miserable tender ride into the port, where for twenty minutes Sheila and Shane and forty other human sardines rocked and rolled over ocean waves in an airless orange container, they boarded a hop-on/hop-off bus to travel around the city. As they made their stops, rain pelted their hoods, and crowds pelted their spirits, especially at Edinburgh Castle, where they could barely find their footing let alone find staff members to ask about Shanna. If only they were twenty years younger. Realizing the futility of their mission, they returned to the ship earlier than planned. Though the city was one of the most beautiful Sheila had ever seen, she was damp, tired, and hungry. To make matter's worse, on the return tender ride to the ship, she sat knee-to-knee across from a man whose breath smelled worse than a corpse's. The only bright spot was climbing out of the tender—which, at her age, took the help of two crew members to achieve—and finding ship staff distributing cups of hot chocolate to returning guests. Renny, the assistant waiter from the dining room, was one of them, his darling face pink from the cold.

Sheila smiled when she saw him. "You're a multitasking young man."

"Yes, I do a little bit of everything around here." His gold radiance was as vibrant as ever.

She wrapped her stiff fingers around the cup of heat he handed her. "Ah, that's much better."

After they drank their hot chocolate and discarded the paper cups in the trash barrel outside the gangway, they ascended to the checkpoint and proceeded through security. Back in the warmth of the ship, they headed to the elevators.

"I don't think I can take another day of that." She was referring to both the weather and the tender ride.

The elevator door dinged open, and they stepped inside, but not before anxiety blanched Shane's face. "But we have to go to the Scottish National Gallery. That's how Shanna spent the second day in Edinburgh, or at least it is if she stuck to her schedule. We have a much better chance of finding someone who spoke to her there. That's where she would interact with—"

"Shh, shh, you're right." Sheila rubbed his arm. She hadn't meant to worry him with any plan deviation. Although he didn't always vocalize it, she knew finding Shanna occupied his every waking thought. Probably his sleeping ones too. "Don't worry. We'll go back tomorrow. I'll be better after a yummy dinner and a long night's sleep."

"Yes, good, that will help." Though his color returned, his hand still trembled when he pushed the elevator button for deck ten.

"Wait, darling." Sheila pressed the number five button as well. "Let's stop and get you some coffee and a snack. You look like you could use more than Renny's little cocoa treat."

The midship of deck five was a glitzy shopping promenade. Its stores displayed high-end purses, clothing, and jewelry. So far, Sheila had only graced its glossy tiles once: on day two during their full day at sea. Although she had enjoyed seeing the pretty displays, she hadn't enjoyed the pushy salespeople outside.

This afternoon the shops were closed. They wouldn't reopen until the ship left port. Outside the boutiques, returning passengers, many of whom could be heard complaining about the tender rides, were milling about. Sheila and Shane had to sidestep and skirt in order to reach the bar beyond the last shop.

Nearby, in a circular foyer with paneled walls, a man in a suit and tie was arranging framed paintings on easels in the center of the room. Other artwork leaned against the walls. A few small tables, flanked by leather chairs, completed the cozy decor.

"I'll be over there," Sheila said, leaving Shane's side.

While he fetched the coffee, she browsed the paintings. When she stepped back for a better view of a mother and daughter strolling on a beach, she collided with the man setting up the room.

"Ooof," she cried, losing her balance. Had he not caught her, she would have fallen on the marble floor.

Tall and slim with hair the color of the sand along Loch Ness, he made sure she was upright before letting go. "Are you all right?" His accent sounded Scandinavian.

"Yes, I think so. Thank you for keeping me from shattering a hip." Breathless from the scare, she started brushing at the man's suit. "I'm so sorry, my raincoat got you wet."

He smiled. "My clothes are fine. It's me who should apologize. I should have watched where I was stepping." His name badge read *Josef* and indicated he was from Sweden.

Sheila waved a hand at the paintings. "What are all these for?"

"The ship's auctions. There'll be two this sailing."

Shane joined them and handed Sheila a sleeved cup of coffee. Steam wafted from the sip hole. "These are for the auctions, Shaney. I wonder if Shanna attended the ones on her trip." At the thought, she thrust the coffee back at Shane, secured her soggy umbrella under her arm, and fished through her purse for her phone, her cold finger joints stiff and uncooperative. Finally, she retrieved it and pulled up Shanna's picture. "Do you recognize this woman?" Her breathing was still uneven, but this time from hope.

The Swedish man narrowed his eyes in concentration, and when he did, a mole revealed itself on his forehead, just below his side-swept bangs. "Indeed I do."

For the first time all day, Sheila felt a spark of vigor. "She's our daughter. We're looking for her."

"On the ship? Now?" He seemed confused. "I remember her from a past sailing."

"Yes, yes, that's her." Sheila's excitement grew.

Shane, who had been looking beyond Josef at the paintings, seemed similarly revived. "What do you remember?"

The man shifted a still-life painting on its easel. He hesitated. "I remember she didn't think much of our artwork. Why do you ask?"

"Because she might have gone missing from your ship," Shane said. "We're looking for her."

Josef's hand lingered on the framed painting. His expression saddened. "I'm very sorry. Truly I am. But you should be talking to our ship's security staff, not me."

"We have, but they were no help." Sheila tried to keep the pleading out of her voice. "Please, any details you can give us might be helpful."

The auction attendant pushed back the flap of hair on his forehead, his mole visible once again. "Well, the only reason I remember her is because she was…" He paused, as if trying to choose his words carefully. "Well, she and her companion were strolling around the paintings, pointing and—"

"Companion? She was with someone? Who? What did he look like? Was it before or after dinner?" Sheila's questions poured out so quickly the man took a step back.

Shane placed his coffee on a nearby table and pulled his notebook and pen from the pocket of his raincoat. He started writing.

"It was late afternoon," Josef said. "I remember because I was very hungry and thinking about dinner. I'm not sure he was actually her companion at that point though. Maybe that was a bad choice of words. In fact, I think they had just met."

"What makes you say that?" Sheila asked.

Uncertainty waffled on his face. "Maybe I should direct you back to security."

"Please. Why do you think they had just met?"

"Your daughter was shaking her head at one of our paintings when the man I mentioned came up behind her. He pointed to it, and whatever he said made her laugh. Then he did the same with some of the other artwork, and she laughed even more." Josef again seemed to search for the right words. "I don't want to offend you, but their behavior was rather rude, condescending even, like they were making fun of the paintings."

Sheila rushed to her daughter's defense. "Shanna is an art restorer in Boston. I'm sure she didn't mean to be uppity. She just has high standards when it comes to art."

Josef seemed to consider that. "I suppose that would make her an excellent critic."

"But again, what makes you think they'd just met?" Sheila asked.

"The man appeared to be introducing himself. He extended his hand, and your daughter shook it."

"Did you get his name?" Sheila asked breathlessly.

Shane's pen was poised and ready.

"No. I wasn't close enough to hear every word."

Sheila sighed and sank against one of the leather chairs. She'd been on her feet too long.

"But when I walked over to ask if I could answer any questions for them, I heard his voice. He sounded Australian. Or maybe from New Zealand, I'm not sure, but I would guess Australian. He mentioned his interest in art, and he suggested your daughter visit some museums with him. Said he was a frequent visitor to the UK and would be happy to show her around. He seemed to be flirting."

"Was that in Edinburgh? If so, which day?"

Though Shane had asked the question, Sheila knew that if Shanna had stuck with her plan of visiting Edinburgh Castle and other tourist sites on day one, and the museums on day two, she must have met the man on their first evening in Edinburgh. That would fit with Victor's account as well, because although the waiter hadn't remembered which day in Edinburgh he had first seen Shanna dine with the spiritually smelly man, he remembered it was that city.

"Hmm, let me think." Josef put a finger over his lips and looked up at the domed ceiling. "I remember your daughter said she had visited Edinburgh Castle and was looking forward to seeing the museums." His eyebrows shot up. "So yes, that would mean it was day one."

Sheila pushed away from the chair and squeezed Shane's arm in excitement. "That's now *two* crew members who saw Shanna with Mr. Smelly. Plus, now we know they met in the late afternoon on the fourth day of the cruise." Were her knees thirty years younger, she would have leaped onto the table and boogied.

"I'm sorry?" Josef blinked. "Mr. Smelly?"

Sheila touched her nose. "Our waiter said Shanna met a man who didn't smell right."

Josef's nostrils twitched. "I didn't notice any odor."

"Not that kind of odor."

Shane paused his pen. "Can you tell us what this man looked like? Just to make sure it was the same man our waiter saw?"

"He was around your height." Josef glanced at Shane, who stood five feet, nine inches. "But he was muscular. Dark hair, blue eyes, a broken nose poorly set, like a boxer might have. I would guess him to be in his mid to late forties."

Though Josef didn't share Victor's dreamy look, to Sheila, the descriptions sounded similar.

"Thank you so much, Josef. You've helped us tremendously." She hugged the Swedish man in gratitude. At first he seemed embarrassed, but when she blinked away tears, he clutched her hands. "I hope you find her." His expression suggested he meant it.

She and Shane departed. In their excited haste, they left their coffee behind, but she no longer needed it. She had enough adrenaline in her blood to wake up an army.

"We need to see security again," she said. Shane nodded, and after sixty years of marriage, she had no doubt he knew exactly what she was thinking. "We have to insist they show us the video footage. Not only to see what Mr. Smelly looks like, but to see if and when she left the ship with him."

In front of her, Shane kept nodding like a bobblehead, his notebook and pen still clutched in one hand, his umbrella in the other. He marched past the boutiques toward the elevators so swiftly she nearly had to run to keep up with him. But she ignored the pain in her feet. She ignored the heaviness of her still-damp raincoat. She ignored the pressure of a bladder long past its empty date.

Because they now had a solid lead. Victor had mentioned a man, and now with Josef they had a second witness.

They knew three things: Mr. Smelly had been flirting with Shanna; he had voiced an interest in art, which was the only thing that would win Shanna over so quickly; and he had probably visited Edinburgh's art museum with her.

Surely the security team would let them confirm it.

8

THE CAMERA NEVER LIES

SHEILA WAS NEVER one to experience sweaty palms, especially at her age with hands more like parchment paper than flesh, but she wiped them on her linen trousers all the same. At eight thirty in the morning on day five of their cruise, she and Shane were back in the security office on deck two. After a heated discussion the evening before, followed by a call to the captain, the chief of security had finally relented to showing them the security footage from Shanna's trip.

Seated in the same bland room at the same round table with the same three uniformed officers, they waited to begin. Shane was to her left, his notebook and multi-tool pen on his lap. On a fresh page, he had already documented the date, time, and occupants in the room. To her right was the Croatian security officer, Niko, or Officer Gorgeous as she had taken to calling him in her mind. Personalized nicknames were easier for her to remember. Actual names sometimes slipped through her mind like confetti, especially in times of stress. Ivan, the head of security, AKA Officer Sourpuss, leaned against the wall, his arms crossed and his rimless glasses perched low on his nose. His grumpy gaze never left the McShanes. The third security guard, Tad (Officer Floppy Ears to Sheila), balanced sideways on the edge of the table next to Shane, one skinny cheek on, one skinny cheek off. In the middle of the table sat a laptop, from which Tad was accessing a file.

Sheila had imagined they would be watching the footage in a room full of monitors: six, eight, twelve screens displaying different parts of the ship on CCTV. When she said as much to Ivan, he snorted. "This is not crime show on TV. You are civilian. You get USB flash drive and laptop." With the Ukrainian accent, his irritation seemed even more pronounced.

"I'm grateful for anything you'll show us," she said, her voice more timid than provocative at the moment. "Thank you for letting us see the footage."

Officer Sourpuss rubbed his knuckles over his salt-and-pepper hair. "Well, it is not like you gave us much choice. Last night, you make threat to jump overboard and swim to American embassy if we do not."

The young Officer Floppy Ears laughed, but upon seeing the glare from his superior officer, he turned it into a throat clearing. His gaze went back to the laptop, where he awaited further instruction.

"That was dramatic, even for me," Sheila acknowledged, "but the information we received about this smell—er, I mean—this strange man who befriended our daughter makes it all the more important we watch your tapes."

Ivan removed his glasses and rolled one of the metal arms between his thumb and index finger. As if Sheila hadn't spoken, he said, "You also threatened to spread word over 'the Twitter' and 'the Facebook' that we refused to help you find 'suspicious man' involved in your daughter's disappearance. Threats are not a good way to make friends, Mrs. McShane."

Redness glowed around the security chief's body, an angry, crimson aura Sheila hadn't seen since her son's childhood tantrums. But Officer Sourpuss wasn't finished. "You also said if we did not allow access to video, you would make us look worse than airline who drags passenger from seat."

Sheila smoothed her cardigan and inhaled some much-needed chi. "We just—"

"Want to find our daughter." Shane pulled a folded piece of paper from his blazer pocket and smoothed it open on the table. It was Shanna's excursion itinerary, which, of course, matched their own.

For the first time, Niko, AKA Officer Gorgeous, spoke. "We want the same. But what my superior officer means is that it would be best if we work together."

Though she was tempted to remind him that was exactly what she and Shane had asked for on day one, she held back. Instead, she fluffed her wispy but coifed hair and smiled. "Then we're in agreement on something."

"Come on." Ivan flicked his hand at Tad, as if he had no more time to waste. "Let us get rolling."

Officer Floppy Ears nodded. In his British inflection, he said, "To ensure the privacy of past guests, I put together a video that includes only the footage of your daughter getting on and off the ship. That took time, of course, and that's why we couldn't show it to you last night when you asked."

"Asked. Ha," Ivan muttered. "More like demanded."

Sheila twisted her faux pearls. Footage only of Shanna coming and going? She didn't like the sound of that. "But what if something happened on the ship that we should know about?"

"Nothing happened on ship." Ivan's retort made Sheila jump. "As I already told you, both we and land authorities went through video footage many times. This," he waved his fingers at the laptop, "is pure courtesy. We know your daughter did not go missing from ship."

"But—"

Shane put a hand on her arm. She bit her tongue and exhaled any chi she had collected. She nodded at Officer Floppy Ears. "Thank you for putting this together."

Tad smiled. "You're most welcome. I handle all the CCTV work." His coloring was particularly purple this morning, indicating he was in tune with their needs. Maybe, as his name suggested, he was a gift from God, after all.

Officer Sourpuss was a different matter. Not wanting to inflame him further, lest he scoop up the laptop and bolt out the door, she framed her next question delicately. "Two of your crew members remember seeing Shanna with the same man, a dark-haired man with an Australian accent. Remember I mentioned him to you last night? Did you know about him, and if so, did you question him?" She kept her tone as non-accusatory as possible. If Ivan's aura glowed any redder, he would need sunscreen.

"Your daughter talked to many people on ship. We questioned who we needed to." Ivan approached the table. "You want to tell me my job too?"

Shane stopped writing and put a protective arm around Sheila. "Please don't speak so harshly to my wife. She only wants to know what happened to Shanna. We both do."

As before, Officer Gorgeous smoothed things over, his English flawless and his orange halo exuding warmth and confidence. "My boss means no disrespect. He feels terrible your daughter is missing. We all do. We investigated your daughter's disappearance thoroughly. He speaks merely out of frustration." Niko glanced up at his superior.

Ivan rammed his glasses back on, nodded, and, like a fed-up Ukrainian grandmother, muttered a guttural *achhh*. Still, there was something in his expression that suggested Niko's words were true, that the security chief's irritable behavior stemmed from his inability to find Shanna for them.

Officer Floppy Ears broke the silence. "Ready?"

Sheila pried her hands from her slacks, unaware until now how tense her body had become. She lowered her shoulders and rested her palms on the table. Next to her, Shane withdrew his arm and raised his notebook and pen. His troubled gaze caught hers, and she imagined that he, too, was bracing himself to see Shanna on camera.

And indeed, when their daughter first popped up on the laptop screen, Sheila caught her breath at the sight. Grainy footage or not, other than photographs and a home video, it was the first time she had seen Shanna in almost two months. There she was—the back of her, anyway—in muted color, holding her key card in front of the security camera at the ship's checkpoint, just as Sheila and Shane had done in both Inverness and Edinburgh.

Tad's finger hovered above the laptop's touchpad. "Are you okay, ma'am? We don't have to do this if it's too difficult."

"Yes we do," Sheila and Shane blurted simultaneously. Nothing could keep them from watching this footage. Sheila added, "I'm fine. It was just a shock."

"Okay then. See here?" Officer Floppy Ears pushed the laptop closer to the McShanes.

Sheila reached for the reading glasses in her purse and slipped them on for a sharper image.

"This is your daughter getting off on day three in Inverness. You can see she is leaving alone."

Sheila nodded. In the video, Shanna wore skinny jeans with a dark raincoat. Her long reddish-brown hair, blown out straight, swished over her shoulders as she descended the gangway. She disappeared from view.

Shane held up a hand and asked Tad to pause the video. He wanted to document everything. Watching him write, Sheila saw he recorded the stop, Shanna's clothing, the time stamp on the video, even a brief description of the crew member who checked her out. When he finished, Officer Gorgeous took over for Tad, his seat at the table affording him a better view of the screen. "Here your daughter is returning from Inverness. Alone again."

Sheila watched the video as Shanna removed her cross-body purse from around her neck and shoulder and placed it on the x-ray belt. When she displayed her key card to the scanner near the crew member behind the security podium, he waved her through the metal detector. Seconds later, she was out of camera range.

It was enough time, however, for Sheila to gauge Shanna's mood. To those who didn't know Shanna, her affect on the screen would seem flat, but to Sheila, despite the video's subpar quality, Shanna's expression looked relaxed, as if she had experienced a good day at Loch Ness. Sheila said as much to Shane, and he jotted down her thoughts.

When Shane finished writing, Niko continued. "Next we have

day one in Edinburgh. As before, your daughter gets off and on alone."

Dressed again in her raincoat and skinny pants but this time with her hair in a ponytail, Shanna no longer looked content. At least not upon her return to the ship. Her raincoat dripped water, and her face was pinched, probably less from the rain and more from the rocking, cheek-to-cheek tender ride she had just endured.

"And here she is leaving the ship alone on the second day in Edinburgh." Officer Gorgeous pointed at the screen unnecessarily.

"Look, Shaney. She's wearing a hat and no raincoat. There must have been sunshine that day."

Against the wall, out of Sheila's line of vision, Officer Sourpuss sighed heavily. She imagined him checking his watch.

When Shanna stepped onto the metal plank to exit the ship, Sheila called out, "Wait."

Startled, Niko paused the video.

She pulled the laptop closer. "Look. Look at that man."

In the frozen image, a man in a long-sleeved but tight-fitting T-shirt scanned his key card to leave the ship. Sheila pointed to the screen, her finger trembling. "He has dark hair. He's muscular. He looks about your height, Shane." She turned toward her husband, her eyes wide. "That's Mr. Smelly."

Tad crinkled his nose, which, unlike his floppy ears, was proportional to his face. "Mr. Smelly?"

Officer Sourpuss stomped up to the table. "I have no time for this."

Sheila held her ground and forged on. "He's the man I told you about last night and again just a few minutes ago. Please, Officer Niko, replay the tape, but slowly this time." The mysterious man's back was mostly to the camera, and she hoped for a better view of his face.

Niko shot a glance to Tad and then to Ivan, who was now pacing the room. She supposed they thought her a silly old woman. Maybe she was, but she had to at least try. To his credit, Officer Gorgeous obliged, but he had barely pressed *play* when Sheila shouted for him to stop the tape again.

The man she was convinced was Mr. Smelly had turned to look at something over his shoulder, making three-fourths of his face visible on the screen. Worried she might not get a better view, she pulled out her phone, tapped on the camera, and snapped a photo of the frozen image.

"No, no, you cannot do that." Officer Sourpuss rushed up to the table and thumped the wood with his fist. "Delete photo."

When Tad saw the man on the screen, he nodded vigorously in agreement. "Privacy issues, you know. We have a responsibility to our guests. This man is not a suspect. He is simply another guest on the cruise."

"But have you spoken to Victor, our waiter? Or your auctioneer attendant?" Sheila fumbled with her phone, her reading glasses slipping down her nose. "They—"

"No," Ivan barked. "Delete photo now or I turn off rest of footage. Nothing here says that man knows your daughter. They passed through at same time, that is all. Watch more and you will see."

"Okay, okay. My heavens, I'm sorry." Sheila deleted the photo, and when Officer Sourpuss asked to see proof that she had deleted it, she showed him her phone. What he didn't know, however, was that while they were crabbing at her, she had copied the picture before she got rid of it. A simple press on the screen and a click on the *copy* icon did the trick. As soon as she and Shane left the security department, she would paste the photo into an email to herself and log onto the internet to send it. Who was the silly old woman now?

Although the room seemed twenty degrees hotter, order was restored, and all eyes returned to the screen. Sheila's chest rose and fell in rapid breaths. She placed her hand against her breastbone to calm herself. The three officers might not think the man was a suspect, but she most certainly did. Though she couldn't make out his aura on a video, she trusted Victor's gut that something was off about him. She thought she even smelled it.

Niko restarted the footage. The next shot was of Shanna returning from her second day in Edinburgh.

"See?" Tad said. "Your daughter returned alone that day."

Sheila peered intently at the screen. Several guests streamed in around Shanna, splitting off into separate checkpoint lines, but there was no sign of Mr. Smelly. Had Shanna not visited the museum with him? Had the auction attendant heard wrong? Maybe Mr. Smelly was simply another guest who shared a few meals with Shanna. Maybe she, Sheila McShane from Sherry, New Hampshire, was a silly old woman, after all.

Still, even with the shadows and poor lighting at the checkpoint area, Sheila could tell Shanna looked happy as she placed her purse and a plastic shopping bag on the x-ray belt and walked through the metal detector. Once she passed through she was no longer on camera, but it was enough time for Sheila to catch the smile on her daughter's face. She nudged Shane. "Look at her eyes. They seem dreamy." Something had put a spark in her normally undemonstrative daughter. Was it a day full of Scottish museums or was it something more?

They watched the rest of the footage in silence, Shane's pen in constant motion, his hand resting only to signal Niko to pause the video so he could catch up with his notes. During the Liverpool stop, Shanna was again recorded getting off the ship alone and returning alone, her expression neutral both times. Next up was Belfast. On that day, Shanna's hair was combed out straight and the raincoat back on. As always, security scanned her key card, but this time, just before she stepped onto the gangway to exit, she turned and looked over her shoulder. A smile lit up her face.

"Stop," Sheila ordered.

Niko obliged.

"Do you see that?" She pointed to her smiling daughter, paused at the top of the gangway. "She's looking at someone. She seems happy. Radiant, even. Maybe the Australian man is a few guests behind, hidden from camera view."

Officer Gorgeous started the film again. "But look. She now turns and walks away. If she was leaving with someone, wouldn't she wait here in the corner? There's plenty of room to stand. Instead she exits and walks down the gangway."

Sheila was not convinced. "Maybe she wanted to wait outside. See how happy she looks, Shaney?"

Shane looked up from his notebook and nodded.

"She's probably just excited for a lovely day in Belfast," Tad said, rather stupidly, Sheila thought. "Look here." He pointed to the screen. "You can see several people getting off behind her before the video shifts over to her afternoon return. None of them are the man you saw before."

"Maybe he's farther back. Maybe we would see him if you hadn't chopped the film off so quickly."

Tad started to respond, but Niko cut him off with a head shake and moved on. "Here is your daughter returning from Belfast."

Immediately Sheila ordered him to pause the video again. Unease simmered in her belly. "Something's not right." Behind her, Officer Sourpuss emitted another guttural *achhh*. She ignored him. "Shanna looks bothered. She's upset about something."

Niko sat up fully and stretched his shoulders, his short-sleeved uniform pulling taut across his chest. "Her head is down. You can barely see her face as she walks through the metal detector." Even he, in all his officer gorgeousness, seemed to be losing patience with her.

"Maybe so, but she seems bothered. Don't you think so, Shaney?

Shane studied the screen. He squinted, even though his eyesight was fine. No one's optometrist was more impressed than Shane's. "Maybe. But you're better at gauging emotion than I am."

Feet shuffled behind her, but again she ignored the obvious impatience in the room. She and Shane would likely only get one shot at this. "What could have upset her? What was her plan for the day? Check the itinerary."

Shane moved into action, his skill set being called upon. He scanned their daughter's itinerary. "She took a historical bus tour around Belfast in the morning, just like we plan to do. Then she was going to stop at the Ulster Museum to see paintings by..." He ran his fingers along the text. "Paintings by Mainie Jellett, the first Irish painter to delve into Cubism."

"So she could have joined Mr. Smelly after her paid excursion, either for lunch or a visit to the museum."

Ivan, still behind her, sighed so heavily his breath ruffled her hair.

"That's a bit of a leap, ma'am," Tad said, his voice gentle but also condescending. The fact he was almost young enough to be her great grandson made his tone all the more irksome.

Even Officer Gorgeous placated her. "Maybe your daughter just had a bad day. Got caught in the rain, didn't get to see the paintings she wanted to, lost some money." He leaned in toward the screen. "But honestly, ma'am. I don't see that. I just see a weary woman putting her purse on the security belt and returning to the ship."

Sheila's fingertips fluttered lightly against her neck. Maybe they were right. Maybe she was reading too much into it. "Resume the tape," she told Niko.

In Dublin, Shanna was seen getting off and on the ship alone again. Though Shanna seemed content, Sheila swore her daughter was on guard. When she scanned her key card and slipped her purse over her head to place it on the security belt, she seemed to be looking around the checkpoint, as if watching for someone.

Of course, the three security officials wouldn't see that. But they didn't know her daughter. She did. And what might seem subtle and inconsequential (silly, even) to them held relevance for her. The tiniest details mattered. They were all she had to go on. She voiced these thoughts to Shane so he could jot them in his notebook, even if the officers thought her a silly old woman.

The next stop was Cork. There, Sheila sensed more discomfort in her daughter, not in the morning, for Sheila could only see Shanna from behind as she departed the ship, but upon her return. There was a firmness to her jaw and a frown line in her forehead. Sheila recognized that look. It meant Shanna was working through a problem. She mentioned her concerns to Shane, and he recorded them.

Officer Sourpuss paced back and forth behind her. She understood the head of security was a busy man. She understood he took their sleuthing as an affront to his skills. But what she could not understand was how anyone could be so callous over a missing woman. Didn't he have any daughters? A wife? A sister?

Port Zeebrugge in Belgium was the next stop, from which Shanna had booked an excursion to Ghent, Belgium. It was what Shanna had been most excited about. "Just imagine, Momma Girl, I'm going to see *The Adoration of the Mystic Lamb* in person." That rare burst of animation had ended in a giant mother-daughter hug. Sheila hadn't known what the Mystic Lamb was, but she reveled in Shanna's enthusiasm all the same.

Sure enough, as Shanna exited the ship at Zeebrugge, a sideways turn of her face showed excitement. With her wide-brimmed hat in place and her purse slung over her shoulder, she stepped on the gangway and into the sunshine. But when the video showed her return hours later, something seemed off. She was dressed in the same capri pants, v-neck tee, and gray hoodie as she had been that morning, but this time her head hung so low only her chin was visible. Her hat and hair covered everything else. When she looked up at the checkpoint guard to scan her key card, she turned sideways so that all the camera caught was her hat and long hair. She did the same when she removed her purse and placed it on the security belt. Then she lowered her head, stepped through the metal detector, and slipped out of sight.

Why such a hangdog return? Was she sad? Was she crying? Was she simply deep in thought? None of the passengers behind her was Mr. Smelly, but still, was he there? Had he hurt her? Something felt off to Sheila. Very off.

A coldness settled over her. "Did you notice how she never looked up? Something is wrong, I know it."

Officer Floppy Ears had moved to the side now. He scratched his neck. "Her head was lowered in other shots too."

"Maybe so, but not like this. Something isn't right, I'm telling you." She asked Officer Gorgeous to play it back. He obliged, but not before she caught him glance at his watch.

She studied the video again. Shane, too, had stopped writing and watched closely. It looked like their daughter, but something seemed different. They watched it again, but still, Sheila couldn't put her finger on what bothered her. It wasn't just the poor view of Shanna's face. It was something else. But what?

Frustration bubbled up inside her. She wanted to see it a fourth time, but Officer Sourpuss grumbled and rumbled behind her. Finally, she waved Niko on, and he played the video on to the last shot of Shanna, which was her leaving the ship in Amsterdam. As with the other departures, her exit shot was only of her backside, but the skinny jeans, raincoat, long hair, and familiar suitcase seemed to identify their daughter.

When the tape was over, Ivan closed the laptop. "So you see, your daughter left ship in one piece. Nothing happened to her, at least not on our ship."

For the first time since they had started the footage, Sheila leaned back in her chair. Her vertebrae creaked in protest. She looked up at the ceiling, but her stiff neck refused full extension.

Shane tucked the notebook, pen, and Shanna's itinerary back inside his blazer pocket. When he stood up, he winced, as if the tension had stiffened him too. Helping Sheila to her feet, he thanked the three security officers for their time and shook each of their hands.

Sheila nodded her appreciation as well, but while Niko and Tad offered their empty—but doubtless well-meaning—platitudes of hoping they find Shanna, a disquietude took root in her gut, one that would not be quelled by a peanut bar in her pocket.

What was it that was upsetting her so? Was something off about the footage? Or was she simply hoping there was, because to do otherwise would be to admit there was nothing more to be learned from this trip? According to the video, Shanna had gone missing in Amsterdam, somewhere between her leaving the ship and taking a cab to the airport, just as the ship's security team seemed to think. But Sheila's intuition insisted Shanna disappeared from the ship itself. As Shane would be the first to confirm, the odds of her disappearing in the short trip to the airport were extremely low.

Under Tad and Niko's guidance, they weaved their way through deck two's corridors to the elevators. Still lost in thought, she shook her head. Those things might be true, but they were not the reason for the storm in her belly.

It's that man, her intuition told her.

The man who didn't smell right to Victor.

Her intuition had rarely been wrong in the past. She'd known Shane had been injured while skiing in Vermont even before she got the confirmation call from the lodge. She'd known Shanna would be born on February twentieth even before her contractions had started. She'd known Dr. Shakir would be mauled in the Running of the Bulls in Pamplona even before he returned home with his ribs wrapped in a bandage. (To be fair, anyone could have deduced the stubby man would not fare well.)

And she knew now that everything boiled down to Mr. Smelly. Find him, and they would find their daughter.

If the security team thought seeing the footage would end Sheila and Shane's investigation, they thought wrong. In fact, the opposite had occurred, for now she had a photograph of the man. No matter what the cost, she would log onto the ship's internet, paste the picture into an email, and mail it to herself. Then she would start showing Mr. Smelly's picture around.

They reached the elevator. When the door dinged open, Tad held it open for them, a cheerful expression on his dopey face. "Here we go then. Please, keep me informed if you have any concerns."

With renewed determination she stepped inside and clapped her hands once. "Thank you, boys." To Shane, she said, "Come on. Let's catch the next tender into Edinburgh. We need to ask the museum guides if they've seen Shanna or Mr. Smelly."

Before the elevator doors closed, she caught the disbelieving stares of Officer Floppy Ears and Officer Gorgeous.

She smiled sweetly at them and patted her hair. Oh no, boys, she thought. The McShanes are not done looking for their daughter. Not by a long shot.

9

MIND YOUR STEP

A FEW MINUTES after they left the security department, they made a stop in the Shipmate Bar across from Guest Relations. There, Sheila paid for five minutes of ridiculously expensive internet time to paste Mr. Smelly's photo into an email and send it to herself. She also took her phone out of airplane mode to check for new text messages on their emergency data plan. Despite her age, she had taken to smartphones like nuns took to prayer. She read books on the device, searched for recipes, even pulled up lab results from her annual physical with Dr. Shakir. In fact, the one thing she used it for least was a phone. Even with her gnarly fingers, she texted her kids and the gals from work more often than she called them.

She could do without the spam texts from unknown numbers though. She got so many of those, and today was no different. As soon as she took her phone out of airplane mode and connected to the internet, a string of texts appeared. Two were from Gloria, one was from Pastor Tim, and one was from a spammer. *Send hekp restorinb just judges pa*, it said.

"Heavens," she said to Shane, who was tapping his thigh, seemingly eager to be on their way. "If spammers are going to waste my time, the least they could do is make sense."

Ignoring the messages for now, she saved Mr. Smelly's image to her photos. When she finished, they exited the ship via the gangway and caught one of the transport tenders. Twenty minutes later they stepped onto the concrete quay of New Haven Harbor near Edinburgh.

Oh, what a difference a day made.

Gone were yesterday's morose clouds and chilly drizzle. In their place was brilliant sunshine, a cerulean sky, and just enough coastal breeze to lift Sheila's tresses and dry the perspiration dotting her hairline. Even the squawking seagulls seemed to be celebrating. With their energy, Sheila felt a renewed hope and purpose.

In the brightness she squinted up at Shane. "You were right about needing our hats."

"The raincoats are too much, though." He repositioned his fedora and took in the surroundings. She could almost see his navigational calculations: sea to the north, restaurants and shops to the east, taxi stand to the south. Other passengers from the orange sardine can of a tender spilled out around them. Some headed into the stores along the quay, others to the string of waiting cabs.

"It's the only coat I brought on the trip." She unzipped the jacket. "We can carry them if we get too warm."

A fat seagull rested on the edge of the quay, soaking up the sun.

"It's a sign," Sheila whispered.

"What was that, dear?"

"God's giving us a sign. Based on what she was wearing in the security footage, Shanna had cold and rain on her first day in Edinburgh and sunshine on the second, just like us. He's telling us we're on the right track."

Shane was too deep in his navigational planning to respond. He studied the back of the ship's daily schedule, which showed a general map of Edinburgh and a few highlights of the city. His scrunched handwriting shaded every free area on the page. Such had been his nightly ritual on the cruise. Every evening after turn-down service, he found the next day's planner on the bed, alongside two pieces of chocolate and a towel animal sculpted by Raoul. While Sheila took pictures of the towel monkey (or dog or mouse),

Shane studied and marked up the planner. If the ship's captain ever gave a pop quiz, Shane would ace it.

"New Haven used to be a fishing village," he told her now. "It's one of several ports for cruise ships around Edinburgh."

"That's nice, but we should catch a cab before—"

"We were originally scheduled to tender into South Queensferry. You'll remember that from the fine print in one of our pre-departure emails."

No, she would not remember that. She didn't busy her head with such details. Just deliver her to dry land and keep the ship from sinking, that was all she asked. But since there were still enough taxis at the stand, she was happy to let Shane continue. After all the bathroom waiting he did for her, she owed him.

"Of course, there's Rosyth Dockyard too. As you might recall, I mentioned it was once a naval base, big enough for twenty-two battleships if need be. Then there's the cruise port at Leith. It's been around since…" Shane's voice trailed off, his gaze settling on the dwindling number of taxis. "Oh no. We better hurry or there won't be any left."

Seeing Shane leap into action was an endless source of entertainment for his family. He looked like the cartoon Roadrunner. One moment he was still, the next he was darting off to his destination.

His quickness snared them the last of the taxicabs. Behind a congenial driver, the two of them rode to Waverley Station, where they caught the same hop-on/hop-off, double-decker bus as the day before. Today, however, with the sunshine and warmer temperature, they climbed the tiny staircase to sit in the bus's open top. With the wind threatening their hats and the sun warming their faces, the city unveiled itself in all its medieval wonder. Sheila could hardly believe it was the same city as yesterday.

"Oh, Shaney, the view is so much better up here." As the bus picked up speed, she quit fighting the wind and removed her hat, letting the gusts have their way with her hair. City scents of diesel, fresh bakeries, and intermittent bursts of nature teased her nostrils.

Shane cranked his head from side to side. "Edinburgh's topography is very unusual. I've never seen anything like it."

She knew what he meant. One moment the bus seemed to be driving down a typical street, trees and shrubs on one side, stone buildings on the other. The next she would discover it was not a street at all, but a bridge, beneath which more buildings, lush parks, and avenues weaved. In her funk the day before, she hadn't appreciated the grandness of it all. They had simply peered through a rain-streaked and foggy bus window until they reached Edinburgh Castle. But today, up on the top deck with no roof to confine them, she felt like she had stepped out of a black-and-white movie into a full-color one.

As they drove along Princes Street, its business district on one side and tree-lined gardens on the other, Shane identified the landmarks.

"That's the Scott Monument, and that fellow in the center is Sir Walter Scott." He pointed to a statue inside the monument's open-air vestibule. Sheila's eyes traveled above the cloaked figure, all the way up to the stone edifice's Gothic tip, which, according to Shane, rose over two hundred feet. How he knew that, she wasn't sure. Maybe he read it on the ship's daily planner or the complimentary bus map. Or maybe he simply knew it, like he knew how far down the earth's core was or how far the earth was from the moon.

Their intended stop was the Scottish National Gallery, about midway through the eighty-minute bus tour, but given their enchantment with the city, they opted to go all the way around on the tour first before getting off there. That still left plenty of time to query people at the museum, and, though unlikely, the drive might trigger something new in their minds.

The bonus of the extended bus ride was a breathtaking view of Edinburgh Castle. On top of Castle Rock, the medieval fortress rose magnificently against a deep-blue sky, its structures and walls bordered by precipitous cliffs. Though Sheila and Shane had toured its grounds yesterday, they hadn't appreciated it from afar.

"It's built on the remains of an extinct volcano," Shane

explained. "There's been a royal castle there since the twelfth century, but people have inhabited it since the second."

Sheila rubbed his cheek and snuggled into him. "My husband. The smartest man in the world."

A few minutes later he raised an arm. "Look. There's The Scotch Whiskey Experience." He wiggled his eyebrows, making Sheila laugh. How different their first trip to Europe would be if its mission were not so somber.

He talked. She listened. In traffic-heavy stops and starts (both vehicular and pedestrian), the bus drove down the Royal Mile, where densely packed medieval buildings housed modern-day restaurants, hotels, and shops. From there, they passed along George IV Bridge, and when they caught a glimpse of the cobblestone road and colorful buildings of Victoria Street, Sheila clapped her hands in delight. "It looks like a winding rainbow!"

All the while, horns blared, pedestrians clamored, police cars bleated. Even the musical cadence of the sirens was different from those in New Hampshire. *Everything* was different from New Hampshire. The sights, the sounds, the smells. Sheila took it all in, imprinting the city on her mind and drawing its rhythms and nuances into her soul.

She was so engrossed in the journey, she could hardly believe it when they arrived back at the Scottish National Gallery. "Have we already gone around one and a half times?"

Shane assured her they had. As the double-decker bus maneuvered its way to the curb to drop passengers off, one bus in a sea of buses, Shane explained that the National Galleries of Scotland consisted of three separate museums in different parts of the city: one for modern art, one that showcased the history of Scotland, and one for old paintings. That last one, the Scottish National Gallery, was Shanna's museum of interest. Their daughter specialized in late medieval and early Renaissance work, particularly with religious symbolism.

When they stood to depart the bus, Sheila climbed down its narrow stairwell with surprising agility. All the adrenaline had loosened her joints. On the sidewalk, in a swarm of other tourists, she took in the massive pillars and stately architecture of the gallery. Its inside walls held the treasures of Monet, Rembrandt, Raphael, and more, all for whom Shanna could no doubt offer detailed biographies and facts.

"Come," Sheila said with nervous excitement. "Let's ask every docent we see if they recognize Shanna. She would have stayed here for hours. Someone is bound to remember her." As they passed between tawny pillars toward the entrance to purchase tickets, she added, "But first I need to use the bathroom."

～

LIKE THE CITY of Edinburgh itself, the Scottish National Gallery was nothing short of a visual feast. On the lower level, from one arched doorway to the next, crimson rooms showcased gold-framed paintings and ivory sculptures. Decorative crown molding lined the domed ceilings, and jade carpeting cushioned the floor. From the brochure Shane had picked up at the entrance, similar rooms of blue and emerald were upstairs.

Throngs of visitors perused the collections. Some strolled past rather quickly, lingering only briefly to gaze at richly robed figures brought to life on canvas. Others preferred deeper contemplation and sat on padded benches in the center of the room. Meanwhile, Shane and Sheila weaved their way around in search of room attendants to ask about their daughter. So far, in addition to the woman at the entrance who hadn't recognized Shanna or Mr. Smelly, they had found two docents, one near the first gallery and one near a statue of two women with their arms entwined. No recognition of Shanna on either of their parts.

Sheila refused to get discouraged. Her bladder was good to go, and a pastry from the café on the ground floor had neutralized her blood sugar.

"Oh look." She pointed to another room attendant near one of the arched doors and headed in that direction, Shane at her heels.

Out of nowhere, a group of students swarmed in from another hallway and blocked her way. She fussed at the interruption, worried the docent she had spied would leave before they reached her. One of the students must have seen her frustration, because he grabbed a couple of his pals and pulled them out of the way.

"Well, isn't that lovely of you." Sheila patted the blond youth's arm. "And who says all teenagers are terrible."

"Um…thank you?" he said.

When they escaped the students, Sheila was relieved the room attendant was still near the doorway. "Excuse me. We were hoping to ask you a few questions."

"Certainly." The matronly woman's accent was Scottish, and when Sheila showed her Shanna's picture and explained their situation, the attendant lifted her heavily lined eyebrows. "Aye, I do remember her."

"You do?" Sheila steepled her hands and said a silent prayer of thanks. Shane fumbled for his notebook and pen, raincoat slung over his arm.

"Aye, your daughter sat in this room for a long time, taking notes, drawing sketches, asking questions. Not easy to forget someone so in love with the art."

"Yes, that's our daughter." With jittery fingers Sheila swiped her phone screen until she came to the picture of Mr. Smelly, the one she had taken from the security footage and copied before Officer Sourpuss made her delete it. Though not a fully frontal shot, his face was discernible. "Was this man with her by any chance?"

The attendant pulled the phone closer. Her cheeks flushed. "Aye, he was. Quite a looker, that one."

Sheila glanced at the man. They would have to agree to disagree on that point. All she saw was a crooked nose and a dark heart.

"He would come and go." The docent pursed her lips, as if trying to remember. "Enjoyed the artwork, he did, but maybe not so much as your daughter. It wasn't so busy that day. I could hear most everything they said."

Shane flipped open his notebook. In his haste to start writing, he activated the gadget pen's laser pointer. Its beam landed inches from the attendant's eye. "Forgive me," he said, his face contrite over his fumble.

"Did our daughter seem interested in the man?" Sheila asked.

"That's an odd question, isn't it then?" The woman brushed back her feathery bangs. "They seemed happy enough. He made her laugh a few times, told her they could grab a pint in Old Town to see more of the city. But mostly your daughter seemed focused on the paintings. She asked me a lot of questions, that one."

"That sounds like my Shanna." Although Sheila admired her daughter's passion for her work, it had done no favors for her love life. "Did he seem troubled by her inattention?"

The boisterous student group moved along on their way. Sheila waited until they were situated on the other side of the room and their voices lowered to a more reasonable decibel. When she returned her focus to the attendant, her peripheral vision caught a red-haired man slinking past the arched doorway. When she looked fully in that direction, he was gone. Something stirred in her gut.

"What was your question again?" The docent stole Sheila's attention back. If the woman was annoyed by having her time taken, she didn't show it. On the contrary, she seemed to enjoy the company.

"I asked if the man seemed troubled by my daughter's disinterest?"

"Troubled? Nah, I wouldn't say troubled. Maybe more bored than anything, at least after a while. But he seemed enthralled by her descriptions of how she would restore the paintings." The attendant studied the artwork hanging on the blood-red walls. "Bit strange, really. They all look fine to me."

"Our daughter is an art restorer," Shane clarified. "She sees flaws others don't."

"Ah, that would explain why the Aussie man loved it, I guess. Even so, he started to look a bit bored, like he wanted to get movin'." The woman leaned in closer. Her dark blazer showed flecks of dandruff. "Truth be told, most women would enjoy his company, you know what I mean? But your daughter, she told him to go ahead on his own. Said she was headed to the Trinity Altarpiece for a long look."

"Did he leave?" Shane scribbled everything down in his notebook.

"He did, but only after your daughter agreed to have dinner with him on the ship. Guess that means they were on a cruise?"

Sheila nodded. When the attendant said that was all she remembered and that Shanna had left shortly after for the Trinity Altarpiece in another part of the gallery, Sheila thanked her profusely.

Thrilled with the new information, Sheila and Shane shifted their draped raincoats, linked arms, and climbed the stairs to see if they could glean anything more from the attendants on the other levels.

"Here's what we know." Sheila leaned into the banister to steady herself. "The ship footage showed Mr. Smelly leaving with Shanna on the second day in Edinburgh. Whether the security officers think they left together or not doesn't matter. We know they did since they were in the museum together, right?"

Shane nodded.

Sheila opened her mouth to say more, but between the stairs, the crowds, and her excitement, she was too winded to speak. She waited until they reached a gallery room, this one with royal-blue walls, mustard wainscoting, and Impressionist paintings. After a few moments of rest, she continued. "Clearly Shanna enjoyed his company. She's an introvert, but she's not shy, nor is she tactful. She would have asked him straight out to leave if she didn't want him tagging along."

The two resumed their stroll through the gallery rooms. "According to the ship's auction attendant, the Australian man knows art," Shane said. "Plus, the attendant downstairs mentioned he was interested in Shanna's art restoration. That would be attractive to Shanna."

"Exactly. For her, his art knowledge would be a far better aphrodisiac than a drink in Old Town."

"Hold on a moment." Shane steered them to a corner and paused. He pulled his notebook back out of his blazer. With the raincoat still folded over his arm, he flipped through his notes. "We know Shanna got back on the ship alone in Edinburgh, but..." His gaze skimmed over his notes. When he found what he was looking for, he continued. "But she looked quite happy when she got back on board, remember? You said her eyes seemed dreamy."

"Which means she enjoyed her time with Mr. Smelly and was planning to have dinner with him as he'd asked. That would confirm what Victor already told us."

Shane ran his finger over the small page. "In Liverpool, she got off and on alone, but in Belfast, before she got off, she turned and looked over her shoulder. She was smiling. You said she looked radiant, and she did. She looked beautiful." Shane's voice hitched. He glanced up from his notes and blinked.

Sheila's own throat grew tight. "Yes, but when she returned from Belfast, she seemed upset."

"So we need to find out what happened that day to upset her. She was enjoying the man's company, so what changed? What happened between day five of the cruise—the second day in Edinburgh—and day eight, when she returned from Belfast?"

Pondering their daughter in silence, they resumed walking from room to room, paying little attention to the paintings, looking only for docents to query, but none of them recognized Shanna or the Australian man with the boxer's nose, at least not with any certainty. Soon, Sheila was too tired and too hungry to go on. She nibbled a few bites from her peanut bar for sustenance until they could have a late lunch. Still, she felt the museum trip had been a success. They now had another piece of the puzzle. The mysterious man had used his interest in art to woo their daughter.

At the stairs, Sheila once again took Shane's arm, and together they began their descent amid a swarm of tourists.

"Tomorrow is a full day at sea, correct?" she asked

Shane nodded.

"Then let's spend the day trying to figure out what might have gone wrong. We're onto something with this man, I just knoooooo—"

Sheila's last word morphed into a cry of surprise as a hand shoved the small of her back. She and Shane went tumbling down the stairs. Arms, legs, and elbows thumped off steps. Head, hands, and feet bounced off other tourists. A few museum-goers joined the flight, but most managed to move out of the way. Despite their speed, Sheila felt like she was in slow motion. Through it all, dispersed voices called out:

"Somebody help them."

"Oh my God."

"Call for help."

Finally, with only a few steps left, they stopped rolling. A group of men had practically caught them in their arms. Behind the men a crowd was gathered.

"Jeez, are you two okay?"

"Do you need an ambulance?"

"Is there a doctor here?"

Sheila opened her mouth, tried to call Shane's name, could not.

"Ma'am, can you hear me? Are you all right?"

"Beetle Bug, are you okay?"

The fear in Shane's voice startled her out of her shock. She turned her head and saw him seated next to her, though how they had gotten into an upright position, she didn't know. She embraced him, every part of his body familiar and safe. "I think so, oh honey I think so. Are you?"

Shane nodded. He straightened his arms and legs as if proving they still worked. Sheila did the same. A wince at a stiff knee here, a crack of neck there, but everything seemed to comply.

She looked at Shane's bare head. "Your hat," she said, still dazed. "It's gone." She saw it at the bottom of the stairs.

At the same time, she spotted the red-haired man she'd seen earlier. He was gathered with the other huddled tourists but showing none of their concern. Upon locking eyes with her, he formed an imaginary gun with his thumb and index finger, his bare arm blotchy with hives. He pointed the fake barrel at her.

Then he turned and walked away.

10

THE ELEPHANT IN THE ROOM

AFTER THE DRAMA at the Scottish National Gallery the day before, including both their momentum in finding clues about their daughter and their momentum in falling down the stairs, Sheila and Shane looked forward to a quiet day at sea.

She could not get the red-haired man at the museum out of her mind, the one she had seen at the bottom of the stairs. She was convinced he had pushed her. She swore she had felt a hand on her back, but Shane assured her she was reading too much into it. The shove on her back had likely been an overeager tourist, and in her confusion from the accident, she had only imagined the finger gun. "We simply lost our footing in the crowd," he said. "Luckily people were there to shield our fall. Had they not been, we'd be in the infirmary today." But Sheila swore the man looked familiar. If only she could place how and why. As was happening more and more frequently, her brain refused to make the connection. How frustrating it was to get old. She decided a rest day at sea was exactly what her thought wheels needed.

Finding the breakfast buffet on deck fourteen too noisy and crowded, they carried their plates of waffles and fruit down to the solarium on deck twelve.

When they reached it, Sheila said, "I see we aren't the only ones who had this idea." With chlorine fumes stinging her eyes and a cacophony of conversations buzzing in her ears, she scanned every table around the indoor pool. All were taken. Most of the deck chairs too.

Shane pointed to a cluster of pod chairs, similar to those in the library. Like cars of a Tilt-A-Whirl, the chairs swiveled in different directions, but the majority faced the rain-streaked windows, beyond which the turbulent sea melded into a cloudy sky. "Maybe those two in the corner are empty," he said. "Even if there's just one, we can squeeze in together. It's too cold to sit by the outdoor pool."

They doddered over, Sheila feeling like a creaky bag of bones, and rounded the first chair. Inside its cushioned paradise, a middle-aged man in nothing but a Speedo snored soundly. A military thriller lay face-down on his hairy belly.

"I wonder if he knows they sell clothing on deck five," Sheila said.

She moved onto the remaining seat, which directly faced the corner. In order to see if it was occupied, she had to swivel it a few inches. When she did, she inhaled in surprise. Her plate slipped from her hands and whacked the pool deck. Cantaloupe cubes skittered across the wooden floor.

She scurried away, shocked by the carnal act she had just witnessed between a skeletal woman with bleached-blond hair, a rotund man with a combover, and a towel sculpture elephant. "Oh no, Shaney, you don't want to see that—"

Too late. Shane peered around the corner. His head jerked back, and his eyes widened to comical dimensions. He mumbled an incoherent apology, and when he hustled back to Sheila, his foot slipped on her scattered melon pieces. His arms flailed and his steps stuttered, heightening the comedic show. Luckily, he neither fell nor dropped his breakfast plate in the process.

Like two octogenarian Charlie Chaplins, they scampered out of the solarium, giving no thought to spilled food or stiff bodies. Escape was their only objective.

After climbing one flight of stairs back to the buffet restaurant, they were too speechless and breathless to greet the hostess again. Not until they sank into an empty table, its surface sticky with syrup and orange juice, did they make eye contact.

Sheila giggled. Shane followed suit.

"And to think I thought those towel animals were just for show," she said. "Who in their right mind would use them for...for...well, for *that?*" She pressed her palms against her flushed cheeks, too embarrassed to even utter the words.

Shane coughed, his laughter dying down. "Imagine what Raoul would think of his towel creations falling victim to such erotic misdeeds."

"Just when I think I've seen it all. Wait until I tell Dr. Shakir and the gals about this one." She shook her head and forked a piece of Shane's watermelon, since he was the only one who still had his breakfast. "Makes for quite a story. Maybe we should call the local news."

"Maybe we should call PETA. Certainly that qualifies as abuse."

They chuckled all over again.

AFTER BREAKFAST, the McShanes waited outside the elevator bank to return to deck ten, not for their stateroom, but for the library. Quiet and calm, it had become their favorite place on the ship, especially since the weather was too chilly and wet to sit outside. Thanks to the heavier pedestrian traffic on sea days, three minutes had passed with no whoosh of an incoming elevator.

"I suppose we could take the stairs. It's only three flights down." Sheila rubbed her bruised elbow and massaged her sore neck, compliments of yesterday's fall.

Shane seemed no more enamored by the idea than she was, his hand on his hip, fingers making circular motions around the joint. He glanced at the stairwell to their left, its brass handrail being polished by an industrious crew member. "I hate to disrupt his work."

"Yes, that would be rude." A flimsy excuse, but she seized it.

Shane turned back to the elevators. "Always thought it was ridiculous to skip a thirteenth floor. Silly superstition messes with logical design."

"It's called triskaidekaphobia, dear."

As if Sheila had just scaled the rock-climbing wall up on the sports deck, Shane's eyebrows shot up. She gave him an affronted look. "You're not the only one who knows big words." She neglected to mention the only reason she knew the term for severe fear of the number thirteen was because one of Dr. Shakir's patients had it.

"Never underestimate a woman who can fold a fitted sheet." Shane's expression shifted to engineer mode. "It's estimated that eighty-five percent of buildings omit a thirteenth floor. Architecturally—"

The elevator arrived.

Saved by the *ding*, Sheila thought with a smile. A swarm of guests got off, some dressed in swimwear, others in more suitable attire for the northern climate.

Once on deck ten, they veered left toward the library. On their past visits its concierge desk had been empty. Today, a man in a burgundy blazer and tie sat behind it. Sheila acknowledged him with a nod, and he, busy with an older couple leafing through brochures, did the same.

As would be expected on a sea day, the two tables and most of the seats were taken, including the white pod chairs that resembled the ones in the solarium. Sheila recalled the morning's encounter with the amorous couple and shuddered.

"We may have to read somewhere else." Shane tilted his head toward the occupied chairs.

A hand holding a baseball cap dangled from one of the pods. Recognizing its source, Sheila approached it in time to hear a prepubescent voice say, "Donations are always appreciated."

She circled around and peeked inside the chair. Carson Quick, the twelve-year-old magician, grinned up at her. Across from him, in another pod seat, sat two wide-eyed girls. "OMG, how did you do that?" one squealed.

"A magician never tells." Carson winked at Sheila.

"Aren't you a cheeky one?" she said, smiling.

When the girls giggled and darted off, claiming they had no money, Carson's grin flattened into a defeated sigh.

Shane strolled over and joined them. "Well, if it isn't the great Carson Quick." Her normally frugal husband pulled out his wallet and plucked a five-dollar bill from the fold that held his American money. Sheila's eyes widened as much as Carson's. "Amaze me, and Mr. Lincoln's all yours," Shane said.

Carson burst up from his chair and offered it to Sheila. "You got it, sir." Shane took the one vacated by the girls. Warily, they sank into the cushioned pods. Sheila decided the real magic would be getting them back out.

"Pick a card and sign it, Mister..."

"McShane."

"Mr. McShane." Carson extended his deck toward Shane, along with a black marker. Shane selected the four of diamonds and signed it.

A few minutes later, after shuffles and distractions and impressive sleight of hand, the same card came out of Carson Quick's mouth, without ever having been seen going in.

The McShanes cheered and clapped in genuine astonishment. True to his word, Shane handed over the five-dollar bill, but when Carson offered him the soggy remains of the spit-out card, Shane declined.

After Carson departed, Sheila beamed at her husband. "That was sweet of you. A real twenty-first-century payout."

Shane gave a sheepish grin. "I have a soft spot for young entrepreneurs."

Despite not having selected any reading material, they remained in the pod chairs. You don't need a book to nap, Sheila thought sleepily. An hour later a blast of music from the atrium five decks below startled them awake. After a few thrusts and false starts, they managed to escape the pods. In various degrees of limping, they ambled down the narrow corridor toward their stateroom. Like newborn colts, their bruised muscles and stiff joints needed a little time to find their rhythm.

When they neared cabin number 1176, four rooms in front of their own, Sheila slowed. It was the same stateroom they had heard raised voices coming from a few days before, the one with the messy couple who had berated poor Raoul. Sheila had locked eyes—or rather one eye—with the woman. Beyond that, a penciled-in eyebrow and blond curls were all she had glimpsed.

Now, however, the door was propped open, Raoul's cleaning cart blocking its entrance. Sheila stopped and looked inside.

"Don't snoop, honey."

Shane's words were nothing but window dressing, for he too had stopped to peer inside. How could they not? Wreckage like that was hard to ignore.

As before, trash and food littered the room. A half-eaten piece of pizza lay face-down on the bed, next to sheets so twisted they looked like white licorice. A squashed chicken strip hovered precariously over the edge of the desk, and an overturned coffee cup lay on the carpet, brown liquid soaked in around it. Clothes cluttered every surface, including the ceiling, where a lacy brassiere was stuck on the ornate metal leaves of the light fixture.

"Oh, how awful." Sheila clucked her tongue and shook her head.

Tousled-haired and agitated, Raoul stepped out of the bathroom, his arms full of sopping towels, some stained bronze with makeup. At least Sheila hoped it was makeup. Raoul's muffin cheeks were flushed and his forehead sweaty. Incomprehensible muttering slipped through his clenched jaw. When he saw the McShanes, he froze.

After a beat, he hurried his stout body to the cart blocking the room and stuffed the towels into an attached laundry bag. "I'm very sorry. I should not have left the door open." Although an industrious green aura still emanated from him, a gray cloud of anxiety stole its thunder.

One of the wet towels fell out of the overstuffed bag and landed on Sheila's feet.

"Oh, madam, forgive me." The Venezuelan man snatched a

fresh towel, pushed the cart out of the way, and appeared to be about to mop up her shoes.

She put a hand on his shoulder. "Please, dear, don't worry about my shoes. These could withstand a tsunami."

Raoul straightened, his anxiety so high it transferred to her.

"You shouldn't have to deal with this." Heat rose up her neck and into her face. "Speak to your supervisor about these people. Guests or no guests, they have no right to treat you or their cabin this way."

"No, no, I must not cause trouble. I worry they are doing this on —" Raoul cut himself off. He raked a hand through his coarse hair, as if fearing he had said too much.

"You worry what?" Sheila asked. "You're worried they're doing this on purpose? Is that what you were about to say?"

Raoul's expression suggested that was indeed what he was about to say. He shook his head. "I don't know anything. All is good."

"What are you worried about?" She grabbed his hand and squeezed. "Losing your job if you make waves?"

Raoul looked torn, as if wanting to talk but fearing he should not. He glanced each way down the corridor, then stepped back and lowered his voice. "They have already complained to my supervisor that I left them soiled towels and dirty coffee mugs to save cleaning time." He shook his head so vigorously his cheeks wobbled. "But I did no such thing. Never would I do such a thing. I'm very careful and neat."

"I know you are. Our room is so clean it sparkles, doesn't it, Shane?"

A murmur of agreement from behind.

Raoul lowered his gaze to the towel still in his hands. He twisted it around his thick hand. "I think they are making their room very messy so it's impossible to keep clean. I think they want to make something bad happen to them and blame me."

"Why would they do that?" Shane asked. Although by outward appearances, her husband could seem indifferent to human emotion, he was anything but. Sheila sensed his concern for Raoul was every bit as acute as her own.

Raoul chewed his lower lip but said nothing.

"It's because they want to get a free trip, isn't it?" From the look on Raoul's face, Sheila had guessed correctly. "On our first day at sea, we overheard them telling you they got a free upgrade to a veranda room because of an issue with a past sailing. Looks like they're shooting for a suite next time."

"But I will lose… No, I should say no more. This is not your concern. You are here to find your daughter, not worry about me." Raoul stuffed the towel into the laundry bag and then fisted his hands so tightly his knuckles blanched.

"You'll lose your job," Sheila said, finishing the sentence he had left hanging.

His cheeks sagged. "Yes, madam, I surely will."

"Not with us as witnesses."

"But how can you prevent that? You cannot stop these people from making up such stories."

Shane ran his hand along the door frame, his gaze on neither Sheila nor Raoul. "People like this can't be reasoned with. Other methods are required."

"Methods? What methods?" Raoul's tone took an uncertain turn.

Sheila scrutinized her husband, her own curiosity roused.

But Shane didn't answer. He turned and walked away, not glancing back until he reached their stateroom, hands patting his blazer in search of his key card.

11

TAXI!

On day seven of the cruise, Sheila and Shane waited for their tour bus to depart Chester, England, where they had spent a pleasant morning touring the medieval city. Sun streamed through the windows onto their seats and bathed them in welcomed warmth.

All was not sunshine and roses though. Two tourists hadn't yet returned to the bus.

Parked on an unpopulated street, flanked by a parking garage on one side and an industrial building on the other, Sheila scoured the area for them. Unfortunately, she was not sure what they looked like. She and Shane had sat near the front of the bus, paying little attention to who was behind them.

"You don't suppose the guide will really leave them, do you?" Her fingers clasped and unclasped the buckle on her handbag.

"He has a schedule to keep." Shane glanced at the glowing numbers on his watch. "The couple was supposed to be here ten minutes ago. People need to be better timekeepers."

Earlier that morning the ship had docked in Liverpool. From there, Sheila and Shane had departed by bus for their Sampling of Chester excursion, the same one Shanna had booked. Their plan was to then spend the afternoon in Liverpool, just as Shanna had, assuming she hadn't strayed from her itinerary.

Were the bus parked a block or two over, the view would be far more exciting. Their walking tour of the old, walled city had taken them past a collection of architectural eras, including early Roman ruins with Gothic and Victorian restorations. They visited Town Hall and Chester Cathedral, inside of whose dark-paneled walls Handel had once rehearsed parts of *The Messiah*. They had laughed as Chet, their bug-eyed tour guide, led them to a sandstone gateway with a colorful clock and spun tales of rivalry between the English and the Welsh. "The Eastgate Clock faces every direction but west," he had joked, "because we haven't got time for the Welsh." They had even enjoyed thirty minutes of free time to explore the gift shops on Eastgate Street, where Sheila found a blown-glass beaver for their waiter, Victor, to add to his peculiar collection. While they weaved in and out of shops, a man with his hair in a bun played guitar in the pedestrian mall. When Chet rounded up the excursion guests to return to the coach, Sheila had tossed a one-pound coin into the singer's guitar case.

Back on the bus, Chet was no longer smiling and telling jokes. He stood at the front near the driver, nervously checking his watch and peering through the windows for the truant couple. A short man in his fifties with a gravelly voice and missing eyelashes, he had recognized Shanna from her photograph the moment Sheila had shown it to him earlier that morning. Though he hadn't recognized Mr. Smelly, he remembered their daughter with an odd exuberance.

"Oh, she was a pretty one, that gal," he had said. "Quiet though. Didn't say boo the whole time we walked through the town." While he spoke, he rubbed his protruding eyelids, as if they harbored an insatiable itch. The silence that followed was equally disconcerting, a weird smile on his face, the back of his hand going from one eyelid to the other. But other than ascertaining the reason for his lack of eyelashes, Sheila and Shane had learned nothing new about Shanna. Aside from her quiet nature—which, if she had no questions about Chester art to ask, fit their daughter—Chet had noticed nothing strange, nor did he remember seeing anyone who looked like Mr. Smelly. "A gal like that should have a man by her side," he had added, with another seat-squirming grin.

Three hours later and two passengers short, Chet blinked his buggy eyes at the coach driver. "It's been fifteen minutes. We have an afternoon group waiting back at the ship. We'll give these two five more minutes, then we're gone."

From the second-row window seat, Sheila opened her mouth to speak. Shane shook his head and mouthed the word *no*. Her words spilled out anyway. Worrying about others was her nature. "How awful for them to return and find no bus waiting. How will they get back to the ship on their own? It's too far for a taxi."

Chet swiveled around to Sheila, his pinched grimace making his eyes even more pronounced. "They'll have to figure that out. They can take a train."

"But will it get them back before the ship sets sail at six?"

"We sent the ship's rep out to look for them. That's the best we can do." Chet's attention was back on the parking lot beyond the coach window.

"But—"

"Ah, there's the rep. She's come back alone." To the bus driver, Chet said. "It's been twenty minutes. We can't wait any longer."

"Oh, that poor couple." Sheila closed her eyes. How scary to be left behind in a foreign country. Shanna's face swam before her.

The ship representative boarded the bus. "I couldn't find them anywhere," she said.

Sheila recognized the woman from the breakfast buffet. Last evening at dinner, Victor had told Sheila and Shane that when a crew member had a free shift, he or she could tag along on an excursion if there was room. "We get to see parts of the world we never thought we would see."

Chet flapped his arm at the driver. "We're off, then." Moments later the bus was in motion, leaving a couple stranded behind in Chester, England.

Shane squeezed Sheila's thigh. "Try not to worry about them. They'll be fine. Focus on Shanna instead."

Two hours later, after a nap on the bus and a buffet lunch on the ship, Sheila and Shane disembarked once again, this time on their own to explore Liverpool. Shanna had scheduled nothing specific for The Beatles' hometown, other than to walk along the waterfront and visit the Liverpool Cathedral, the fifth largest cathedral in the world.

Having more than three decades of age on their daughter, they didn't feel a several-mile walk was in their best interest, especially not with Sheila's troublesome feet and the fall down the stairs the day before. Getting old set limits both she and Shane had trouble accepting but nonetheless had to. One could stay active. One could eat well. One could meditate. But old age would always come knocking.

As such, they had to make a decision: stroll along the sparkling waterfront or visit the cathedral? They decided to skip the waterfront. What could squawking seagulls and moored sailboats offer them in the way of information? The cathedral seemed a better bet. So they bypassed Albert Dock with its bevy of restaurants, shops, and carnival rides, and crossed a heavily trafficked road toward the heart of the city.

"Do you think the cathedral is too far of a walk for us?" Sheila barely reached the curb before the pedestrian light turned red, everyone else outpacing them.

Shane unfolded his paper map and leaned against a storefront, seemingly oblivious to the swarm of tourists passing by in both directions. Like a New World explorer, he scanned and assessed and pondered. When he finished, he squinted against the sun and glanced up at her. "It's about a mile. Think you can handle that?"

One at a time she flexed her feet in her supportive shoes. Only a twinge of discomfort followed. "I think so. I walk farther than that at home."

Navigating a circuitous route, Shane led them to Duke Street. "This will take us straight to the cathedral."

Despite the cooler temperature, they opted to walk on the shady side of the street, where three-story brick buildings protected them from the sun's glare. Before long, restaurant and shop signs changed from English letters to Chinese ones.

"We must be in Chinatown," Sheila said with some excitement. But as the blocks went on, her eagerness turned to trepidation. With each step the sidewalk grew more deserted. Soon they were its only strollers. Cars buzzed by, but with less frequency than she would have liked.

Doubt constricted her throat. "We seem to be out of the tourist area."

"It shouldn't be much farther now. Maybe five more blocks."

A feeling of being followed overcame her. She glanced over her shoulder but saw no one. Only shuttered buildings and quiet restaurants with posters of rice and noodles in their windows.

"Shouldn't we be able to see the cathedral from here?" Her voice betrayed her anxiety.

"Not from this angle."

Shane opened his map to show her, but she pushed it away. "Close that. Makes us look too much like tourists. I trust your instincts."

They walked another block. Footsteps tapped behind them, Sheila was sure of it. When she turned around, she saw nothing but empty sidewalk, darkened by the shade of the buildings. No one on the sunny side of the street either.

"Did you hear that?" she asked her husband.

He shook his head, but his quickened steps indicated he too felt an intuition of danger that his rational self would no doubt deny.

Tap tap tap.

"There it is again." Sheila gripped Shane's arm. "Someone's following us." She looked behind her but for the third time saw no one. Still, she upped her pace until, despite the pain in her feet, she was practically speed walking.

"Look, that street two blocks down is busier." Shane's voice was breathy and winded. "The cathedral is just beyond it."

Tap tap tap.

This time they both spun around. A flash of red hair and a bare arm disappeared into a restaurant. A bell tinkled above the door, proof their eyes hadn't deceived them.

Sheila's stomach swirled. "We've seen that man before."

"Based on a swatch of hair and an arm?"

"He was at the gallery in Edinburgh." Sheila's fingers fluttered to her neck, and her voice shook. "He's the one I told you about. I saw him. He was at the base of the stairs. He made a gun with his fingers. He pushed me, I just know it. I—"

"Okay, okay, dear, I believe you." Shane put his arm around her and guided her onward, all the while looking over his shoulder. Though over the years he claimed not to understand her sensitivities, she knew he had learned not to discredit them.

Another tinkle of a bell behind them. They pivoted around and watched the man with red hair exit the restaurant, his head down low and his face mostly hidden. Still, she knew it was him. She could tell from the hives on his blotchy arms.

He was not more than twenty feet away.

And he was walking in their direction.

"Let's go." Shane's voice snapped Sheila out of her stupor. He pulled her forward in the direction of the cathedral. She tried to match his gait, but she was already walking as fast as her arthritic feet would allow.

The footsteps marched closer.

She didn't dare look over her shoulder. She focused only on crossing the last long block, beyond which lay the cathedral off to the right. Gone were the Chinese restaurants. In their place, residential buildings.

But still no tourists.

The man's footsteps were so close now she swore she could feel his breath on her neck.

Shane broke away.

"What are you doing?" she cried.

She soon had her answer. Her husband had moved to the curb and was waving his arms maniacally at an approaching cab.

"Taxi, taxi," he shouted. Within seconds the cab pulled up. Shane opened the back door and almost pushed Sheila into it. As he followed, he looked over his shoulder, as if fearful the man would climb in with them.

He didn't, but as the cab pulled away, Sheila looked through the rear window at him, barely five feet away. No imaginary gun this time, but his new warning was equally frightening: a slow drag of a finger across his neck.

The cab driver turned the corner, and the man disappeared from view. Sheila faced her husband, his skin pale and his hands trembling. Her own body shook more than the plastic hula doll on the cabby's dashboard.

When she finally caught her breath enough to speak, she said, "Someone's sending us a message."

Shane wheezed and secured his seatbelt. "Consider it received."

INSIDE THE DREAMSCAPE Dining Room on deck four, Sheila slurped French onion soup as if her life depended on it. Maybe it did, because after the fright on Duke Street a few hours before, she needed something to warm her unshakable chill. The brandy outside the casino upon their return had failed to do the job. Now it was up to the steaming broth.

She regretted not making it to the Liverpool Cathedral. Now they would never know if anyone there recognized Shanna. But the encounter with the ginger-haired man had left them too rattled to do anything but return to the ship. Their only recourse was that Shanna would not have lingered in the cathedral given her short time in Liverpool.

A glance at Shane revealed he was in a similar state. Neither his complexion nor his aura had returned to normal. Both were shades of gray. He used his fingers to break off a string of cheese in his French onion soup.

Hoping to take her husband's mind—and her own—off the Duke Street encounter, she mentioned the couple who was left behind in Chester. "Do you think they made it back to the ship in time?"

Shane chewed and stared blankly out the window at the sea beyond. Whether he heard her question or not, she didn't know, because his subsequent response was to a question she had posed earlier. "Maybe you're right. Maybe we should tell the security team about what happened in Liverpool. Officer Tad told us to keep him informed of things. Probably just to humor us, but we should still do it."

A waiter carrying two silver platters smelling of seafood approached the table next to them. After he had served a big-haired woman and her companion, Sheila said, "No, you were right the first time. It's best not to cry wolf yet. We need something more concrete. They already think we're senile and foolish. If we tell them a red-haired man with bad skin is following us, they'll add paranoid to the list too."

Shane's gaze was back on the lump of cheese in his soup. He swirled it around with his spoon, his mind deep in thought. "It might be even worse than that if we say something. What if they tell us we need to leave the ship for our safety? Use the episode as an excuse to get rid of us?" His spoon fell from his hand and clattered against his wine glass. "I'm not going anywhere."

"Me either. Because we're on to something." Sheila leaned in, her cardigan bunching up around her place setting. "You feel it too, don't you?"

"Even more than I did yesterday, when I was simply going on your intuition that the Australian man had something to do with Shanna's disappearance."

"And now?"

"And now I know you're right. Or at least right about someone taking her. Why else would that red-haired man follow us? Maybe he was a mugger, but..."

"But?"

"But he seemed more interested in intimidating and scaring us than taking our money. Why would he do that if he wasn't connected to Shanna somehow?"

Tingles of fear, but also excitement, danced up Sheila's spine. "So you agree it's the same man I saw at the gallery in Edinburgh?"

"I don't know, but I have no reason to doubt you."

"Which would mean our fall wasn't an accident." She gulped

three mouthfuls of wine. "Do you think Hivey Red is on the ship with us?"

"Hivey Red?"

"Can you think of a better description with those blotchy hives on his arms?"

Seeing that his wine glass was empty, Shane reached for his water instead, his tremor so marked Sheila worried the liquid would spill. "I don't know if he's on the boat. I don't know what he wants. I can't make sense of any of this. He could have really hurt us." With each sentence, his agitation grew. "I don't—"

"Shh, shh." Sheila cupped her hands over his and helped him guide the quavering water glass back to the table. "We'll sort it out."

Shane stared up the ceiling, his lined face distorted and stressed. Sheila hadn't seen him this upset since June thirtieth, when they had gone to pick Shanna up at the Boston airport and discovered she hadn't returned from Amsterdam.

"Darling, we'll figure it out," she repeated.

With his head still tilted back, he closed his eyes. "I couldn't save you, Beetle Bug. If that man had attacked us, I wouldn't have been able to save you." He finally lowered his gaze. She was startled to see tears in his eyelashes. "I'm too old. I couldn't save you."

"Oh honey." From across the table, she rubbed his arm. "You'll always have my back, just as I'll always have yours. We might be old and creaky, but together we could row this ship to Belfast with our bare hands."

He blinked, and after a beat, he laughed. Sheila sighed in relief.

"The inaccuracies of your statement would require too much time to recite." He squeezed her hand. "But I'll take it."

In mutual love they smiled at each other across the table, each their own person yet somehow connected. Were it not for Renny stopping by to refill their water, they might have stayed that way forever.

"Can you send Tina over?" Sheila asked the young assistant. "My husband could use some more wine."

A short time later the brisk and efficient sommelier hustled over. Her expression was pinched, and Sheila was confused by the brown color emanating from her. Normally the woman radiated a strong and disciplined blue.

"What can I help you with?" Other than Officer Sourpuss, no crew member had spoken so brusquely.

Shane ordered more wine for both of them. When he finished, Sheila risked asking the sommelier if she remembered anything about Shanna since they had last spoken.

Tina shifted from one hip to the other, as if her feet were on fire.

Growing annoyed at her attitude, Sheila pressed on. Surely the woman could spare three seconds. "You see, according to the security footage, the day Shanna returned from Belfast—which is our stop tomorrow—she was bothered about something. I know it's asking a lot of you to remember, but even the smallest detail might help us. For example, did you see her with a man with red hair and hives—"

"I told you, I know nothing about your daughter."

The woman spun around and clipped away so abruptly Sheila's mouth fell open. When she finally collected herself, she scrunched up her nose and grimaced. She swore the woman's sour brownness still clung in the air.

12

NO PEACE UNTIL THEN

GIVEN the drama in Liverpool the day before, Sheila hadn't expected to enjoy the coach tour through Belfast as much as she did. She had assumed she would be too preoccupied with Shanna's disappearance and Mr. Smelly's (or Hivey Red's) role in it, but her surprises on that eighth day of the cruise were threefold.

First, the Belfast tour guide recognized Shanna. "Aye, I remember her well," the stocky, sixtyish man said, his Northern Ireland accent so thick Sheila had trouble deciphering it. "She sat up front like the two of you. Asked me questions about our art museums."

Second, he also remembered Mr. Smelly. "He had a boxer's face and an Aussie's speech, that one did, but he was not as infatuated with our fair city as your lassie was."

Third, Sheila fell in love with Belfast, far more than she would have imagined.

During the three-hour coach tour, their exuberant guide rallied them with tales of Belfast's past, present, and future. When they were driving along Queens Road past a former shipyard, he pointed to an angular building with metallic siding that shimmered like shards of ice, even on a cloudy and drizzling day. "That's

Titanic Belfast. You can learn all about the doomed ship in there
after yer tour if you have the time." He scanned his bus audience
and raised a bushy eyebrow. "Hope yer own ship fares better than
she did."

A titter went through the excursion group.

He pointed to another building along the waterfront. "And that
yellow-and-gray-striped buildin' there is Titanic Studios. Anyone
know what was filmed there?"

In his rapid rogue, Sheila barely understood the question, but
someone else did, because a voice from the back of the bus shouted,
"*Game of Thrones.*"

"Ay, yer right. A pint of Guinness to the man in back." The
guide made a *cheers* gesture with his arm as if clinking a glass in a
toast.

A few minutes later Belfast's residential areas, with their
picturesque stucco and stone homes and luscious landscapes, equally
wowed Sheila and Shane. The shrubbery and lawns were so
vibrantly green they almost fluoresced, perhaps making the frequent
rain worth it.

The upscale neighborhoods gradually shifted to working-class
homes, where row houses connected to each other like brothers in
arms. This led to the best part of the tour, at least in Sheila's mind:
the Peace Lines, or Peace Walls as their tour guide called them.

A series of barriers, constructed with either bricks or steel and
ranging from a few hundred yards in length to over three miles long,
the Peace Walls separated the Catholic neighborhoods from the
Protestant ones. Some climbed as high as twenty-five feet. Others
were shorter. Political images and peace messages colored their
facades, the vivid graffiti bringing people together through art.

When the coach stopped to allow the excursion guests time to
sign their own messages of peace, Sheila didn't hesitate to grab her
umbrella and a marker from the tour guide and leave the warmth of
the bus. Neither did Shane, but although Sheila quickly found a spot
on the wall next to a cluster of purple and pink hearts, Shane was
more methodical in his choosing. With the planes of his face shifting
in mental calculation, he finally zoomed in on a spot. He nodded at

her. "This should fall at eye level for two standard deviations of the population."

Sheila thought for a moment about what to write. She decided on something simple. "Hate will destroy us. Love will save us."

When she looked up from her work and saw Shane's message, her eyes moistened. Written in her husband's scrawled penmanship were the words: "Peace for the world. Peace for my daughter. But until I find her, there will be no peace for me."

"Oh Shaney." Sheila raised her umbrella to cover his hat, water dripping from its brim. They huddled in silence for a moment, drinking in a sight they would likely never see again. Then he ushered her back onto the coach.

When the bus was once again on its way, headed to the Botanic Gardens in south Belfast where the Ulster Museum was located, Shane's peace message echoed in Sheila's brain. He and Shanna had always been close. The two were of like minds, Shane with his numbers and precision, Shanna with her logic and pragmatism. "Mom," she would say, with unintentional condescension, "you can't let emotions make your decisions. Eliminate them first, then decide."

Sheila would chuckle. "Oh dear, it's cute you think that's possible. It's even cuter you and your father think you only make decisions based on logic."

Engrossed in her thoughts, Sheila missed out on most of what the tour guide said about the Botanic Gardens. She caught something about twenty-eight acres and being near Queen's University. The next thing she knew, Shane was helping her off the bus. For their sixty minutes of free time, they planned to walk along the park's perimeter with its fragrant flowers and lush greenery, and then visit the Ulster Museum.

Earlier, she had learned from the tour guide that Shanna had wanted more time in the museum. She had asked that the bus leave without her, stating she would take a cab back to the ship. Sheila and Shane, however, didn't need an afternoon to observe art like their daughter. They merely wanted to ask the museum staff if they remembered anything about her.

As they approached the massive gray museum, trepidation stiffened Sheila's gait. Her eyes scanned the tourists for flashes of red hair and irritated skin. Though she saw no signs of Hivey Red, anxiety plagued her nonetheless. To distract herself, she again recalled something from the security footage they had watched a few days before.

"Remember how Shanna paused at the top of the gangway as if she was waiting for someone to join her? How happy she seemed?" she asked Shane.

He nodded, his gaze on the red-bricked residential units across the street.

"And how she looked bothered when she returned? As if she was upset about something?"

"Of course. We talked about that before we fell down the stairs in the Edinburgh museum. I couldn't really tell from the footage, but if you say she was upset, that's good enough for me."

Sheila smiled. Logic without emotion, my hiney, she thought. If his faith in her intuition was not illogical, she didn't know what was.

"We need to find out what made her go from radiant to bothered," she continued. "I don't think it was anything on the coach tour. Our guide said Shanna and Mr. Smelly left happy enough. He said Shanna tipped him five euros and mentioned wanting to see some paintings in the museum."

"The works of Mainie Jellett." Below a stone awning at the museum's entrance, Shane held the door open for her.

"So she left the coach tour happy but came back to the ship bothered. What happened within those few hours to change her mood? Was it a bad cab ride back to the dock? Did she not see the paintings she wanted? Or did something happen inside this place to upset her?"

"Let's find out."

In contrast to the cozy environment of the Scottish National Gallery, the Ulster Museum's interior was industrial, with massive rooms, high ceilings, and bleached walls that connected via glass-bordered hallways and walkways.

"It's brutalist," Shane said, slowly turning around full circle.

"I'm sorry?" Sheila studied a prehistoric raptor suspended from the ceiling. Before entering the museum, she had been thinking art in a traditional sense, with paintings and sculptures, but according to the guidebook dispensed to them at the ticket booth, the museum also displayed historical and natural science exhibits. Had they more time, she knew Shane could spend hours in the facility. "What did you say about brutality?"

"Brutalist. The architectural style is brutalist, especially on the outside. Exposed concrete, massive, rugged, raw. The inside was renovated decades ago though. It's softer now."

Sheila shook her head and narrowly sidestepped an escaped toddler, his mother running in hot pursuit behind him. "How you know all these things is a mystery to me."

"While you're tapering toilet paper into a V, I'm reading the ship's daily planner."

Shane's lopsided grin told Sheila he was teasing her, but she supposed he had a point. Think of all the opportunity for learning she had lost by being neat.

Shane did another three-sixty turn in the open space. With an expression of regret, probably wishing he could explore the dinosaur and mummy exhibits, he unfolded the museum map and searched for the Mainie Jellett collection.

After a few wrong turns, five map checks, and a bathroom stop, they finally found the work of Mainie Jellett, along with several other artists. Rows of track lighting illuminated the paintings, which were hung on the walls at various heights from the wooden floor.

As with the previous museum they visited, tourists milled about with different degrees of interest. Some strolled from painting to painting, casually taking them in. Others came to a standstill, arms folded, gazes locked on a canvas. A couple people sketched. Though Sheila found the work pretty, her feet were tired, and her joints ached. On top of that, the museum air dried out her eyes, siphoning away precious moisture an eighty-year-old woman with mild cataracts could hardly spare. When an attendant entered the room, she sighed in relief.

"Excuse me, miss, could you help us?" Sheila took in the tall woman's red aura, bobbed hair, and manicured hands, each finger-nail painted with yellow polka dots on a crimson base.

"Certainly, ma'am. What is it you need? A wheelchair?"

Sheila's eyes widened. "Goodness no. We're perfectly capable of walking."

"No offense meant." The woman's smile flashed a generous ridge of gum line. "You just looked to be limpin' a bit."

Sheila puffed air out of her nostrils. Why did people with red auras always feel the need to be right? Just like Officer Sourpuss. Then again, that very nature was why they emanated red hues in the first place. "I'm fine. My feet are a little sore, that's all."

"If you say so, ma'am." The words danced playfully in the Irish accent.

Sheila debated further discourse but decided there was no point. Instead, she shifted her raincoat to her other arm and pulled her phone from her handbag. Going through the motions that were by now rote, she showed the young woman first a picture of Shanna and then the picture of Mr. Smelly, explaining that their daughter was missing and they were in search of her.

That last bit of information seemed lost on the woman. In fact, Sheila was not even sure the attendant had heard, because when she saw the picture of Mr. Smelly, her pink gum line popped back into view, and her eyes sparkled like the eyeshadow embellishing them. "I do remember those two."

"You do?" Sheila's hopes lifted. To her left, Shane fumbled for his pen and notebook from the inside pocket of his blazer.

"Yeah, that guy's hard to forget." The attendant ran two polka dot fingers over her chin and poked the tip of her tongue out. What the gesture meant to convey, Sheila didn't care to know.

"But what about our daughter? Can you tell us anything?" Shane's uneven tone suggested he was similarly bemused by the colorful woman.

"She was in this room a long time. That's why I remember her so well. Was interested in Mainie Jellett."

"Yes, that's her." Sheila's pulse quickened.

"While she stared at the paintings, I heard that handsome man asking her questions about her job in the museum. An art restorer, isn't she?"

"Yes, in Boston."

"They talked about that for a while, him asking her how she would restore this one if it were torn or that one if it should get soiled." The attendant's hands waved breezily at the paintings around her. "But then he made her mad."

"How? What did he say? What did he do?" Sheila asked quickly.

The woman leaned in. Shane scribbled madly. "He asked her about forged artwork."

"Forged artwork!" Sheila's raised voice drew looks from museumgoers. She dropped her volume, but her words still quivered in surprise. "Are you saying some of these paintings are forged?"

The attendant laughed, her hair swishing around her chin. "Of course not, don't be silly. He was only trying to get a rile out of her, you know? She's a serious one, your daughter."

Sheila said nothing. She couldn't argue with that description.

"He asked your daughter if she would ever forge a painting. He said to her," the attendant put her hands on her hips, slim in a pencil skirt, and dropped her voice to sound like a man's, "'You know, just to see if you could get away with it.'" The woman giggled again. "Then, when your daughter looked annoyed, he said, 'If someone offered you loads of money to make a fake painting or fix up a stolen one, you'd really say no?' He was kiddin', of course, but your daughter would have none of it."

"Of course she wouldn't." Sheila stuffed her phone back into her purse with more force than necessary. "She's a serious art restorer."

As if it had finally dawned on the woman that Shanna was missing, her face softened, and the gums disappeared. Even the shimmering redness around her eased up. "Of course she is. I didn't mean to imply otherwise. I hope what I've told you will help. That's all there is, really. After that they left, but she still looked a bit peeved."

In equal parts fatigue, excitement, and grief, Sheila said, "Thank you. You've been a big help."

With only ten minutes remaining until the bus left, they retraced their steps to the museum exit. On the walk back, the rain beat a steady rhythm on the umbrella. Beneath it, Sheila pondered what they had just learned. Joke or no joke, Mr. Smelly had questioned Shanna's ethics. Was that why she had looked bothered on the return from Belfast? She was a stickler for rules, no question about that, and she took nothing more seriously than art and her work with it.

Or was it something simpler? Had she just grown tired of his company? Shanna's good intuition disappeared when it came to choosing men. Her longest-running boyfriend had been arrested for accounting fraud, after all. Was it simply a matter of girl meets boy, girl grows disillusioned with boy, girl avoids boy for the rest of the cruise?

But if that were the case, her daughter would have returned home. Clearly something or someone had kept that from happening. Although Sheila had no proof, nothing concrete on which to hang Shane's fedora, she knew in her heart it was the spiritually smelly man in the picture on her phone. How had the Belfast tour guide referred to him? She thought for a moment and then remembered: a man with a boxer's face and an Aussie's speech.

But how—or if—he was tied to Hivey Red, she had no clue.

13

A SNAIL FOR YOUR THOUGHTS

FOR THE THIRD time since Sheila had given the blown-glass beaver to Victor, he thanked her. "I will treasure your beaver forever, madam. You are so very kind to think of me." Then he served her appetizer, the one she still couldn't believe she had been bold enough to order, and stepped back from the table. "You have made an excellent choice tonight. You won't be disappointed."

She stared at the unusual plate. Like the waves outside the dining room windows, second and third thoughts washed over her. "Oh dear," she managed to say.

Six small wells with six small creatures looked up at her, each snail drowning in a buttery sauce flecked with parsley and seasoned with garlic.

"Oh dear," she repeated.

Across the table, Shane chuckled. "Bon appétit." He dipped his spoon into his French onion soup, the same appetizer he had ordered four nights out of the last eight. "You've always been braver than me."

Waiters passed by, less hurried than usual, and diners—fewer than typical—clinked silverware and chatted about their day in

Belfast. Classical music wafted from hidden speakers and softened the already warm atmosphere.

"I…" Sheila poked one of the shells with her fork. "I don't know how to eat this."

Victor clapped his hands once, and within seconds Renny, the assistant waiter, arrived at their table. Sheila had taken to calling him Cutie Pie. Surely he wouldn't mind such a complimentary name from an old woman, especially when his gold aura welcomed attention and admiration.

"Please show our guest how to eat her appetizer." To Sheila, Victor said, "Everyone needs to learn the first time, but you will soon be a pro at it. How wonderful of you to try it." His lyrical Indian accent was smoother than whipped butter, and his aura a kindhearted orange.

Not wanting to disappoint him, she put on a brave face. "We learned new information about our daughter today, so I'm feeling especially adventurous." She raised her arm in triumph and nearly stabbed Renny with her fork.

Victor had turned to leave, but he pivoted back toward the table. "You did?" After adjusting his black-framed glasses, he clasped his hands and held them at his chin in anticipation of their news.

As Renny used tongs to anchor a snail's shell in one hand and a tiny fork to pluck out the meaty body with the other, Sheila filled Victor in on their findings from the day in Belfast. Meanwhile, Shane slurped his soup. A tiny string of cheese dangled from his chin, and Sheila reached over and dabbed it away.

When she finished her story, Victor inhaled sharply. "So the museum employee recognized both your daughter and Mr. Smelly?"

Shane raised his eyebrows at Victor's use of the nickname but kept eating. Sheila, on the other hand, was not at all surprised Victor had adopted the name she had accidentally let slip out. After all, he was the one who first mentioned the Australian man had smelled off. She and Victor had such a strong spiritual connection that were he not from another continent and a different gene pool, she would swear he was her long-lost son.

"Yes, she recognized them both," Sheila responded. "And she

told us Mr. Smelly irritated Shanna with talk of art forgery and theft. Got our daughter all riled up about it. That's probably why she came back from Belfast looking bothered on the security footage."

Victor pressed his hand against his hip. A linen napkin was draped over the same arm. "Hmm, you just made me think of something."

"I did?" Sheila looked up hopefully.

"Yes. Let me fetch my orders, and I will return when I get a chance."

As he left, Renny plucked out the fifth snail. She had yet to eat any of them. "Would you like to remove the last one yourself, miss?"

Before Sheila could respond, Tina, the sommelier, flew past their table in a tight, swishy gait. Given both Sheila and Shane had declined wine that evening, Tina didn't acknowledge them, but in her haste she almost bumped into an occupied table. Her expression was as taut as her hair bun, and the brown color emanating from her was darker than the previous night.

Sheila returned her attention to Renny and smiled slyly at what he'd said. "*Miss?* No one has called me 'miss' since well before you were born. You're such a cutie pie and no doubt a terrific flirt. You probably have a dozen girlfriends back in Pakistan." When she went to take the tongs and snail fork from him, she noticed his yellow aura of confidence fade. His countenance, too, was darker. "Oh my, what's wrong? Have I hurt your feelings?"

He scanned the room as if looking for someone. "Not at all. It's just, well, normally what you say about me is true. But there is a woman on this ship who will have none of it."

Renny's confession got Shane's attention, and for the first time he rested his spoon against his crock of soup and made fleeting eye contact with the assistant waiter. Analytical engineer or not, the man enjoyed a bit of gossip.

"Oh *pfft*." Sheila plucked the last snail out of its shell with gusto, as if she had been doing it all her life. Unfortunately, all six creatures were now ready to eat. "I don't believe any woman could resist your charms."

"This one can." He looked around and lowered his voice. With his hands clasped behind his back, he leaned his trim frame over the table. "What is strange is, I would swear on my grandmother's grave she likes me. She smiles when I approach her, or at least I see it in her eyes, but—" He stood abruptly, as if realizing he was sharing too much information with a guest. "I'm sorry. Please forgive me. You must get back to enjoying your dinner."

"No please," Sheila said, "I want to hear more." Her statement was in part true. The other part was pure stalling, anything to postpone her first bite of the rubbery mound on the end of her fork.

"You might as well confess all, son." Shane returned to his soup. "She'll figure it out, anyway. I don't know how, but she will."

Renny bit his lower lip. He took a few steps back to the waiters' station, grabbed a silver pitcher of water, and returned to their table. As he refreshed their glasses, he said, "You see, as soon as I start speaking, telling her how pretty she is today, how nice her nails look, how smooth her skin is, she goes all stiff and her smile disappears." Renny pointed to Sheila's fork. "She's like a snail that returns to its shell."

Sheila lowered the fork and sat back in her chair, its plush fabric heaven on her stiff spine. "My dear boy, maybe you've got the wrong game plan."

Renny's hand slipped on the pitcher. Condensation dripped off its base and onto the patterned carpet. "What do you mean?"

"Believe it or not, not all women want to hear how pretty they are or how smooth their skin is," Sheila said. "Take my daughter, for example. That wouldn't work on her at all." Across the table Shane smiled, as if a memory of Shanna had drifted into his mind. "If you tell her she's pretty, which she is, of course, she'll puff out her cheeks and roll her eyes. But," Sheila paused for emphasis. "If you tell her she's one of the smartest people you've ever met, or that her skill with a paintbrush is unrivaled, or that her attention to detail is amazing, well then, my young cutie pie, she'll melt."

Renny straightened his posture and tilted his head, as if such a thought had never occurred to him. He gripped the water pitcher with both hands and stared out at the sea. "This woman is all those things. Well, not the part about the paint brush, but she is very efficient and very smart. That is why I like her. She's different from the others."

Sheila lifted her palms in a *voilà* fashion. "There you have it then. Switch up your compliments and you'll have a date with this woman in no time."

A smile lit up his angelic features. "I will, miss, I will. Thank you so very much." He looked down at her escargot. "Please, I have taken too much of your time. You have not even tasted your appetizer yet." He made a slight bow and hurried away. Even from behind, his aura radiated joy.

By now, Shane had finished his soup. "Your meal will be here soon, and you haven't even touched your little mollusk friends." His tone was teasing, and in the cute smirk on his face, she once again saw not the wrinkles, droopy eyelids, or age spots of an old man, but the boy she fell in love with decades ago. A boy who had awkwardly complimented her pretty face, smooth skin, and quick wit, and she had not minded any of the three. "I knew you'd change your mind about the escargot."

"Care to wager on that, dear husband?" Sheila leaned forward, grabbed her fork, and popped the rubbery blob into her mouth. She chewed. She contemplated. She swallowed. What she tasted was butter, garlic, and seasonings. What she felt was a firm, gelatinous mound.

"Well? What's the verdict?"

She wiped her mouth. "I believe I've just eaten a pencil eraser drowned in butter."

They laughed, and the laughter felt so good she braved another eraser. While she was chewing, Victor returned to clear their plates. "Your entrées will be out shortly." He looked at the remaining four snails. "You did not like, madam?"

"They were better than I thought they would be, but two is enough. I don't want to be craving sand or sprouting tentacles tonight."

Victor blinked uncertainly, then picked up their appetizer plates and said, "May I tell you now what I remembered about your daughter?"

Both McShanes sat tall in their seats, all teasing and laughter cast aside. Sheila nodded eagerly. Shane reached for his notebook and pen.

"When you mentioned your daughter seemed upset after her day in Belfast, I thought more about her meals in the dining room. Remember I told you I didn't see her much at the end? After further thought, I realized I didn't see her at *all* after Belfast."

"Are you sure?" Sheila hardly dared breathe. That could be important information, because if Shanna had disappeared from the ship, it gave Sheila and Shane a timeframe. Something to help narrow down the day she went missing. Shane documented Victor's words.

"I am now. You see, I remember asking her if she visited the Titanic Belfast. She said no. She said she spent most of her time at a museum. At that point in her meal, she was still happy."

"What do you mean *still*? What changed?"

"She came in alone. She seemed fine, happy, not at all riled up. Isn't that the word you used earlier?" Victor didn't wait for an answer. "But that changed when he tried to join her."

Sheila tilted her body closer to Victor. "Who? Mr. Smelly?"

The waiter nodded conspiratorially, still holding the soiled appetizer dishes in his hands. "Yes, Mr. Smelly, the man with—"

"A boxer's face and an Aussie's speech." Sheila quoted their tour guide from earlier that day.

"He joined her for dinner. Sat right at the table with her. After that her happiness vanished. I simply assumed they had a lover's quarrel. Certainly none of my business. When I returned to take their order, she apologized to me and said she was not feeling well enough for dinner. She got up, and I never saw her again after that."

"Didn't you wonder where she had gone?" Sheila asked, fear taking root in her belly.

"To be honest, I don't think I gave it any mind. If I did, I would have simply assumed she chose to eat up in the buffet for the rest of the cruise or ordered room service. We have so very many passengers, madam. I would have remembered none of these things without your prompting." Victor stared at Shane's feverish writing, his face sagging in guilt. "My deepest apologies I didn't remember this sooner. I've been so rushed every evening. Tonight is less busy." He nodded his head toward the other tables. "Discounts in the specialty restaurants, so our dinner crowd is smaller."

Were Victor's hands not full of dishware, Sheila would have grasped them in gratitude. "You have no reason to apologize. In fact, you've been very helpful. But are you absolutely positive you didn't see Shanna in here the last four nights of the cruise?"

Shane looked up from his notebook, and Sheila waited breathlessly.

The waiter lowered his chin. "I did not. I wasn't so sure before, but I am sure of it now. After that night, I never saw your daughter in the dining room again."

14

THAT'S NO PLACE FOR A PROPHYLACTIC

WITH EVERY STEP toward the library, pain shot through Sheila's feet as if the undersides of her pedal bones were welded to metal balls. The day in Belfast had been long, and she wanted nothing more than to retreat to her stateroom and sleep, but it was imperative she talk to Shane about what she had just overheard. She hobbled along toward the midship elevator bank and spilled into the library beyond it.

She spotted her husband in a wingback chair across the room from the concierge, who was behind his desk discussing future cruise options with a guest. She nodded at the man in passing. She had spoken to him a few days before to ask if he recognized Shanna, but he hadn't. He'd worked a different ship until July. A few other guests were scattered about the room. Maybe, like Shane and herself, they preferred a quiet read over live music, dancing, and karaoke.

By the time she reached her husband, she was breathless. "Oh, Shaney, we have to help him."

He looked up from his book, which was a guide on British art. Though not his usual fare, she supposed it was his way of connecting with Shanna. Despite her urgency to convey her news, she was touched by his attempt.

"Help who?"

"Raoul. Those terrible people. They're——" She stopped to catch her breath and pulled her cardigan around her. A thicker wool, it was the warmest of the three she had brought.

"Here, sit down, dear. You look exhausted."

He reached out a hand to her, but she shook her head. "No. If I sit I'll never get back up. It's that couple again."

Shane closed his book and shifted to the edge of his chair. "Uh oh, what have they done now?"

"They're just awful. They claim they found a used condom under their bed, and they're blaming poor Raoul."

If Sheila thought the room had been quiet before, it was now a soundless tomb. Everyone was looking her way, the concierge included. His expression said, "Well, that's one I haven't heard before."

Shane pushed himself to a stand. "Is he still in their room?"

"No, he was leaving when I passed by. Once again I couldn't see what they looked like, but I heard them hollering. Despite Raoul's protests that the condom wasn't his—and of course it wasn't—they wouldn't believe him."

Shane's cheeks colored, and his hands tightened on the book. "They're looking for a free cruise at Raoul's expense. And by expense, I mean losing his job."

"Please, we have to help him. I know he doesn't want me to talk to his supervisor, says it will only make things worse, but I don't see what else we can do." She took a deep breath to calm herself. "He has a family back in Venezuela. We can't let him lose his job."

"Can I help you?" The concierge joined them, his burgundy blazer bearing the logo of the *Celestial of the Seas*. His name badge and accent confirmed he was from England.

Sheila glanced back at his desk. The man he had been speaking to was gone, and the few other guests in the room had returned to their reading, though Sheila suspected they were still listening.

"We're fine, thank you," Shane said.

"Are you sure? If you're having difficulties with a stateroom attendant, I can talk to——"

"No," Sheila blurted. She lowered her voice and added, "Thank you, but our stateroom attendant is lovely."

"I see, well…" An uncomfortable silence followed, and then, as if eager for something other than used condoms to discuss, the concierge pointed to the book in Shane's hands. "You're reading up on British art, I see. There are still some lovely museums to visit in the last four days of your cruise. In Belgium as well, which is our last stop before returning to Amsterdam."

Shane nodded. Sheila was still fretting about Raoul. How she hated to see a good person wronged.

"In fact," the concierge continued, "if you visit Ghent rather than Bruges on our last day, which, given your…" he cleared his throat and looked embarrassed. "What I mean to say is, since the coaches can't go into the old part of Bruges, there is much more walking involved in those excursions than the Ghent ones."

"We're going to Ghent." Sheila was too distressed about Raoul to be offended by the concierge's assumption they were too old to enjoy Bruges.

The polished man clasped his hands together and brought them to his chest. "Splendid. Then be sure to visit the Ghent Altarpiece in St. Bavo's Cathedral. It's a beautiful collection of several paintings. Sadly, one of them, *The Just Judges*, was stolen decades ago and is still missing." When neither Sheila nor Shane replied, he added, "The whole altarpiece is also called *The Adoration of the Mystic Lamb*."

Sheila jolted in recognition. Though she hadn't forgotten about Raoul, hearing mention of the artwork Shanna had most wanted to see momentarily distracted her. "Our daughter was very excited to see that."

At the mention of Shanna, the concierge's face fell. "Yes, of course, you are looking for her. Here I am prattling on about excursion activities. I didn't mean to sound so enthusiastic in what must be a difficult time for you."

His chagrin touched her. She was about to tell him not to worry, when a couple took a seat in front of his desk. Looking relieved, he wished them well with the rest of the cruise and hurried over to help the couple.

Sheila looked back at Shane, ready to return to the issue at hand. He beat her to it.

"A used condom?" He stroked his chin. "Left by Raoul? He barely has time to eat let alone get frisky in a stateroom." He stared up at the ceiling, his thought wheels churning. Then he reshelved the book, grabbed Sheila's elbow, and guided her back toward their cabin. "Since we're exploring Dublin on our own tomorrow, I'd like to make a little stop. For Raoul."

"A stop? What kind of stop?"

As was his quiet way, Shane said nothing more, but as they stood outside their cabin door, riffling through pockets for their ever-wandering key cards, Sheila once again wondered what exactly he had in mind.

15

THE COMPETITION GETS FIERCE

As THEY SET out for Dublin on the ninth morning of their cruise, Sheila and Shane chose seats near the front of the bus, just as they had with all the other excursions. It was easier for them to get on and off, and so far passengers had been cordial about giving up the spots. This morning they ended up in the fourth row, but as the coach pulled away from the port, belching a plume of diesel fumes in its wake, Sheila took one look at the couple in front of them and wished they had opted for the back instead.

The woman was thin, with curly, bleached-blond hair. The man was heavyset, with a 1970s combover. The scent of morning-after hangovers clung to them both.

Sheila nudged Shane. From low in her lap, she pointed to the seatbacks in front of them. At first Shane shrugged, a questioning look in his eyes. He seemed eager to get back to the city map the coach driver had given him. But when Sheila mouthed the words *towel animal* and *solarium*, he dropped the map and his face shifted into a sour grimace that mirrored her own.

"Let's make sure to avoid that seat on the way back," he whispered. "No telling what might be left behind."

Sheila smirked. "They're the color of sulfur."

"I don't smell anything but whiskey and diesel."

"No. They're the *color* of sulfur, not the smell. Like a mustard color."

"Should that mean something to me?" Shane's attention was back on his map, and his voice no longer whispered.

"A mustard aura means anger and irritability. Maybe their towel animals jilted them." She laughed quietly, but her chuckling abruptly halted when the woman turned her head sideways and a penciled-in eyebrow came into view. In a tizzy of recognition, Sheila pinched Shane's sleeve. When he didn't respond, she tugged the fabric so hard the map nearly slipped out of his hand.

"What is it?" He sounded annoyed.

Barely able to contain her agitation, she cupped a hand over his ear and whispered, "It's the couple from stateroom eleven seventy-six. The messy couple who's so awful to Raoul."

That got Shane's attention. He stared at the back of the two heads in front of him. "Are you sure?"

Sheila's thighs bounced up and down on the seat. She whispered, "I recognized her overly plucked eyebrows when she turned sideways. Between those and the bleached-blond curls, I'm positive she's the woman I saw through the door crack. I should have known they were the towel weirdos. If only I'd made the connection sooner. I'm going to give them a piece of my mind."

She leaned forward, but Shane held her back. He shook his head. "Not yet. I'll handle it."

Though his focus remained on the couple, he didn't respond to Sheila's whispered inquiry as to what he had in mind. Instead, after a few moments, he returned to his Dublin map and with his fancy pen circled various sites in the city, drawing arrows this way and that.

Seeing he had no intention of taking the discussion further, she looked out the window at the gray skies and city traffic. Her ire at the couple eased to a tepid simmer, though her worry for Raoul remained. After fifteen minutes of driving, each street more historical in age and more packed with tourists than the last, the bus came to a stop on a divided road. To their right was a lovely park. To their left, a string of brick and stone buildings, seemingly a mixture of business and residential units.

Their driver stood, yanked a creaky lever, and opened the bus door. "This is where ya can pick up the hop-on/hop-off buses." His Irish brogue was much easier to decipher than the Belfast tour guide's had been. "I'll be in the same spot at four o'clock to take ya back to the ship. If you're running late, it's easy to catch a cab in Dublin to the port. But I hear yer boat's leaving at six, so unless ya want to stay all night and drink with me, ya best be back before then."

A collective chuckle went through the bus. Someone called out, "Heck yeah, man."

Sheila wasn't interested in drinking. She wasn't even particularly interested in Dublin. Though beautiful and bustling, it wasn't enough to entice her to leave the warmth of the bus for a brisk, windy day all on their own, which was how Shanna had planned to spend the day, at least according to the itinerary she had shared with them. It was much easier to drive place to place in a toasty coach. Feeling particularly achy today, she hadn't yet worked out the muscle kinks from their fall down the stairs four days before or their tense scare in Liverpool two days after that. Plus, although she took frequent walks back home in New Hampshire, she hadn't walked this much in ages. The throb in the balls of her feet could attest to that. A trip to her podiatrist was a must when they returned home.

Hopefully with their daughter.

That thought, no matter how futile or naive it might be, was what propelled her out of her seat behind Shane and into the aisle of the bus, where she waited to get off. Between the knowledge gained in Belfast and Victor's recollection of not having seen Shanna beyond that stop, Sheila thought they were on the right track. No, it went beyond thought. She *felt* it. Felt it like she felt the ache in her spine, the rocks in her feet, and the mounting fatigue in her soul. Even if it meant encountering Hivey Red again, she wouldn't give up.

As guests filed off the bus, the coach driver held up a hand. "A fair bit of warning, ya hear? There are several hop-on/hop-off bus companies in Dublin, each one hungry for tourists. Be on the lookout for a bit of scrappy competition."

When they stepped off the bus into the gusty cold, Shane tugged the collar of Sheila's raincoat, urgency in his voice. "The orange line. We have to catch the orange bus line. That was the one Shanna planned to use because they have live guides. She didn't want a recording."

"Yes, I remember. The orange line."

Barely had she uttered the words when a trio of young people raced toward them. Each held a clipboard, and each wore a jacket the same color as their hop-on/hop-off bus company. The woman in orange was in the lead, her flaxen ponytail whipping side to side and her tortoiseshell glasses slipping down her nose. She narrowly missed a large family hailing a taxi cab near the curb, but she was able to sidestep them. The two young men, one in purple and one in blue, were not so lucky. By the time they dodged the horseplaying kids, the woman in the orange jacket had already skidded to a stop in front of Sheila and Shane. Both McShanes stepped back in bewilderment.

"Hi, are you looking for a bus?" The young woman was nearly breathless from her sprint. "I'm with the orange line, we pick up every ten minutes at thirty stops and have live guided tours and—"

At that moment the young man in the purple jacket swooped in, followed closely by the one in blue.

"Take the purple," the youngster barked, his thick hipster hair billowing out in the wind. He jerked his head toward the woman in the orange jacket. "They say every ten minutes, but they don't mean it. We—"

"Look, look!" interrupted the young man in the blue jacket. He pointed at an approaching bus. Unlike his competitor's hirsutism, his early-pattern baldness withstood the wind nobly. "One of our buses is pulling up now." He waved his arm in a frantic motion, as if to pull Sheila and Shane forward in its momentum.

"Oh dear, the bus driver wasn't kidding." Sheila took another step back, both from the youths' onslaught and from the blast of cold air that whipped her raincoat. At the moment she didn't care about bus colors or competitive sales. She simply wanted to sit down and be warm. At least it wasn't raining, though the dark, pendulous clouds suggested it might. "Look Shane, the blue one is here already."

Shane stared at the blue double-decker bus. He shook his head. "Shanna took the orange. We need to—"

"No, not the orange," Hipster Purple repeated. He scowled and flapped his hand in a manner that suggested the orange line was operated by baboons. "They say every ten minutes, but they don't—"

"Yes, yes, they don't mean it. We heard you the first time." Sheila hadn't meant to snap, but her chill got the best of her. She pulled up her hood and cinched it around her neck to block out the wind, knowing it would flatten her hair but willing to risk it. Had Dublin skipped all the way into December without telling anyone?

She glanced at Shane again, longing in her eyes for the warmth of the blue bus, but he shook his head again. He moved closer to the young woman with the orange jacket. Behind her designer glasses, her eyes lit up in victory.

Sheila sighed. "Sorry boys. My husband is right. We need to take the orange line for our daughter. You see she—"

Hipster Purple and Baldy Blue had already darted off to other targets, but not before Hipster Purple flashed a cocky smile over his shoulder and yelled, "No worries. We'll be seeing you soon enough when the orange bus doesn't show."

The woman in orange shook her head. "Don't listen to them, you've made the right choice." With her Irish accent, she was as chipper and chirpy as a canary, a canary who had just bested two male cats. "We're the only one with a live guide on every bus."

"So you said." Sheila shivered and shoved her hands deeper into her pockets, her handbag holstered in the crook of her arm. "Surely it isn't always this cold in Dublin at the end of August?"

Orange Jacket grinned and shifted her clipboard to the other hand. "It's a bit nippier than usual, but it can get pretty cold this time of year."

"Will the bus be here soon?"

"Three minutes."

"Three minutes until the next bus." Shane's statement was more a confirmation than a question. He blew air into his cupped hands, and his face sagged when a purple bus pulled up to the curb.

Three minutes didn't give much time for questioning, Sheila thought, so she exposed her hands to the cold and withdrew her phone from her purse. While Shane gave Orange Jacket the hop-on/hop-off vouchers from their Dublin On Your Own excursion in exchange for tickets, Sheila pulled up Shanna's picture. They had planned to do most of their querying at the National Gallery of Ireland where Shanna would have spent the bulk of her time, but it didn't hurt to ask this young woman about Shanna as well, no matter how slim the odds.

Orange Jacket gave Shane a map of the orange line's route and was pointing out stops when Sheila held up her phone. "Do you recognize our daughter? We think she took this same excursion back on June twenty-sixth. She's…" Sheila swallowed a lump. "She's missing. She never came home."

The young woman froze, her finger suspended midair above Shane's map. "Oh how terrible." Her concern seemed genuine, and that warmed Sheila a bit. While Orange Jacket studied the photo, Sheila looked at the commotion going on behind the young woman. Hipster Purple and Baldy Blue were charging a group of tourists who had just rounded the street corner. Meanwhile, another blue bus pulled up to the curb. A group of fortunate travelers, those with blue line tickets, climbed into its warmth, save for those who braved the open-air top.

Through her glasses, Orange Jacket squinted at Shanna's picture, and when Sheila swiped the screen to Mr. Smelly, the woman tilted her head. After a beat, she lifted her face and gave a nod of recognition.

"You remember her?"

"I remember them both." Orange Jacket seemed as surprised by that as Sheila and Shane were. "It's because I'm an art student, that's why. While your daughter waited for the bus, she told me she worked as an art restorer. We talked for a long time."

"You mean you talked for three minutes? Three minutes while you waited for the next bus?" Sarcasm flattened Shane's words. He searched the busy, divided street, but no orange bus materialized. Sheila knew he was as eager for news about Shanna as she was, but nothing irritated him more than getting behind schedule, whether his schedule or somebody else's.

"Er, yes, um, just a minute." Orange Jacket grabbed her phone and made a quick call. She nodded and disconnected. To the McShanes, she said, "I've just spoken to my colleague one stop over. He said the bus will be here soon. Three minutes tops."

Shane scrunched his lips but said nothing. He pulled out his notebook and pen. Traffic whizzed past them, and pedestrians jostled noisily on the sidewalk. Some entered buildings on that side of the street. Others crossed over to the park.

Sheila shoved both her phone and her hands back into her coat pockets and rigidly braved the wind. "How did our daughter seem with that man?"

"He wasn't with her at first."

"He wasn't?" While Sheila questioned, Shane scribbled.

"No. She and I were having a nice chat about art, about a seventeenth-century painting she was restoring back in Boston. That's when the man on your phone joined us. He'd just gotten out of a cab."

"So he knew she'd been dropped off here by the cruise coach?"

Orange Jacket shrugged. "I dunno, but I imagine so. It's the most common spot for ships to drop off their guests. At first I thought maybe she was waiting on him, but when she saw him she stopped talking. She didn't look happy to see him."

A shiver ran through Sheila. "Did my daughter seem scared of the man?"

"Scared?" The young woman stared off toward the park, as if replaying the scene in her mind. "Not really. She just kind of stiffened, like she didn't want to see him. She seemed more annoyed than anything. He's a very handsome man though."

"He's a very smelly man." Sheila plucked a tissue from her pocket and honked her nose.

Orange Jacket seemed unsure how to process that last bit of information. "Um, yes, well, they were waiting for the next bus, just like you two are doing, and—"

"Let me guess. It was coming in three minutes."

"Shane," Sheila said, using the same tone she reserved for children tearing up Dr. Shakir's waiting room.

Shane returned to his note-taking, but by the way he rocked his body back and forth, she knew he was antsy. Who could blame him? Though it was nothing short of miraculous to find a hop-on/hop-off employee who recognized Shanna, they were freezing their keisters off. Like her own, Shane's nose started to run. She handed him a tissue.

"At that point, your daughter mentioned she would catch a different bus on her own. She started to speak to one of the guys from the purple line." The art student expelled air as if the idea were preposterous. "The man in the photo pulled her back. Not roughly, mind you. More playfully. Then he mentioned your daughter was a renowned art restorer, which I already knew, and we got to talking about art again."

"And Shanna—that's my daughter—seemed interested?"

"Somewhat, but I could tell she wanted to leave. She kept craning her neck to see if the bus was coming. But then he started talking about his art collection, and that got her attention again. He seemed rather pleased to have such a captive audience, and he got a little braggy, truth be told."

"What do you mean?"

"Just a sec." Orange Jacket raised one hand to pause the conversation and answered her phone with the other, the clipboard back under her arm. "Gotcha. Thanks, James." She disconnected and beamed at the McShanes. "The bus got delayed by traffic rerouting, but I promise it'll be here soon." When she saw Shane's cynical gaze shift to an approaching purple bus, her face tensed in anxiety, especially when Hipster Purple strolled by like a peacock in full plumage.

"That makes purple bus number two since you folks have been standin' here," he said. "But don't worry. I'm sure your orange bus will be here any minute." He chuckled and whistled his way back to a fresh batch of tourists.

Orange Jacket chewed her lip, glancing back and forth between the newcomers and the McShanes, as if debating whether to risk losing their commission for that of more tourists. When she saw cash exchange hands with Hipster Purple and Baldy Blue, she shrugged and returned to the conversation.

"What were we saying? Oh yeah, he seemed braggy. Saying things like 'you wouldn't believe some of the paintings I have' and 'no one can compete with my collection, stuff people haven't seen for years, art collectors would drool like poodles.' You know, that kind of thing. I can't remember exactly. It's been two months. But I remember he cut himself off, kind of froze, like he'd said too much, you know?"

"And then?" Sheila shifted from one aching foot to the other.

"And then they waited a bit longer for the bus."

"Three minutes, I imagine," Shane said.

Sheila grunted at her husband. For the most part, he was the easiest man in the world to live with, but when he got on about something, heaven help her, he wouldn't let it go.

"Wait." A tiny warning bell dinged in Sheila's brain, but she couldn't define it. "He said he had art that people hadn't seen in years? Didn't my daughter press him on that?"

"Sure she did, but then the orange bus came." Here Orange Jacket paused for effect and winked cutely at Shane. Sheila was amused to see him blush. "He put his arm around your daughter and escorted her to the bus."

"Did she resist him?" Sheila tried to piece it together. Clearly the man had bothered Shanna, but it appeared she wasn't afraid of him.

"Not really, but she didn't look happy to be in his company. He was kind of a chatterbox."

"Something my daughter is not," Shane finally offered.

"Unless it's about art," Sheila clarified.

"Unless it's about art."

"The last time I saw them was on the top deck of the bus near the back. Like I said, your daughter seemed unhappy, but then he said something that seemed to surprise her. Alarm her, even. That's why I kept staring. Well, that and because the guy was cute."

"What did he say?" Sheila's own alarm rose.

Orange Jacket frowned. "I'm sorry, they were on the bus. There's no way I could hear them."

Finally, the orange bus pulled up and screeched to a stop at the pickup point.

Orange Jacket beamed, her cold-flushed cheeks rising to meet her stylish frames. "You see? That wasn't much of a wait at all."

Shane scoffed, but he thanked the young woman for her help. Sheila embraced her, the crisp fabric of the orange jacket tickling her nose. "It's like God sent you to us. You have no idea what a big help you've been."

And she truly had been, even though Sheila didn't know what all the new information meant. For the next few hours, she was lost in thought, trying to decipher it. She barely took in the historical sites from the lower deck of the bus. She barely registered their quick stop for a sandwich and soup in a quaint Irish pub. She barely examined the art work they passed by in the museum, where they had learned nothing more about Shanna. And she barely perceived the gift shop in which she browsed, while Shane visited an electronics store across the street. What he was hunting for she had no idea.

The only thing she could seem to concentrate on were those alarm bells in her head. She ruminated and churned and cycled her thoughts, trying to snag a piece of the puzzle. If Mr. Smelly had upset Shanna, as Orange Jacket had claimed, why had Shanna returned to the ship in Dublin looking content? Or at least that was what Sheila remembered from the footage. She would have to check Shane's notes to be sure.

What had Mr. Smelly said to make Shanna so appalled? Sheila couldn't fit the pieces together. Then again, maybe in her quest to find her daughter, she was reaching for things that weren't there. Maybe the man had simply made a crude comment or shocked Shanna with an unwanted advance.

She sighed and gave up, and when they got back to the ship,

their assistant waiter, Cutie Pie Renny, was once again handing out hot chocolate from a table near the gangway. As the *Celestial of the Seas* guests returned, the weather still cloudy and brisk, he and a colleague greeted everyone with a bright hello and a toasty cup of cocoa.

"How is my favorite couple?" he asked Sheila and Shane when they reached for the paper cups. Though Sheila suspected he said the same thing to everyone, his cheerful manner warmed her nonetheless. He held up his index finger to them. "Hold on one moment please." After he doled out hot chocolate to the last of the tourists who were on the same excursion as the McShanes, he rounded the table and approached them, leaving his colleague to tend to the task alone. "I have been hoping to run into you. I remembered something about your daughter. Something I wanted to pass on to you. After seeing a couple arguing earlier today, it came to me."

Though Sheila was at the end of her tether, so tired and cold she wasn't even sure she could walk up the gangway, she straightened in anticipation. "What is it, dear?"

"I remember she came back to the ship with a big smile on her face. I know it was Dublin, because she carried a bag from the museum with her. When I asked what made her so happy, because…well…she's not the most smiling of sorts."

He paused, as if maybe his comment had offended her, but Sheila nodded for him to go on. It was true, after all. Like Shane, Shanna's expression was often furrowed and pensive, so lost in thought they both usually were.

"So yes, I asked her why she was so happy, and she said, 'Because I dodged a bullet today.' A bullet? I asked, thinking that was an odd thing to say. She smiled and said something like, 'A bad boyfriend bullet. Someone with bad judgment who wanted me to do something bad.' Then she boarded the ship. I forgot all about it until I saw the couple fighting today." He shrugged, as if embarrassed it might be a pointless story. "I suppose that's not helpful to you, but—"

Sheila was no longer listening. Upon hearing Renny say the word *judgment*, something pinged in her brain.

With quivering fingers, she dug her phone from her purse and opened her messages, not to check for new ones but to read an old one. In her flustered state, it took three tries to find. Finally, there it was. The spam text she had received four days earlier when she used her phone to email Mr. Smelly's photo to herself.

"What's the matter, dear?" Shane's voice sounded a million miles away.

She reread the spam text, or rather, what she had assumed to be a spam text. Thank goodness she had been in a hurry when she first read it and hadn't deleted it. *Send hekp restorinb just judges pa*

Restoring.

Just judges.

Wanted me to do something bad.

And just like that, the puzzle piece snapped into place.

Sheila jumped into Renny's arms, her cup of hot chocolate falling to the cement quay. Clearly, she had startled him, but nonetheless, he smiled at her exuberance and her profuse thanks.

"I don't know what I have done to deserve your affection, miss, but I will gladly accept it." His laugh was genuine.

She released him and turned to her husband. With so much excitement bubbling up inside her, she found she couldn't speak. She swallowed and tried again. Finally, she managed to sputter what she wanted to say. "Shaney, I know why he took her. I know why he took our daughter."

16

LONG LOST PAINTING

INSIDE A MAHOGANY CUBICLE in the Internet Café on deck five, Sheila waited for a website to load. Like an impatient child, she swiveled back and forth in her chair. That text she had received was not from a spammer. It was from Shanna. Her Shanna. Her daughter had been in the process of texting for help before getting cut off, and Sheila hadn't even realized it. The awfulness of that thought nearly closed off her throat.

But she realized it now, and with that discovery she understood what was responsible for her daughter's disappearance. It was a painting. *The Just Judges* painting, the one stolen from *The Adoration of the Mystic Lamb* panels, just as the concierge had told them about. Had he not mentioned it to them back in the library, Sheila might not have made the connection. Of course, that was assuming her conclusion proved correct. But it would. Between the text message and her intuition, she knew she was right.

Behind her a bartender served drinks at a small counter. Meant to be enjoyed in the social section of the café, beverages were prohibited near the computers, at least according to the plastic signs in every cubicle. Some guests, hidden out of sight from the bartender, chose to ignore the warning. They click-clacked their keyboards and took sips of colorful drinks on the sly.

Sheila hadn't yet revealed to Shane her suspicions about what had happened to Shanna. She'd let her bombshell statement outside on the gangway hang in the air unexplained while he ran their belongings to the stateroom. Meanwhile, after she passed through security, physically tired from her day in Dublin but mentally invigorated, she headed straight to the Internet Café, where she had told Shane to meet her as soon as he was done. They had research to do. That was thirty minutes ago. What was taking him so long?

She stared at the screen, willing the website to materialize. The ship's internet service was not only obscenely expensive at seventy-five cents a minute, it was terribly slow. Growing annoyed, she yanked off her reading glasses and sank back against the chair, her feet no longer touching the floor. Finally, a page unveiled before her, the third website she had clicked so far. She glanced over her shoulder for Shane, looking past the other cubicles, most of them occupied. She hated to go further without him. She had neither pen nor paper and risked forgetting the details she had learned so far. She needed her husband, the stenographer, the note-taker, the details man.

Just as she was about to ask the bartender for something to write with, Shane shuffled into the café. From his gait, Sheila knew his hip was bothering him as much as her feet and back were bothering her.

"Did you swim back to New Hampshire before coming here?" Sheila checked the time clock in the corner of the screen, "I'm twenty-five minutes into our hour, and the internet is so slow."

Shane pulled a chair from a free cubicle three desks down and wheeled it over. "I chatted with Raoul for a few minutes." His hand took control of the computer mouse.

"In our stateroom?"

"No, outside room eleven seventy-six."

"That awful couple's cabin? Did you see in the room? Is it still as messy?"

"Yes, no, and probably." Shane stared at the website Sheila had pulled up. "The door was closed. Raoul was about to knock for the room's evening service when I ran into him."

"How is he?"

"Anxious, distressed, overwhelmed."

"That poor, poor man."

"Says his supervisor's looking into the used condom complaint. He's worried he'll lose his job."

"Oh no, that would be terrible." Though consumed with her own daughter's welfare, Sheila had plenty of room to worry about Raoul and his family back in Venezuela.

"Just as he and I finished talking, the couple came out of their cabin and headed down the hall." A muscle twitched in Shane's jaw. When Sheila asked what was wrong, he remained silent. Without further elaboration he shifted gears. "What are you looking at? You left me hanging out there on the gangway. You said you know why that man took Shanna." His tone suggested he was not convinced of Sheila's revelation. "Nothing that young lady told us today at the hop-on/hop-off stop proves he had anything to do with her disappearance."

Sheila pointed at the screen. "See this?"

"It's a group of paintings."

"It's *The Adoration of the Mystic Lamb*. It's in Ghent, Belgium, inside St. Bavo's Cathedral, just like the concierge told us last night. It's what Shanna was most excited to see." She retrieved her phone from her purse, which was wedged behind the computer. Then she pointed to a painting on the screen. "And this is why our daughter is missing. *The Just Judges* painting."

Shane's expression was thick with skepticism. Knowing that would be his reaction, she already had the text message pulled up. Her face drooped in shame when she showed it to him. "I thought it was spam, but I now know it wasn't. It was from Shanna."

Shane grabbed the phone in disbelief. As he read the words in front of him, his facial planes shifted to dismay. "It can't be," he whispered.

Sheila tilted the mobile's screen toward her and reread the message: *Send hekp restorinb just judges pa.* "I think that second word was supposed to be *help*, not *h-e-k-p*, and the next one *restoring*. The last word got cut off, but I bet the text was supposed to say: *Send help restoring just judges painting.* I think Shanna got ahold of someone's phone and was frantically trying to text us, trying to tell us she was restoring a painting and to send help, but she got cut off before she could finish. Why she didn't call 911, or whatever the emergency number is here, I don't know. Maybe she was worried she'd be overheard."

Shane stared at her, his jaw slack and his mouth open. When she pointed to the computer screen again, he returned to it and started reading. She gave him a few minutes to navigate the website in silence. On the page was a collection of paintings in three wooden panels hinged together like a tri-fold display board. Each held medieval paintings of heavily adorned religious figures, save for two nudes in the upper far corners.

"It's called a polyptych." Sheila straightened her shoulders, pleased to be the one with the factual information for a change. "A polyptych is a painting divided into panels. Most art historians think two Flemish brothers created this one back in the fifteenth century. It's survived fires, looting, and war, and it spent much of World War II in a salt mine."

Shane's eyebrows rose, unruly strands poking out like porcupine quills. "Wow, you've been busy. There was a movie about that, you know." His cheeks flushed with the heat of nervous excitement. "A team of servicemen and civilians who retrieved stolen artwork from the Nazis."

"Yes, it had that handsome actor in it, the one Gloria at work is always going on about. This was one of the paintings mentioned in it."

Swiveling his chair closer—and by default, given the small space of the cubicle, pushing hers farther out—Shane scrolled down the screen to learn more about the many panels of the polyptych.

She jabbed another finger at it. "See? Right there. That's the painting we need to focus on. The other website I was on mentioned it too."

Shane squinted at the small print on the screen, but while he made do without reading glasses, she slipped hers back on and slid her chair closer to the screen, which, of course, shoved his farther out.

With the commotion of the musical chairs, the man in the next cubicle poked his head out. Sheila mouthed an apology and continued. "It mentions that in 1934, two parts of a panel were stolen: *The Just Judges* and *Saint John the Baptist*. The Saint John one was returned shortly after, but *The Just Judges* was not."

Shane swiveled his chair closer. Hers pushed back. With the mouse, he scrolled farther down the screen to a bigger picture of *The Just Judges*, which showed several robed men on horseback and three castles in the background. "Was it in the salt mines?"

"No." Sheila's short-term memory was impressing even herself. "In 1945, an art restorer created a copy of it, and that's what's in the panel to this day."

"So it's still missing?"

"Yes, look here. It says the Ghent Altarpiece—which is another name for *The Adoration of the Mystic Lamb* panels—is very coveted. Over the years it's suffered thirteen crimes and seven thefts. Its latest restoration was just this past decade."

Shane read on. Out loud he said, "The two stolen panels were removed from their frames in April 1934, but the other panels were left untouched." As always, when fascinated about a topic, Shane's posture was rigid and his eyes electrified. No old man there. He whistled softly between his teeth. "A ransom for one million Belgian francs was demanded, but the Belgian minister wouldn't pay. Negotiations went back and forth by letter, in which the Belgian government insisted the artwork was a national treasure and shouldn't be subjected to ransom. Then, in October, the thief returned one part of the panel, the one of John the Baptist, but not *The Just Judges*."

Sheila's teeth chattered, both from cold and nerves. "Does it say who the thief was?"

"Some man named Arsène Goedertier claims to have taken it. Says he told his lawyer he was the only one who knew where the panel was and that he would die with the knowledge."

"And I assume he did, since the panel is still missing."

"He did indeed." Shane read on silently, his lips moving. When he finished, he said, "Officials looked for it relentlessly, including x-raying the entire area of St. Bavo's Cathedral up to ten feet deep. It's never been found. To this day, there's a police detective on the case. What we'll see when we visit the cathedral in Ghent is a copy of it."

"That's still three days away." Sheila sighed and massaged her trembling hands, the dull ache from Dublin's cold still deep within her joints.

"You're shivering." Shane removed his navy blazer and draped it around her shoulders. Gaze back on the computer screen, he brushed his hand toward it. "This is fascinating information—stolen paintings, missing panels, and all that—but I don't know. It's difficult to believe our daughter is caught up in this."

"Then how do you explain that text message? Can you really say it's a coincidence? Just some spam message that happened to have the words *just judges* in it?"

Shane scratched his chin, seemingly unsure how to respond.

She pulled his blazer around her, its fabric scented with the same drugstore aftershave he had been wearing for years. The familiar smell and the warm weight of the jacket calmed her. "Don't you see? It always comes back to her art. Josef, the Swedish man who works the auction, said Mr. Smelly was discussing art with Shanna during the Edinburgh stop."

"All that proves is they both have a love of art."

"Yes, but then the museum attendant we spoke to at the Scottish National Gallery said something unusual. What was it again?" Sheila tapped her forehead, frustrated she couldn't remember. So much for stellar memory. "Help me, please. Look in your notes."

Shane reached over to his jacket, Sheila still wearing it, and gently lifted the left side of it to retrieve his notebook and silver pen. The man in the next cubicle got up and left. A woman took his place. Sheila waited in silence while Shane flipped through his note-book. Their internet minutes ticked away, though she supposed it no longer mattered. She had learned what she needed.

"Ah, here it is," he said. "She told us the Australian man was 'enthralled' by Shanna's descriptions of 'how she would restore the paintings.'"

"Yes, that was it. He was enthralled by her restorations skills."

"That still doesn't—"

"Yes, yes, I know." Sheila waved her hand at his notebook. "Now, find your notes from the Ulster Museum in Belfast and read back what that docent told us yesterday, the woman with the polka dot nails and shimmering eyelids."

He flipped some more pages. "She said the Australian man told Shanna: 'If someone offered you loads of money to make a fake painting or fix up a stolen one, you'd really say no?'" As Shane read the words, his speech slowed down, and his tone quieted. He looked up at Sheila. "Can it really be?" She heard both hope and uncertainty in his voice. The notebook shook in his hand.

She shifted her bottom on the seat. "And remember, Belfast was the day she came back looking bothered. Maybe it wasn't only his company that bothered her. Maybe his talk about art theft and forgery made her uncomfortable. Scared even." Sheila grew dizzy at the thought.

"Which brings us to today." Shane's expression wavered, as if wrestling with the desire to be on the right track but also acknowledging the lack of concrete proof beyond a few unethical comments by the Australian man and a garbled text message.

"Which brings us to today," Sheila repeated. "The young woman from the orange bus line told us…" She fluttered trembling fingers at his notebook, her failed memory humbling her again. How grateful she was for her husband's attention to details.

He flipped forward to his Dublin notes. "She said the man told her and Shanna: 'You wouldn't believe some of the paintings I have' and 'no one can compete with my collection, stuff people haven't seen in years.'"

"Bingo." Sheila's dizziness worsened. Her trembling too. She recognized the onset of low blood sugar and reached into her cardigan pocket for her peanut bar. They hadn't yet eaten dinner. To tide herself over, she pulled the last half from its wrapper and started munching, careful not to let the bartender see her with food near the computer. "The woman in the orange jacket also said Shanna looked alarmed on the bus by something Mr. Smelly had just said. That much I remember." Sheila took another bite, her shakiness dissipating.

"What do you think he said that alarmed her?" Shane looked as though he knew but wanted Sheila to voice it first.

"Isn't it obvious? I think he either wanted her to forge this painting or restore the stolen one, probably the latter since the text mentions the word *restoring*."

Shane pursed his lips and exhaled slowly. "It seems hard to believe…" The computer screen flipped to a spiraling screensaver, so he touched the mouse to revive it. The Ghent Altarpiece came back into view.

"Between that text and my gut, I know I'm right." When he said nothing, she added, "Remember that time you lost your blueprints for that downtown footbridge and fountain park? How you were in an absolute panic because you were supposed to present them to the board the next day? You searched everywhere. We all did. Remember what happened?"

"You said you would sleep on it."

"And?"

"And the next morning you told me they were at the library, back in the stacks where I'd been researching historical documents the day before. You said it came to you in your sleep."

"And where were they?"

His lips curled sheepishly. "In the library stacks."

"Well, there you have it. My intuition. I could give you a dozen more examples, and you know it."

"Some would say they were coincidences and nothing more."

"Do you want to stake our daughter's life on that?"

Shane's face paled to a ghastly gray, and Sheila felt bad for provoking it.

She squeezed his hand to comfort him. "It sounds crazy, yes, but I truly believe Mr. Smelly found the missing panel, and he needs

Shanna to restore it. I don't know why. Maybe it was damaged; maybe all the years in hiding destroyed parts of it. And I don't know why *her*. Maybe because that time period is her area of expertise and maybe his usual restorer wasn't up to the task. But I do know the chances are slim he would just happen upon our daughter on a cruise."

"Astronomically slim."

"Clearly we're on to something." She rolled up the sleeve of Shane's blazer and her cardigan beneath it and pointed to a fading bruise on her forearm, compliments of the fall down the stairs back in Edinburgh. "We've had two run-ins with Hivey Red. That can't be a coincidence too."

"But how does he tie in?"

"I don't know, but just because we suspect Mr. Smelly doesn't mean others aren't involved."

"I suppose that's true. Or maybe it's not the Australian man at all. Maybe it's the red-haired man, and we're headed down the wrong path thinking her disappearance involves the Ghent Altarpiece. It could be something else entirely."

"No, I'm sure Ghent is the answer. When she returned from that city, there was something on the security footage that bothered me. It still does."

"What?"

Sheila grunted in frustration. "I don't know. I'd need to see it again."

Exhaling, Shane planted his hands on his thighs and sank back against the chair. "So where do we go from here?"

"We need to show security the text message—maybe they can trace it—and get them to let us rewatch the footage, especially Shanna's return from Ghent so I can see what it is that's nagging me."

"And then?"

"And then we keep doing what we're doing. But the real focus will need to be in Ghent, at the cathedral where *The Adoration of the Mystic Lamb* is."

Looking overwhelmed, Shane bit his lower lip. Then a wave of relief seemed to wash over him, and for the first time he voiced what neither of them had dared discuss. "If your theory is true, that means our Shanna might still be alive."

17

A SUBTLE DIFFERENCE

FOR SHEILA, being confined once again inside the bland, airtight room of the ship's security department was like bad déjà vu, but it needed to be done. After leaving the Internet Café an hour before, they had rushed to Guest Relations on deck three and requested (demanded?) to speak to one of the security officers. Their wish had been granted.

As before, they sat at the round table next to Officer Gorgeous from Croatia and Officer Floppy Ears from England (or Niko and Tad as Shane kept reminding her, lest she inadvertently say the nick-names out loud). Also as before, their boss, Officer Sourpuss from Ukraine (AKA Ivan), paced the gray tile flooring and rotated the arm of his rimless glasses between his fingers. She wondered if contact lenses wouldn't be a better choice. At least those he would have to leave in place. Though all three men expressed skepticism, Niko and Tad made an effort to smile.

Tad had already recorded the cell phone number from where the strange text had been sent and promised to see if they could get an identification or location from it. "Don't get your hopes up though," he had added. He also said Sheila was inferring too much from the text message, and his colleagues seemed to agree.

"Let me get straight." Officer Sourpuss's free hand raked his crew-cut. "You want to see security footage again. Instead of enjoying nice cruise, you want to continue wild turkey chase."

"Yes, because—"

Ivan made a weird zipping noise with his mouth and silenced Sheila. So red was his aura she was surprised it didn't reach out and slap her. She reminded herself his hostility was a defense mechanism for his frustration over his inability to find their daughter, and thus tried to ignore it.

"And you think you know who took your daughter and why."

"I do." Sheila cleared her throat. Despite her bravado, her voice trembled. How much from nerves and how much from hunger, she wasn't sure. Dinner had still not happened. They were too excited about their Mystic Lamb finding to stop in the dining room, and she had polished off the rest of her peanut bar in the Internet Café. It was imperative she see the footage again now though. Something about Shanna coming back from Ghent was not right, and Sheila worried if she waited until after dinner to figure out what the anomaly was, she might miss it. At the moment, her neural connections were prime rib. After dinner they could be hamburger. "Yes, I do," she repeated. "I already told you who took her."

"Ah yes, so you said. Man with Australian accent took daughter to fix stolen lamb painting or paint fake one."

Next to her, Officer Gorgeous and Officer Floppy Ears squirmed at their superior's gruffness, but she wasn't fooled by the junior officers. Their own expressions might be sympathetic, but their silence translated into: "These old people are senile."

She straightened in her chair. "It's called *The Adoration of the Mystic Lamb*."

"Oh sorry." Ivan whipped open his arms in mock apology, the glasses in his hand hitting the wall. "We would hate to make error."

Shane placed his notebook on the table. When he raised his head, his face was that of an old dog about to pounce. In a flat but surprisingly effective tone, he said, "Sarcasm is a sign of insecurity. It's a tactic of bullies. Why don't you pocket yours and hear my wife out. It's of no effort to you to play the footage again. The sooner you do, the sooner we'll be out of your hair."

Officer Sourpuss huffed, but before he could say anything, Officer Gorgeous pushed up from the table. "It's no problem, sir. I can show them the footage again if they think it will help."

Sheila studied the handsome man with his dark eyes and blessed bone structure. His discomfort was palpable, but she appreciated his response.

A grumble simmered from somewhere inside Ivan's throat, but finally the Ukrainian nodded. To Officer Floppy Ears, he said, "Go get laptop with footage you make."

Tad seemed about to protest, as if he too thought a repeat viewing was a waste of time. Or maybe he worried it would only humor an old couple in their ridiculous folly. Eventually, however, he stood and departed the tense room, his ears the last thing to leave.

While they waited for Tad to return, Sheila's muscles quivered. As if sensing her fragile state, Shane put a hand on her arm and squeezed it reassuringly. The other hand tapped his notebook until Officer Floppy Ears returned with the laptop and zip drive. He set the unit on the table and started the footage.

Despite her inner chill, sweat beaded Sheila's forehead. Her hands shook and her vision tunneled, all signs of low blood sugar. *Just a few more minutes*, she told herself. *Just see what it was about Shanna's return from Ghent that set off your radar.* When Shanna's image came on the screen, Shane's grip tightened around Sheila's forearm.

"Okay." Ivan slipped on his glasses. "There is daughter boarding ship. There is daughter getting off in Inverness. There is daughter getting back on ship after day in Inverness." He continued in that fashion with each stop. Sheila ignored his condescending display because it was only the Belgian stop that concerned her. Next to her, Officer Floppy Ear's mustardy color of annoyance and unease matched her own. With a tissue from her cardigan, she mopped her brow and the back of her neck.

On and off her daughter went. Every time she exited, she scanned her key card. Every time she returned, she removed her cross-body bag and purchases and laid them on the x-ray belt, scanned her key card, and stepped through the metal detector. From there she disappeared from view. Reddish-brown hair in a ponytail, reddish-brown hair down. Sun hat on, sun hat off. Raincoat zipped, raincoat opened. When Shanna returned from Belfast, Sheila again saw the bothered look on her face. According to the docent at the Ulster Museum, that was the day Mr. Smelly first mentioned stolen or doctored art. That was probably why Victor hadn't seen Shanna in the dining room after Belfast. She wanted to avoid Mr. Smelly.

"And here daughter gets off in Dublin. And here daughter comes back." Ivan's monotone droned on. "And here she gets off in Cork. And here she comes back."

The next stop was Zeebrugge, Belgium, from whose port Shanna had taken a coach to Ghent, at least according to the itinerary she'd shared with them. Sheila stiffened and tuned everything else out. The crooks of her arms were wet with perspiration, and her heart pounded a thready beat.

"Here she leaves ship for day in Belgium. Here she returns."

Sheila's breaths shallowed. With her eyes inches from the screen, she watched Shanna return from her day in Ghent. Her hair was long and loose beneath her wide-brimmed hat, and her capri pants, v-neck tee, and gray hoodie matched her clothes from the morning. As noted on their first viewing, her head was down, and her face was further hidden by the hat, save for her chin. She removed her purse and placed it on the security belt. Then she scanned her key card, stepped through the metal detector, and slipped out of sight.

What is it, what is it, what is it? Sheila asked herself over and over again. Something was different from all the other days that Shanna had returned, but what?

What is it? What is it? What is it?

"Stop," Sheila cried out. She rose to her feet so swiftly a gray veil clouded her vision. She blinked it away. "Play that again."

Officer Floppy Ears squeezed the edge of the laptop. "Mrs. McShane, I think we've watched this enough—"

"Again," she demanded.

Officer Gorgeous clasped his hands tightly over the table, his knuckles blanching white. She didn't care if the handsome Croatian was frustrated or annoyed. She didn't care if any of them were frustrated or annoyed. She needed to see it again.

"*Achhh*, play one more time for her." Ivan turned to Sheila, who was growing more and more unsteady on her feet. His expression was unexpectedly concerned. "But this must be last time. Is too much for you."

Sheila nodded. She flexed the knobby joints of her hands and pitched her upper body toward the screen. She needed to sit, but her excitement wouldn't allow it. Tad rewound and played Shanna's return from Ghent one more time.

With the eyes of a sentinel, she watched Shanna step off the metal gangway into the security area, remove her purse, scan her key card, step through the metal detector, and disappear.

The purse.

The way Shanna removed her purse.

"Oh dear God, that's it." She slapped her hands on the table, making Shane jump and all three of the security officers jerk their heads her way.

"Play it again and watch how she removes her purse and puts it on the x-ray belt."

Tad complied, his fingers fumbling, and all five sets of eyes stared at the screen.

"Now," Sheila barked, "go back and replay the other days she returns and watch how she takes off her purse and puts it on the belt."

Officer Floppy Ears glanced up at Officer Sourpuss. After a brief hesitation, the boss nodded. Tad rewound farther back and replayed a few return trips.

"See how she removes her purse?" Sheila's heart galloped a thousand beats per minute.

"You better sit down, Beetle Bug."

Sheila ignored the tug on her sleeve. "She always has the strap slung over her left shoulder while the purse itself hits at her right hip. But look. On the last day in Ghent, she has the strap slung over her *right* shoulder, and the bag itself falls on her left hip."

All three officers looked at her as if she had lima beans pouring out of her nose. Shane peered at the screen and requested that Tad play the Ghent return one more time. When he did, Shane slowly nodded. He glanced up at Sheila, his skin ashen. "I see it too, but what does it mean?"

Ivan sighed. Officer Floppy Ears rolled his eyes and shook his head. Only Niko stared at the screen, a flat expression on his pleasant face.

"Maybe daughter's other shoulder has bruise, that is all," Ivan said.

Shane grabbed the edge of the table and hoisted himself to a standing position next to Sheila. "What does it mean?" he asked again.

Sweat trickled down Sheila's face. Her limbs oscillated like the tiny fan she once used for her hot flashes. Her vision doubled, then tripled. As she grabbed the chair to lower herself onto it, she tried to speak. Only a tinny version of her voice trickled out. "It means that's not our daughter."

The gray veil covered her eyes again, only this time it stayed. She felt herself sway. Like a balloon losing helium, she floated down. She was not even sure she made it to the chair before her world went black.

18

BRING ON THE SUGAR

SHEILA'S EYELIDS OPENED. Two heads peered down at her, one crinkled with age and worry, the other marked by youth and floppy earlobes. The latter was speaking on his phone. From a wobbly distance, she heard him request a medic and a gurney.

She tilted her body from side to side and discovered she was lying on the floor. "No, no, I'm fine." She tried to sit up. The movement was too sudden, and dizziness forced her back down. She rested her head on something soft. Shane's absence of a blazer suggested that was the pillow's source.

"Be careful, dear." Her husband's speech was tight with concern. "You fainted."

"I just had too much excitement on an empty stomach, that's all. Shakey Sheila just needs some sugar."

She felt skittish and confused. When she pressed her hands onto the tile floor in an attempt to push herself up again, Officer Sourpuss's command startled her back down. "No. You stay on floor. Please do not risk injury. It is good fortune Niko caught you before your head hit something."

Niko lowered to her side. She glanced up at him, her vision still a game of craps on whether one, two, or three of him appeared. He seemed unsettled. "I'm afraid we shouldn't have allowed another viewing of the footage. It's getting you too worked up."

She batted at his face. "Thank you for catching me. You look like an actor. Have you ever been in movies?" *What am I saying?*

Officer Floppy Ears looked at Shane. "You see? She's confused. Her low blood sugar made her see things on the video that weren't there."

The comment sobered Sheila, and she suddenly remembered what prompted her woozy descent to the floor. "You don't believe that's not my daughter?" She turned to her husband. "They don't believe me, Shaney. You do, don't you? Please tell me you believe me."

Shane's body rocked side to side in a crouched position, and he squeezed and patted her hand as if not sure what to do. "Shh, shh, it's not a matter of believing you." His usual calm was gone. Instead, he rubbed his forehead and continued to rock on his heels. "It's just with the hat on and her head down, it's too hard to tell. It looks like her, but…"

"You see? Even husband knows this is crazy game."

Ivan's comment seemed to be what Shane's frazzled state needed. He stopped his rocking and swiveled his head up toward the security boss, making firm eye contact. The protective old dog was back. "I said nothing of the sort. With my wife it's a matter of instinct. If she thinks that isn't our daughter, then I know her well enough to know it's worth you men looking into."

"Us? Looking into?" Officer Sourpuss ran a hand over his mouth. "How many times I must say we did all we could?" Sheila had recovered enough to see a forest green of insecurity dampen his red aura.

Tad weighed in. "We've already spent a great deal of resources on investigating your daughter's failure to return home."

Sheila noticed he didn't say "your daughter's disappearance." He probably thought Shanna stayed on in Amsterdam on her own free will. It would certainly look better for the ship if she had.

Officer Floppy Ears continued. "We, along with the European and American authorities, concluded she left our ship on the last day of the cruise. I'll check on that text message, but you have to let this go. Look what it's doing to you." He gestured toward the floor, as if she were unaware she was still on it.

Sheila beseeched Officer Gorgeous. "Do you feel the same? Have you given up on my daughter?"

Niko glanced at Tad and then Ivan, as if not sure what to say. His body visibly sagged in relief when a uniformed medic pushing a gurney burst into the room and interrupted them. Moments later a supine Sheila was launched through a series of bland corridors to Medical Services, located on the same deck as security but on the other end of the ship. Once there, she was transferred from gurney to bed, its back raised at a forty-five-degree angle. Though similar to any other hospital bed, the room that housed it was smaller.

Officer Floppy Ears accompanied them, and a nurse materialized as well, her name tag reading *Pearl, RN* and *Norway*. Her uniform's epaulet displayed two gold stripes on a red background.

Before she could greet Sheila, Tad whispered something in the woman's ear, making Sheila long for bionic hearing. After several seconds the nurse nodded in understanding but said, "You'll have to run that by the doctor. It's not up to me."

"What's not up to—"

Pearl cut Sheila off with a smile and introduced herself. "I understand you fainted. How are you feeling now?" As she spoke she rolled up Sheila's cardigan and the blouse underneath, and then slapped a blood pressure cuff around her arm and clipped an oxygen probe on her finger. Luckily it was the arm without the bruise from the fall down the stairs. Sheila didn't wish to explain that.

"I'm fine. I just need to eat. I don't need to be— Ouch!" Pearl had just pricked Sheila's finger with a tiny needle.

"Just checking your blood sugar. Then we can get you some juice. Here, put this under your tongue, please."

Sheila had barely opened her mouth when the cold metal of a thermometer sneaked its way under her tongue. Once in place, Pearl tore off the blood pressure cuff, its Velcro *rrrrrip* echoing in the windowless room. With speech impractical, Sheila answered Pearl's questions with a series of nods and head shakes. "Have you ever fainted before? Are you diabetic? Do you have heart problems? A history of strokes? Blood clots?"

When the thermometer was removed with a normal reading and the oxygen probe pulsed a healthy oxygenation level, Sheila folded her arms over her chest. "See? I'm perfectly fine. Just let my sweet husband help me to the dining room." She hoped the nurse hadn't noticed the shakiness of her voice.

A bosomy woman in a starched officer's uniform entered the room. "Yes, yes, I'm sure you'll be fine. But let's have a look-see, shall we?" With long chestnut hair that covered her name tag, she looked to be in her forties. Like Pearl's, her epaulets displayed a red background but with three gold stripes instead of two. "I'm Dr. Sinclair. Nice to meet you, Mrs. McShane."

Officer Floppy Ears trailed behind the doctor and motioned her back to the door. Dr. Sinclair obliged and pulled the door halfway shut. Through the gap, Sheila saw the two whispering.

Why is the young British officer still here? she wondered. A second later Officer Gorgeous paced by the door as well and joined Tad and Dr. Sinclair in their tête-à-tête. Good grief, was Officer Sourpuss tagging along too, twirling his glasses and growling like a panther? Although she appreciated the security team's concern, the sooner they left, the better.

Despite her ongoing shakiness she tried to clear her head. She needed to talk to Shane alone about the security footage. If that wasn't Shanna coming back from Ghent, then who was it? More importantly, where was her daughter?

A plastic cup of orange juice plopped into her hands. With a tremor that rivaled Katherine Hepburn's, Sheila lifted the foil seal and chugged the sugary liquid. When she finished, she rested her head back against the pillow and waited for the sustenance to work.

Dr. Sinclair had reentered the room and was listening to Shane explain what happened in the security department. He then recited Sheila's medical history, which, other than arthritis and weak bones, a prior appendectomy, and mild allergies when New England's pollen count peaked, was perfectly fine. At least the physician had closed the door on the security officers.

When the doctor approached the bed, Sheila handed the empty juice cup to Pearl, who was jotting notes on a clipboard. "Thank you, sweetie. I feel a thousand times better." She smacked her lips, as if to prove it.

Dr. Sinclair chuckled. "I imagine you do. Your blood sugar was only fifty-six. That's quite low."

"I know it is. I'm a receptionist for a family practice doctor. But it's been even lower."

"I'm surprised you weren't seeing flying orangutans."

"Are you from Australia?" Sheila asked, holding still while Dr. Sinclair checked her ears with an otoscope.

"I am. Is it my accent that gives me away or the Vegemite in my pocket?"

Like a gullible child, Sheila checked the woman's pocket. This made the doctor chuckle again. "I'm teasing, of course."

Sheila blushed. Now Dr. Sinclair would think her a foolish old woman too. Meanwhile, Shane paced the room, his expression worried, but less so than before. Pearl was taking notes in the corner.

"Are you the only physician on the ship?"

"I am, but we have a terrific nursing and medic staff, and between us, we manage quite brilliantly. No need to worry." Dr. Sinclair placed the ends of her stethoscope in her ears and listened to Sheila's heart and lungs over her blouse. She then moved onto Sheila's belly, pressing it gently in all four quadrants.

"I'm not worried. I'm sure you're all very capable. But it's silly for me to be wasting your time. I'm perfectly fine."

"You clearly keep yourself in good shape. According to your husband, other than ibuprofen for your arthritis and vitamin D for your bones, you aren't on any medications." Dr. Sinclair held each of Sheila's hands in her own and examined the swollen finger joints.

"I'm fit as a fiddle and sharp as a scalpel. So again, no need to waste your time with me."

"That may be true, but we don't want to be hasty. I'd like to run a few blood tests, just to be safe. It's best we keep you in the infirmary overnight for observation."

"Overnight?" Sheila's head shot up from the pillow. "There's no need for that. Tell her, Shane, tell her I'm fine."

Shane looked unsure. His forehead creased, and his hands kneaded each other like dough. "Maybe we should listen to the doctor."

"Preposterous," Sheila said, and then, realizing how that sounded, added, "Nothing against you, Dr. Sinclair. I'm sure you're topnotch, brilliant, top of your class, and all that, but I don't need to be here."

The ship's physician flashed a dental-enhanced smile and was about to respond when someone knocked on the door. "Excuse me a minute."

When Dr. Sinclair opened the door, Sheila did a double-take. Of all people, Tina, the sommelier, was outside the door, her hideous brown aura emanating from her like Pig-Pen's dirty cloud.

Pearl crossed the room. "I'm so sorry, Tina. I forgot about you. I'll be right there."

As Dr. Sinclair held the door open for Pearl and then talked to someone outside the room, her body half in and half out, Sheila grabbed Shane's sleeve and pulled him to her side. His blazer was back on, but its time as a makeshift pillow had left it wrinkled and dusty.

"You have to get the doctor to let me out of here. Tad said something to her and Pearl. Niko was here too, and maybe even Ivan."

"Why does that matter?"

"I think they told Dr. Sinclair to keep me here. Made it sound like I'm a danger to myself so I'll quit wasting their time. Or worse, they know I'm right about that not being Shanna coming back from Ghent. How can they ignore that or the text? Maybe they don't want me fishing further." Sheila's gaze darted to the door. Dr. Sinclair was still occupied with someone outside it.

"But why would they do that?"

"So they're not liable for losing her? So they don't have to explain their shoddy investigation? I don't know, but I have to get out of here. Shanna's life could depend on it."

Her words made an impact, but before Shane could respond, Dr. Sinclair and Pearl burst back in. "So very sorry," the physician said. "We had another patient we needed to deal with. But don't worry. We have plenty of space to keep you for a couple days."

"A couple days?" Sheila gripped the guardrails on the bed. Her suspicions over being purposely confined magnified a hundred times. She looked at Shane in panic.

He gave her a subtle nod, and between that and the look of fear in his eyes, she knew he now shared her suspicions. To Dr. Sinclair, he said, "She can rest in our stateroom. I'll take good care of her."

"What if her fainting was the result of an infection?" the doctor said. She shifted to Sheila. "What if it's the start of something contagious? We can't risk harm to the other passengers." The pleasant smile was back on her face. "Now, where were we? Ah, yes, lab tests."

When Dr. Sinclair turned to the nurse and recited the desired blood work, including cultures to rule out contagious disease, Shane bent down and whispered in Sheila's ear.

"Don't worry. I'll have you out by morning."

19

INTROSPECTIVE FRUSTRATION

SHEILA HAD WORKED as a receptionist at To Your Health Family Practice Clinic for the past thirty-seven years, so she recognized medical gibberish when she heard it.

As she lay on the patient bed in the infirmary, Shane having been sent back to their cabin, she knew the doctor's planned observation for a couple days was hogwash. With a meal tray of grilled chicken and mashed potatoes in her stomach, the vertigo and lightheadedness had long since resolved. The string of blood tests Pearl drew were unnecessary too.

She studied the bandage in the crook of her elbow, a bruise already forming at the site of the needle. The question was, were they keeping her here because security had crafted a story that she was not of sound mind? Or did Dr. Sinclair really think Sheila might be contagious?

Furthermore, if security *had* arranged her confinement—after all, at least two of the officers had been outside her door while Pearl and Dr. Sinclair were assessing her—was it because they truly worried about her mental and physical health? Did Officer Sourpuss believe the strain of her "wild turkey chase" was indeed getting to her? Her fainting in his department certainly supported his case.

Or were their motives more sinister? Did the chief security officer worry about the repercussions for Dreamline Cruises should word get out that their investigation into a missing woman was botched? After her time alone in the infirmary, Sheila was more convinced than ever it wasn't Shanna who had returned to the ship in Belgium. It was a masterful likeness of her, for sure, but it wasn't Shanna.

Emotion swelled within her. If only they had let Shane stay. She and her husband hadn't spent a night apart since Dr. Shakir had sent her to a coding seminar for medical receptionists in Boston fifteen years prior. Of course, with no bed for her husband in the tiny room, she didn't want him sleeping in the chair all night. He would be stiff and achy come morning. He had offered to, of course, just as she knew he would, but Dr. Sinclair convinced him there was no need for him to risk his own health by staying there. "Another contagious guest could come in. I can't risk you catching anything dangerous."

Apparently they could risk it for Sheila though. She shifted her pillow and punched the bedding. The only thing she was infected with was a fervent fever to find her daughter. What if the security staff convinced the doctor to hold her until disembarkation four days from now?

Frustration and fear squeezed her throat. Once again she considered simply getting up and walking out. When she had mentioned as much to Shane earlier, he talked her out of it. "We can't give them more ammunition against you. Rules and rights are different here. They have other passengers to consider, and if they think you might be contagious—"

"I don't have an infectious disease," she had snapped, her eyes threatening tears.

"I know that. You know that. But either they don't or they don't want to admit it."

"Something's fishy, Shane."

"I agree. Don't worry, I'll get you out."

That was the last she had spoken to him before they escorted him out of the infirmary. She had no idea how he planned to spring her, but if he succeeded and they tried to force her back, she would threaten to take to the Twitter and Facebook and all those other sites where everyone knows your business.

Sorrow replaced self-pity, and her chest cinched as if squeezed by a belt. If that wasn't Shanna coming back from Belgium, who was it? And where was Shanna now? Was she alone? Scared? Hurting?

Once again tears threatened to spill, but Sheila tightened her jaw and held them off.

Was Shanna somewhere in Belgium? Was she still in Ghent? Sheila had to pray she was. Otherwise she had no idea how to proceed. She and Shane were far out of their league with this whole awful mess. Based on the video footage, the text, and Sheila's intuition, Ghent seemed to be the key. But if Sheila's theory was correct and Mr. Smelly wanted Shanna to restore the stolen Mystic Lamb panel, would he really hide it in the same city from which it was stolen?

Sheila thought back to the research they had done in the Internet Café earlier that evening. The thief who stole the panel had taken its location to his grave, but before he died, he told his lawyer it was in a place that would arouse public attention were it to be moved. Did that mean it was nearby? Why x-ray the entire cathedral if they didn't believe it might be right under their noses?

She pulled the starched blanket closer to her chin, its cotton fabric smelling as bland as the walls. Intuition and garbled text message or not, she understood the folly of leaping to the conclusion that the Mystic Lamb panel was behind her daughter's disappearance. What if, in her determination to find Shanna, she was inventing mystery where there was none?

"But what else do I have to go on?" she asked herself out loud, the question hanging mournfully in the empty room.

She wondered how long restoration of such a painting would take. Some could take months to years, she knew that from Shanna, but it depended on the painting and the amount of damage. If Shanna had disappeared in Ghent, that meant she had been missing for over seven weeks now. Did the stolen panel require more time than that to repair? Or forge, since that too remained a possibility?

Despite Sheila's stoic efforts, a single tear slipped down her cheek and plopped into her ear. She could not let her mind go there. Would not let it go there. Because if she did, she would never rise from the bed, contagious disease or otherwise.

20

FEET DON'T FAIL ME NOW

THE FOLLOWING morning Sheila awoke with a start to a commotion in the hallway. At least she assumed it was morning. The windowless room in the *Celestial of the Seas's* infirmary made it impossible to tell. But she neither felt ship-rocking nor heard engine-rumbling, so she assumed they were docked in Cork, Ireland for day ten of their British Isles cruise.

Blinking away sleepy eyes and stretching stiff muscles and joints, she wondered what the hallway ruckus was about. Though she saw only an empty corridor beyond her partially closed door, she heard shoes stomping and a frantic plea from a vaguely familiar young voice.

"Please, you have to help them. They're in the elevator. They can't breathe."

"Young man, calm down. Tell me what's wrong." This time it was Pearl's voice, the nurse from Norway, who had checked in on Sheila throughout the night. Within seconds Dr. Sinclair came running down the hallway, her uniform a white blur beyond Sheila's door. Whether the doctor had just arrived or had already checked on patients that morning, Sheila didn't know. She pressed a button on the side rail and elevated her infirmary bed.

"He claims people in the elevator need our help," Pearl said with urgency.

"Yes, hurry, hurry," the boy yelled. "They're clutching their chests and coughing like they can't breathe. Like they've been exposed to gas or something."

"What are we standing here for?" the Australian doctor barked. "Hurry. Show us. And Pearl, call Randy too."

The voices and footsteps faded away. The encompassing silence was so sudden it was noise itself. Sheila didn't know who Randy was, but she suspected he was the medic who had helped her into the infirmary. Or maybe another nurse she hadn't yet met.

"Hello?" She called out tentatively. "Is anyone there?"

Nothing.

She pressed the bed up higher. Should she slip out? Would she be in trouble when the staff returned if she did? She swung her creaky legs over the side of the bed. As soon as her feet struck the metal bed frame, her legs too short to reach the floor, the main infirmary door down the corridor *whooshed* open. Her heart rate spiked, and she tried to pull her legs back up under the covers, but her morning joints refused the swift action.

She had gotten one leg covered when Shane shuffled through the door, his backpack over his shoulder and the long stateroom umbrella under his arm. Rushed determination heated his face.

"Shaney," she cried out in delight. The relief of seeing him eased her movements, and she scrambled back up in bed.

His intense focus didn't waver. He scooped up her folded clothes from the plastic chair near the bed. "Hurry. We need to get you out before they come back."

"What did you do?"

With the fervency of a jailbreaker—and was that not what he was?—Shane tossed the slacks, blouse, and cardigan on the bed and untied her gown.

"How did you—"

"I'll explain later. Just get dressed. They're up on deck twelve, so it'll take them time to get back down, but we need to have you out of here when they do."

Following orders was not one of Sheila's strengths, nor was remaining silent, but on this occasion she did both. As quickly as her limbs would allow, she slipped into her clothing and grabbed her purse. After reassuring Shane she was fine to walk, the two crept out of her infirmary cell and slunk down the corridor, throwing furtive glances at every open door and the hallway behind them. Even after they cleared the Medical Services department, he maintained their brisk pace, leading her up one flight of stairs to deck three, where they proceeded to the gangway.

"Get your key card out," he said, his face still flushed with anxious determination. Sheila saw youthful excitement there too, like a rule-breaker enjoying his caper.

The heavens were smiling on her, because for once she found her key card right away, tucked inside a silk sleeve in her purse. Within moments they scanned their cards at the security checkpoint, and as they made their way down the metal gangway, a gray, drizzling, Irish day greeted them. Shane pulled her raincoat and travel umbrella from his backpack. The pointy one from the stateroom was tucked under his arm.

"We're group eleven." He pointed to a coach waiting in a sea of coaches for the day's excursion. Plump, dark clouds hovered above the parking lot, and wind whipped the tour guides' jackets as they held up numbered signs and corralled their guests.

"How did you get everyone out of the infirmary?" Breathless from their mad dash, Sheila struggled to keep up with him.

Shane handed their tickets for the Taste of Ireland excursion to their group's tour guide. Not until they climbed onto the bus, stored their belongings in the overhead net, and sank down in the second row did Shane answer her. Despite the cool weather, sweat trickled down his temples, and tension strained his face. Slowly, she saw it dissolve.

"I made a little deal with Carson."

"Carson Quick? The young magician?" That explained why the prepubescent voice had sounded familiar.

"None other. Asked him if he wanted to make a buck or two."

"To do what?"

"To run into the infirmary and tell them someone was in trouble in the elevator and needed immediate medical attention."

"But he told Pearl that *two* people were clutching their chests and couldn't breathe, like they were exposed to a gas or something."

Shane chuckled, and the stress in his face dissipated further. A steady stream of excursion guests filed onto the bus. "Guess he improvised. Come to think of it, his story is better than mine."

Sheila rested her head against the seatback and put a hand over her heart. "I need to catch my own breath. That was quite an escape. Nice of Carson to help you."

"Nice, nothing. That little swindler charged me fifty bucks for the job. He said, 'a magician's trunk doesn't come cheap, you know.'"

They both laughed at the child's moxie. Fifty dollars was an extremely steep price for a man like Shane.

With a start, it dawned on her she was not at all presentable for a day in Cork and Blarney. Pearl had given her makeup-remover wipes the night before, and eighty years old or not, Sheila liked to present a pretty face to the world. Her Foxy Glossy hairspray and a toothbrush would be lovely too, but she understood why Shane had hurried them out. Had they stopped at their stateroom, Dr. Sinclair might have summoned her back.

As she dug inside her purse for her zippered makeup bag, her excitement over their escape morphed into fear. "How much trouble will we be in when we get back?" She might not like following orders, but she most certainly didn't enjoy breaking rules.

"Not too much, I think." Shane had already unfolded the map of Blarney provided by the tour guide, his gadget pen at the ready for markings.

"Why not? How can you sound so calm?"

"Because I left a letter at Guest Relations this morning for Dr. Sinclair. I told them it was a thank you note for the excellent care she gave you. In it, I explained how you were sorry to leave without saying goodbye, but that you were feeling great and longed to see Blarney. I also wrote you were an avid poster to Ship Consulter, the online website for cruise ship reviews, and that you might be inclined to mention the excellent care you received by the *Celestial of the Seas's* doctor and how you in no way felt you were being kept there against your will." Looking quite proud of himself, he paused for dramatic effect. "I added, however, that your feelings could change if you were forced to return to the infirmary for a nonexistent illness and normal lab work."

Her eyes widened at his brazenness. "Blackmail?" She grinned, thinking for the millionth time how lucky she was to have married such an amazing man. "What a brilliant idea. What cruise line would want people thinking their crew members confined non-sick passengers against their will? Brilliant," she repeated. "Absolutely brilliant."

She plucked her makeup bag from her purse and got to work.

21

WET AS A FISH

Greens of every shade blanketed the picturesque estates of Ireland's Blarney Castle & Gardens. Emerald grass, avocado shrubs, basil leaves on hunter-green trees, their massive roots furred with luminous lime moss. Pockets of colorful flowers punctuated the verdant display, and stone structures of a medieval castle rose from its fertile grounds, creating an effect so surreal Sheila felt as though she were strolling through the diorama of a fairytale. Shane, too, looked transfixed.

Unfortunately, a downpour threatened full enjoyment of the estate, and despite umbrellas and raincoats, their shoes and the bottoms of their pants were already drenched. Furthermore, Sheila wasn't feeling particularly touristy. Not only was she ruminating about her escape from the infirmary and its potential ramifications, her joints were stiffer than usual, and she longed for a shower. Most days she didn't feel her age. Today she did.

On the coach, Shane had assured her she wouldn't be in trouble for leaving the infirmary. "You can always play the senile card if need be. Say you didn't understand you were supposed to stay. But they have no basis to keep you there, so I think they'll let it go."

She hoped so. Despite only one cup of coffee in Cobh that

morning (pronounced *Cove*, as they had learned from the tour guide), a steady state of nerves made her feel as if she had consumed buckets of caffeine.

Still, as they had traveled from the colorful seaside village of Cobh to Blarney Castle & Gardens, she had enjoyed the tour guide's banter. The middle-aged woman's Irish accent and humor were a gift to the ear, even if she hadn't remembered Shanna or Mr. Smelly.

"Here's a fun fact," the blunt-haired woman had said, speaking into her microphone, her body swaying with the motion of the bus as she stood near the driver. "Ireland is a world leader in pharmaceutical manufacturing. Oh yes, plenty of erectile dysfunction pills got their start on our shores, don't you know. We call it the 'Pfizer riser' around here." Boisterous laughter had flowed through the coach, and Shane had wiggled an eyebrow at Sheila, making her smile.

Now though, as they walked toward Blarney Castle on a muddy path, rain pelting their raincoats and umbrellas, and puddles swallowing their soaked shoes, Shane's earlier levity was gone. Like her, he was eager to get to Ghent, and the two days ahead of them before reaching the city seemed like filler. They had briefly discussed disembarking from the ship early and taking a train to Ghent but quickly dismissed the idea. Deviation from Shanna's itinerary might cause them to miss an important clue, not to mention the ship felt safe to them. Navigating the rail system from Ireland to Belgium on their own seemed fraught with unpleasant hassles, or maybe even danger.

When they reached Blarney Castle, which was a towering rectangle of medieval stone, the line to kiss its Blarney Stone extended well beyond what they cared to wait, particularly with squishy socks and shivering flesh. They stopped a young man who had just exited.

"Is it worth waiting in line to kiss the stone?" Sheila asked him.

He looked them up and down, his shoulders hunched against the downpour and his poncho dripping rivulets of rain. "Um, there are a lot of steps involved, and you practically gotta do a backbend to get your lips on the thing." Though he didn't add he feared they were too old for such a thing, the subtext was clear on his face.

After thanking him, she and Shane decided to skip the stone. The tour guide had told them kissing it bestowed the gift of gab. "I have enough gab for the both of us," Sheila said.

"And then some," Shane added.

A soggy stroll past the castle proved taxing enough. Avoiding puddles on the gravelly path required concentration, and the incessant drumming of rain on their umbrellas made attempts at conversation difficult. Not ready to admit defeat, especially in such beautiful surroundings, the likes of which they might never see again, they continued down a northeast path toward the Blarney House. Touring its premises would grant a reprieve from the rain.

Unfortunately, the walk proved farther than they had anticipated, Shane's site map too wet to be of much use. They barely made it a third of the way before thunder erupted, followed by a crack of lightening in the blackened sky. Within seconds torrential rain poured down upon them. The wind grew equally angry, forcing them to grip their umbrellas with all their might. Pivoting direction, they hurried along the wet path back toward the castle, along with other fleeing tourists. Thanks to her uncooperative joints, Sheila's movement was closer to hobbling than walking.

Out of nowhere, a figure in a hooded rain poncho darted past them. He vanished behind a crop of trees. Sheila wondered where he was headed. Aside from vegetation, there was nothing there. No path to follow, no structure to visit.

She sidled up to Shane and grabbed his arm. Her umbrella would be better supported by both hands, especially with her purse hanging like a weight from her shoulder, but her unease on the stormy path made her want contact with her husband. Praying he knew the way back to the entrance, she pushed on against the elements, her body drenched and trembling.

As if reading her mind, he shouted, "Once we've reached the castle, we'll take the path back to the entrance. We can wait in the gift shop until it's time for the coach to leave."

When they reached the castle complex, however, a succession of thunderclaps blasted their eardrums, and the rain heightened into a blinding deluge. With limited visibility and umbrellas that were no match for the monsoon wind, Sheila's anxiety skyrocketed.

"Here," Shane shouted. "Come in here."

She didn't know where "here" was, but before she could ask, Shane pulled her into a cramped, dank space. Instantly, the rain ceased, at least around them. "Are we in a cave?"

"The dungeon."

"That's supposed to reassure me?" She lowered her umbrella and looked around. Bulbs mounted on a low-lying roof cast subdued light over the uneven, stony terrain. Damp, beige walls closed in on her. Across from the dungeon's opening, a narrow passageway led to a place that could only mean unpleasantness. She shivered at the sight, but when the wind flooded the entrance with more rain, Shane pulled her toward the mysterious corridor. "There's a larger chamber back here where they kept the prisoners. We can sit and rest until the worst of the storm passes."

"Because waiting in spooky prisoners' quarters is so much better than the rain?" Still, like Shane, she closed her umbrella and started down the narrow stone tunnel, keeping her head low. The dirt beneath their feet was mostly dry, save for wet patches dragged in by tourists, but it was uneven enough that she had to be careful where she stepped.

"Don't worry. There'll be other tourists back there."

Shane wasn't often wrong, but he picked a bad time to start being so. When they reached the former prisoners' quarters, there wasn't a tourist in site. Nothing but stone and dirt and the muted drumming of rain.

"See? Much better." He guided her into the wide chamber, its metal doors yawning open for curious visitors.

A jagged rock extension allowed for a place to sit, and despite Sheila's discomfort in the creepy room, she sighed in relief to rest her weary joints. If only she wasn't wetter than a trout. Between the wet fabric of her raincoat and pants and the adrenaline from their flight in the storm, she even smelled like one.

She let her umbrella fall to the dirt floor and flexed her toes inside her squishy shoes and socks. "You're right, my love. This is a good place to rest. Thank you."

Her teeth chattered, and she nearly bit her tongue trying to stop them. At least they were mostly her own, unlike her poor mother who had a set that never stayed put. Still, false teeth or not, the woman had made it to her ninety-ninth birthday. Sheila hoped to do the same or better.

She stared at a small opening across from them, more a defect in the stone than a window. Beyond it, rain pounded mercilessly, and lightning flashed. "Imagine being a prisoner down here."

Shane shook out his umbrella and then closed it again. He leaned his head against the wall. "Not the best accommodations, that's for sure."

"Better than being beheaded, I suppose. Or hanged in the gallows."

"You'll get no complaint from me—"

A noise cut Shane off. Footsteps echoed down the passageway. Slow, shuffling footsteps.

Sheila stared at Shane, her shivering at a manic high.

"Just more tourists escaping the rain," he assured her, though she saw his face pinch with worry.

More shuffling, but no voices. If it was tourists, wouldn't they be talking? A scrape along the wall, followed by heavy breathing.

The coppery taste of fear soured Sheila's mouth. With effort, she stood. Shane followed suit. "A little rain never killed anyone, right?" He spoke lightly, but Sheila heard the tension.

"Of course not. After all, I needed a shower, didn't I?"

They started back out the way they came, umbrellas in hand. Before they could exit the chamber, a shadow filled its metal doorframe.

WHERE THE SUN DOESN'T SHINE

THE HOODED FIGURE stepped into the chamber. Sheila froze and stared at his dripping poncho. Was this the man who had darted past them on the stormy path a short time ago? Had he been following them?

Though much of his face was obscured by the tightly cinched hood, when he raised it she immediately recognized the narrowed eyes, bulbous nose, and irritated skin, even without seeing his hair.

"It's Hivey Red," she gasped to Shane, who was rigid in place next to her.

The man's forehead creased in confusion, but within moments his snarl was back. "Nicknamed me, have ya?" He stepped closer to them, and when he did, Shane positioned himself in front of Sheila.

"What do you want? Why have you been following us?" Though her husband sounded stern, Sheila recognized his fear. He had voiced it to her three days earlier in Liverpool after Hivey Red had pursued them on Duke Street. Her husband was terrified of not being able to protect her.

"Sorry, mate. Nothing personal. Just got a job to do." The man's pleasant Scottish lilt belied the roughness in his eyes. "That's three times now ya haven't taken the hint to back off. Ya will today, though, ya will today."

Three times? Edinburgh plus Liverpool made two. What did he mean, three times? Something blipped in Sheila's brain, but she couldn't decipher it, not when her heart was hammering all the way into her ears.

"We're no threat to you." Shane edged himself and Sheila closer to the stone wall. How they would slip past the man through the narrow passageway that led to the dungeon's entrance, she had no idea.

"Of course yer not. What do you take me for, a fool?"

The man stomped forward and grabbed Shane. "Let's rough you up first, though I doubt either of ya can put up much of a fight." An ugly laugh rumbled from his flabby lips as he shoved Shane against the wall. Shane stumbled to the dirt floor, his eyes blinking in disbelief.

Horrified, Sheila dropped to her husband's side and yelled for help. Would anyone outside the dungeon hear her above the pounding rain?

Hivey Red pushed her aside and wrapped his fingers around the base of Shane's neck, which was covered by his raincoat. Her husband's arms flailed as he tried to push the man off.

Not knowing what else to do, she plowed into the Scottish man with her hundred-pound frame. Her tackle had no effect on him. She grabbed her umbrella and started whacking instead. Head, back, side. The whole time she whacked, she screamed, both in fear and in rage. The only thing her blows managed to do was pull back his hood and expose his red hair.

"Go ahead," he chuckled. "Wear yerself out. That umbrella's about as strong as you are." To Shane, he said, "Are ya ready to give up yer sleuthin' now?" Shane's flailing continued beneath the man's grip.

Sheila's arms quivered from fatigue, and her lungs weakened. "Hold on, Shaney, hold on."

Dropping the umbrella, she kicked a soggy Mary Jane shoe into the crouching man's flank. At first he didn't respond, but as her size-five orthotic made repeated contact with his left kidney, he was forced to let go of Shane. He pivoted toward her with a growl. When he did, her kick smacked him in the nose.

He bellowed in pain, blood sprouting from his nostrils. After his initial shock, he stood, wiped the blood from his nose, and smirked. "Yer a feisty one, aren't ya? Jordan underestimated ya."

Sheila didn't know who Jordan was, but she did know she no longer had any defense against the man. He would crush her with one blow.

She trembled as he stepped toward her, but before he reached her, his eyes widened in astonishment. He bent over and squealed.

At first she didn't understand, but then she saw the source of his agony. Shane had rolled over and snatched his umbrella from the rock it had wedged against when Hivey Red shoved him. It was their stateroom umbrella, the one with a thick metal tip that doubled as a walking stick.

It wasn't being used as a walking stick now though. Instead, the sharp tip thumped Hivey Red's nether regions for the third time.

When the man fell forward, bent at the knees, bottom up in the air, Shane struck a final blow to the family jewels. Hivey Red groaned and rolled over onto his side. His lips puckered and his eyes scrunched together in pain. Into the dungeon dirt he vomited.

"Quick." Shane grabbed Sheila. She scooped up her purse but had no time to rescue her own umbrella.

Together they hurried through the passageway toward the entrance, stiff joints and sore muscles fueled once again by adrenaline.

When they reached the outside, Shane didn't bother to reopen his umbrella, or maybe didn't think to. The couple was focused on nothing but getting back to the estate entrance where they could seek shelter in the gift shop and report the incident to security. At least the rain was no longer torrential.

Twice Sheila looked over her shoulder, and twice she saw nothing but a few tourists braving the weather to visit more of the grounds.

When they finally reached the entrance, their clothes and flesh so wet they might have been mistaken for seals, they spotted their tour guide waiting anxiously by the ticket counter. She zipped toward them. "Oh, thank goodness, there you are. The coach is ready to leave. We've been waiting for you. Come, come."

Without giving them time to relay their recent encounter, she hustled them out to the bus lot, shielded from the rain by her umbrella. Sheila wanted to tell the guide what had happened— security could still catch Hivey Red—but she quickly thought better of it. She and Shane would be questioned. They would get delayed in Ireland. They would miss the ship's sailing in a few hours. They would not get to Ghent.

They had to get to Ghent.

Therefore, she said nothing. She was too winded to speak anyway. When they boarded the bus, a boisterous applause greeted them, startling them both.

"Hurray, they didn't backflip off the castle after all," someone called out. "Irish whiskey for everyone."

Amid more applause, they sheepishly sank into the second row, kindly reserved for them. Too shell-shocked to speak, they didn't even remove their hoods.

"Or get swallowed by the Poison Garden," came another shout. More laughter followed.

More like a poison man with bad skin, Sheila thought, trembling so severely she would gratefully take five whiskeys if they offered.

As the coach drove away and the tour guide resumed her humorous banter, Sheila's heart rate gradually slowed. She finally slipped off her damp raincoat. Her shoes came next, and thanks to her yoga she was able to bend over enough to massage her numb feet through her wet socks.

"Are you okay?" With an ashen complexion, Shane removed his hood and unzipped his raincoat.

"Yes, I think so. You?"

"I'm okay. Now, anyway." He leaned his head back against the seat and took several deep breaths.

The tour guide was saying something about the village of Kinsale, where they would stop for a few minutes of sightseeing and shopping before returning to the ship. Sheila knew hers and Shane's only stop would be a pub.

He rubbed his temples. "I guess this confirms we're on the right track."

"I would say so. Why try to scare us away from 'sleuthin' if we weren't?" Sheila pulled her compact from her purse and inspected herself in the mirror. A streaked face and smudged lipstick greeted her.

"Doesn't prove the Ghent Altarpiece is involved though."

"No, I suppose not." She wiped smeared mascara with a tissue, still tuning out the tour guide's narration.

"It could be a different painting, or maybe even something else, but this man wouldn't be so intent on scaring us off if we weren't getting warm."

"Speaking of, he made it sound like it was the fourth time we've run into him. Do you think he's on the ship?"

"If he is, I haven't seen him." Shane rubbed his neck where the man's hands had squeezed. Whether he really only meant to scare them off or not, the act had terrified Sheila.

"Neither have I, and yet he always finds us, so he must be, right?" Despite the heat in the bus, her chill returned. She tried to summon the blip of memory she had back in the dungeon. Had she seen the man a fourth time? If so, where? Her mind couldn't grasp it.

"No, I don't think he's traveling with us." Shane pulled out his notebook, followed by his pen. Thanks to the raincoat, both were still dry. He jotted something down.

"Then how does he know where we are?"

"Maybe someone on the ship is telling him. It's not that difficult to get from place to place in the UK and Ireland, by plane or car. Much smaller countries than our own."

"But who?"

"If we knew that, our mystery would be solved and we could go to the police. But for now, I don't think we should talk to anyone about what happened."

"Not even the security team?"

"Not even them. I think until we know more, we can't trust anyone, especially anyone who has access to our itinerary."

After Sheila powdered her face and put the makeup bag back in her purse, she closed her eyes, too confused and scared to do much else. She felt better thinking Hivey Red was not on the ship. She hoped Shane was right about that.

"We have to get through tonight and tomorrow, our last full day at sea," Shane said. "Then we'll be in Ghent."

Yes, they had to get to Ghent. Ghent, Belgium held the answer. Sheila was sure of it.

23

I SPY

THE SCENT of tropical coconut oil had never been Sheila's favorite —she preferred an earthy patchouli or soft floral—but she was willing to overlook that detail because the joy of having it rubbed onto her sore back was immensely pleasurable. Shane, at a nearby spa table, his face poking through a padded hole like her own, moaned in similar bliss.

"That must have been a very persuasive letter you left for Dr. Sinclair," she mused. "Getting spa treatments is quite the coup."

A content murmur was Shane's only reply.

The spa gift certificates had been deposited in their stateroom sometime during their Taste of Ireland excursion the day before, compliments of Medical Services. Bribe or no bribe, the McShanes gladly accepted them. After their harrowing experience in the Blarney Castle dungeon, their bodies were in need of some tender loving care. Upon their stuporous return to the ship, they had ascended to their stateroom and collapsed on the bed like zombies, soggy clothing and all. For three hours they slept, rousing only for a late dinner. This morning, Sheila's body felt like it had been in the ring with a bear, and she had the bruises and lumps to prove it. Shane was battered and sore too.

Initially, the two women kneading their flesh had asked about the bruises, at least those that were visible on their backsides, but Sheila explained their accident on the stairs and how easily their tissue bruised. Between the darkened room and the fact the marks on Shane's neck were faint (either Hivey Red hadn't used full force or Shane's raincoat had offered protection) that seemed to satisfy the masseuses. Still, every time Sheila thought about that vile man's fingers around her husband's neck, she wanted to cry.

For now, though, she was at peace. Candles flickered in the dimly lit room, and soothing music with flutes and keyboards played softly. The two women were so quiet they seemed invisible. Only their skilled hands remained. For the next forty minutes, Sheila let herself drift away to a peace she hadn't known since before Shanna went missing.

After the spa visit, with a whole day at sea in front of them, they lunched in the buffet restaurant on deck fourteen, securing a table that overlooked the ocean. Beyond the windows, rippling waves blended into a haze of fog. Despite the cloudy weather, she felt tranquil and grounded, enough so that she could pose the question she had thus far been avoiding. As Shane devoured his Moroccan chicken and rice, she said, "I keep thinking Ghent is where the answer is, but..." She exhaled and took a sip of hot tea for courage. "What if there's nothing there? Do we really think Shanna will just pop up? Maybe we're on a fool's errand, just like the security staff thinks. Then what will we do?"

Shane shoveled in a few more bites, the massage clearly boosting his appetite. After he wiped his mouth, he placed his knife and fork at a ninety-degree angle on his plate. "That's a strong possibility." His eyes grew sad and his voice quieted. "In fact, I think we both know it's the most likely possibility."

Though Sheila had expected the words, they stung nonetheless. "But what if we find someone who remembers her? Or something that lets us keep digging? Do we return to the ship after the excursion or do we stay behind in Ghent?"

"Without our belongings?"

A crew member passed by their table, his expression somber.

When he gave a slight nod to someone Sheila couldn't see, she craned her neck to find out who it was. Spotting no one suspicious, she returned to her salad and soup. She was getting paranoid, expecting to see Hivey Red in every corner. Earlier, she had again broached the idea of telling the security team about what had happened at the Blarney Castle, but Shane reminded her that if the officers sensed they were in real danger, they wouldn't let them off the ship again. That was enough to persuade her to keep the encounter secret. She had to get to Belgium.

"If we don't find anything in Ghent," Shane continued, "we'll return to the ship. But when we disembark in Amsterdam the next day, we'll fly back to Belgium to investigate further instead of flying home. Or take a train."

They sipped their beverages in silence, each staring out at the ocean. Noisy guests in search of open tables passed by with loaded plates, but Sheila hardly noticed them. Finally, she cleared her throat and voiced what she imagined they were both thinking. "It may be a fool's errand, but I can't stop looking for her. Friends tell us we have to accept that our daughter might be gone for good. Authorities say they've done everything they can for now. Dr. Shakir and Gloria tell me I need to prepare myself. But how do I do that? And how do we tell Paul his sister might never be coming home?" Sheila buried her face in her hands. "Just think what it will do to him. She's the only person he's really close to."

"Paul is Paul, you know that. He'll be sad and hurt, but he'll stay busy with his work in Iceland. He doesn't think or feel the way most people do. And that's saying something coming from me."

His words made Sheila smile briefly, but her grief soon returned, both for her missing daughter and for her special son. She understood Paul was different. From her work as a medical receptionist, she knew he was on the autism spectrum somewhere, even though he had never been formally tested. He shared many of his father's characteristics: intelligence, a whiz at numbers and statistics, a need for schedule-keeping and planning. But unlike Shane, who had developed reasonable social skills, their son said the wrong things at the wrong time and was temperamental and rigid. Working as a geologist in Iceland was probably the perfect job for him, though his colleagues likely avoided him. Still, in his own way, he was loving to his family, and he possessed empathy for them, which is why Sheila had finally stopped worrying.

While Shane went to refresh his coffee, she stared out at the rolling sea and recalled their early days. The two of them had tried for years to have a baby. It seemed not meant to be. Then, to everyone's surprise, she got pregnant with Shanna when she was thirty-four years old and beyond the prime baby-making years. Even more of a surprise was Paul, six years later when she was forty. Of course, she understood it now. Both of her children were pragmatic and rational. They probably felt it best to wait until their parents were mature adults and had settled into their careers. She smiled at the thought and could almost see pre-birth sister and pre-birth brother planning the most logical time for conception. Whether or not Sheila would live to see grandchildren was another story. Like so much in life, it was out of her hands.

When Shane returned she looked at him and, apropos of their earlier conversation, said, "I won't give up. Foolish trip or not, I won't give up on our daughter."

Shane reached across the table and squeezed her hand. "Nor will I. No matter how much danger we face."

Their eyes locked for a long moment. "You worried you wouldn't be able to protect me, Shaney, but you did."

"We protected each other."

"You did quite a number with that umbrella. I imagine Hivey Red isn't walking too well today."

"You did quite a number with your Mary Janes."

They shared an intimate smile, and in that moment Sheila found renewed hope. They would continue to do everything they could to find their daughter.

They released each other's hands and finished the rest of their lunch lost in thought. Afterward, they walked through the solarium, hoping for a spot to relax. Unfortunately, all the chairs were taken, including the comfortable but inescapable pods, so they exited to the outdoor pool deck to cross to the other side of the ship. At the high elevation, cold wind stole their breath and whipped their clothing.

Eager to return to the ship's warm interior, they almost missed Carson Quick in the hot tub. The young magician had one of the four Jacuzzis all to himself. When they approached, a fully dressed woman on a beach lounger on the other side of the whirlpool looked up from her book and smiled. Visibly cold, she had a towel wrapped around her shoulders. Judging by her resemblance to Carson, Sheila deduced it was his mother. She said hello to her, but the woman promptly went back to her reading, probably unable to hear anything above the wind and the hot tub jets.

"Oh dear, you must be freezing," Sheila said to Carson, hugging her own body at the sight of his bare torso.

"Not in here." He grinned and splashed the bubbly water. "It's like a thousand degrees."

"You'd be dead if it was a thousand degrees." Shane reached a hand into the water and looked up at the sky, his expression shifting to math mode. "The recommended temperature is between one hundred and one hundred and four degrees. This feels to be in that range. Maybe a degree or two less."

"Is he always this much fun?" Carson raised an eyebrow at Sheila.

Despite her shivering, she laughed. "I heard you earned fifty dollars yesterday."

"Swindler," Shane muttered, but his eyes sparkled in good humor.

"That was quite the performance I heard outside my door."

Carson clutched his chest, water splashing over the side of the tub. "I can't breathe, I can't breathe."

"What did you do when you got to the elevator with the medical staff and there were no dying people inside?" Sheila asked.

"I told the doctor the couple must've gotten better. Then I apologized for wasting their time and asked if they wanted to see a trick. They didn't." Snorting a laugh, he added, "Being a magician is more than the magic, you know." He put his water-logged, pruney fingers together and shook his hand in a gesture of finesse. With a French accent, he said, "Eet eeze all about ze performance."

Shane reached for his wallet and pulled out a ten. "Here. You earned a bonus, kid."

Carson's face lit up. He grabbed the money and stashed it inside the towel he had balled up near the hot tub. "Oh wow, thanks! Because of you, I've almost got enough for my trunk." He glanced over at his mother, perhaps worried she would make him return the money, but she was still engrossed in her book. Sheila wondered how he had explained yesterday's fifty-dollar payout but then realized a boy as enterprising as Carson could easily conjure a perfect explanation.

Back inside the ship's interior, they sidestepped the crowds to the elevator bank and waited their turn to descend to deck ten. Taking the stairs seemed too monumental a task in their aching states, even despite the massages.

On the tenth floor, they headed to their stateroom. A nap was their goal, but they also wanted to keep a low profile until they reached Belgium tomorrow. No sense risking a run-in with one of the security officers or a member of the medical staff. Sheila doubted they would send her back to the infirmary, not after the complimentary spa visits, but she had no intention of finding out.

Once again, as they neared their stateroom, Raoul was standing outside of cabin number 1176. Given his agitated state, the awful couple was inside. Wanting to hear the exchange, Sheila and Shane slowed to a crawl.

"It's all ruined," the woman's shrewish voice yelled through the open door. "Everything. Our papers, our pictures. We spent hundreds of dollars on your ship's photographs—you guys take so freaking many—and your cleaning fluid ruined them all."

"I promise you, madam, I did not leave that bottle open." Raoul's voice rose, and he clutched a chunk of hair near his temple as if he were in pain. "In fact, I didn't leave my cleaning bottle in there at all."

"Those papers were irreplaceable," the man's voice said. "They had to do with my family tree. Don't spew your lies at me."

Sheila whispered to Shane, "The only thing he needs to know about his family tree is that his ancestors were Neanderthals."

"Thanks to you and your ship's incompetence, this cruise has been one disaster after another," the woman whined. "You leave us dirty mugs and used condoms. My husband almost broke his neck slipping on wet stairs. Then you left us stranded in Chester. And now this?"

Sheila and Shane looked at each other, still inching their way down the corridor. This awful, messy couple was the same couple who got left behind in Chester? Having paid little attention to the other guests who toured with them, Sheila hadn't even realized they were on the same excursion. "I bet they missed the bus on purpose," she said.

"Please," Raoul pleaded.

"We demand a refund. Get us your supervisor now."

"Please, let's work this out and—"

"We'll take it all the way to the captain if we have to," the man bellowed, his voice carrying down the long hallway.

Oh, that does it, Sheila thought. Before Shane could stop her, she marched up to the room and planted her feet next to Raoul's. "Don't you dare talk to him like that."

By now Shane was at her side, and for a moment all five people looked back and forth at each other. Sheila peeked inside the room. Beyond the open door, discarded clothes littered every visible surface. On the desk was a collection of strewn papers and photographs, all a big soggy mess. Lying on top of the saturated jumble was a bottle of cleaning fluid, uncapped and tipped over, its pungent chemicals wafting out the door.

"What are you looking at?" the woman with bleached-blond hair and penciled-in eyebrows barked at Sheila. Then the couple stormed out of the stateroom and stomped off down the hall.

"Clean that mess up," the man called over his shoulder. "We're going to Guest Relations to demand compensation."

"And anything less than a free cruise won't cut the mustard," the woman added.

"Mustard. Funny you should say that," Sheila shouted after

them. "Because your smelly auras are the color of mustard." A trio of women passed by as Sheila hurled her insult. They gave her a wide berth. To Raoul, she said, "I'm so sorry they're doing this. We'll stand up for you. We know how careful you are with the rooms."

His cheeks and lips were pinched in distress. "Thank you, madam, but I fear there is nothing you can do. Nothing anyone can do. They have complained too many times now. I don't think my boss suspects I'm behind it, but the bucket must stop somewhere, si?"

"Wrong." Shane's empathic veto surprised both Sheila and Raoul.

"What do you mean?" she asked.

Shane lifted the cuff of his sleeve and removed a small, black disc from his watch. With a mischievous grin, he held the object up.

"What is that?" Raoul's dark eyes grew large.

"That, Raoul, is a tiny camera. Captures up to thirty hours of video. I picked it up in Dublin, and I've been wearing it on my watch ever since. Much less clunky than recording with my phone. You never know when an opportunity might present itself. After you and I last spoke, I followed that couple, and lo and behold an opportunity presented itself."

Stunned into silence, Sheila thought back to their stop in Dublin. She remembered absentmindedly browsing in a gift shop while Shane had crossed the street to an electronics store. Then she thought back to her trip to the Internet Café later that same evening, when she had impatiently waited for him. She remembered him mentioning he had talked to Raoul outside the messy couple's room, just before the two had departed. But he had left it at that. He hadn't mentioned anything about following them, let alone having a hidden camera.

Raoul opened and closed his mouth, no sound coming out. Finally, he managed a weak, "I don't know what you mean, sir."

"I trailed the pair all the way to deck fifteen, up to that staircase that leads to the Sky Deck." To Sheila, Shane said, "Remember that open area at the front of the ship on deck sixteen?"

Sheila did remember. Early in the cruise, the two of them had climbed to it, hoping for a majestic view of the ocean beyond. They had gotten one all right. That and a blast of frigid wind that nearly knocked them into the ocean. It was no wonder the Sky Deck was deserted. At that height one practically needed a parka to withstand it.

"They didn't see me," Shane continued. "I kept out of sight behind a potted tree." He tapped his watch. "But the camera on my watch caught something interesting, something your ship's security camera probably didn't, given its location. I think it'll help you out, Raoul."

"You never cease to amaze me, dear husband. What did you catch?" Sheila tugged one of her dangling earrings and held her breath in anticipation. The stateroom attendant looked back and forth between them, as if afraid to speak.

A smile danced over Shane's lips, his gaze somewhere above Raoul's head. "The woman had a bottle of water. After making sure no one was around—she didn't see me behind the plant or my watch peeking through the branches—she dumped the water onto the stairs and ditched the bottle. Then her husband climbed the steps and purposely fell. Not hard, of course, but he wailed as if he did. Wailed and wailed until one of the ship's crew members came running. By that point a crowd had gathered, and I came out of hiding." Shane held up the tiny camera. "I was planning to give you the evidence, Raoul. Thought it might help you plead your case."

Sheila hugged her husband. "Shane, that's wonderful."

"You mean...you mean..." Raoul stuttered. "You caught the whole thing on camera? Without their knowing?" He looked as if he didn't know whether this was good news or bad, as if trying to decide whether it would liberate him or lead to more trouble.

"I did indeed, but it was in a public place, so don't worry. I don't think I've broken any rules." He winked and held up the camera. "Anybody up for a movie?"

24

AN INFECTIOUS EXPLANATION

In the Dreamscape Dining Room, finely dressed passengers spilled in for their evening meal. Succulent spices scented the air, and as before, Celtic music accompanied the seemingly choreographed moves of the waiting staff. Normally Sheila enjoyed this prelude to dinner, along with any extra time their waiters could spare. Victor and Renny were such nice men, always paying them special attention.

Tonight, however, during their penultimate dinner on the *Celestial of the Seas*, she was impatient for Victor to take their order and be on his way. Shane had been on the verge of telling her about his trip to the security department, where he had handed over the camera footage of the messy couple's staged accident, and she was eager for him to get back to his tale.

"You'll be happy to know, madam, that escargot is among our appetizers again tonight." Victor pointed to the oversized menu in Sheila's hands. Holding it up was her weight-training for the day. "Would you like to enjoy it a second time?"

Haven eaten enough seasoned eraser heads for one lifetime, she said, "Hmm, I'll be boring tonight and start with the tomato and mozzarella salad. For my entrée, I'll have the lemon chicken breast."

"Excellent choices, madam. And you, sir?" A row of teardrop beads from the giant chandelier reflected off Victor's glasses.

"I'll have the same."

"Wonderful."

As soon as their waiter took their menus and departed, Sheila scooted to the edge of the chair and planted her hands on the table, careful not to disturb her elegant place setting. "Okay, spill the beans. I want to hear everything. They didn't notice the bruises on your neck, did they?"

"No. I buttoned my shirt up all the way to hide them. But before I forget, Officer Tad wasn't able to learn anything about the phone number that sent you the text message."

Disappointment washed over Sheila. Before she could say anything else, Cutie Pie Renny arrived at the table with his ever-present pitcher of water. "Good evening, my favorite couple. Did you have a good time at sea today?"

"We did, thank you, dear." Sheila left it at that, eager to get back to Shane's news, but it appeared the waiting staff had extra time that evening, because Renny lingered after refreshing their water.

He shifted his gaze from side to side and leaned in closer. "I wanted to tell you I took your advice, miss."

"You did?" Sheila couldn't remember which advice he was refer-ring to. She was blessed to have plenty of it.

"Yes, I called the woman I told you about."

"Ah, yes, the one who wouldn't give you the time of day."

"Only this time, instead of telling her she was beautiful, I told her she was the smartest and hardest working person on the ship." His smile was angelic, and his eyes sparkled. "Just like you told me to."

"Did you mean it?" Sheila asked. "Because that's important." Shane pushed buttons on his big watch, seemingly preoccupied, but she knew he was listening in.

"Of course I meant it. She is both those things and more."

Sheila smiled warmly. "Good. Then I'm sure she'll date you. Who could resist those dimples?"

His face fell. "I think so, yes, but not yet. She said she was not feeling well and that maybe we could have dinner together on the next sailing." He brightened again. "But that's further than I've gotten with her yet, so I will take it."

He thanked her once more and moved onto a nearby table.

"Another soul my Sheila has helped." Shane raised his water glass to her. The affection in his eyes was touching.

Her hands were back on the table, arthritic fingers splayed. "Now, tell me what happened. I wish I could've gone with you. I would've liked to have seen the look on their faces when you told them about the camera."

"I couldn't risk bringing you along." Shane straightened his silverware. "If I got in trouble, I wanted it all on me."

"Always my sweet man. So how did it go? You're here, so I guess Officer Sourpuss didn't make you walk the plank."

"Not yet. Both he and Tad were there, but your handsome Croatian was not."

"Were they angry with you?"

"Not really. But when I walked in, Ivan grumbled 'what now?' and rubbed his temple so hard I thought he'd hit bone."

"They're not going to charge you with anything, are they?" Fear took root in her gut.

"Ivan sputtered and stomped a bit but then let it go, especially after he saw what was on the camera. And the recording was in a public place on the ship, not a place where one would expect privacy, so I doubt there's much they can do. Besides, the possibility that our daughter disappeared from their ship and they missed it is helping them overlook a lot of our behavior. That and our old age." Shane mimed a doddering, senile old man, which he was anything but.

Sheila took a sip of water, the only beverage in front of her. Tina hadn't yet come to take their wine order. Twice the brusque woman had flown past their table, too rushed to stop. "I imagine Officer Sourpuss will hold a party the moment we leave for good."

"I estimate there's a ninety-seven percent chance of that." He raised his glass. "To Ivan."

Sheila giggled and clinked his glass. "To Ivan." She could tell

Shane had as much nervous energy as she did, both anticipating their day in Ghent tomorrow, fearful of what they might find. Or more accurately, what they might not find. Their nerves were making them giddy.

Shane continued. "Both Tad and Ivan were already aware of the situation with the obnoxious couple. The used-condom business had reached them, as had the couple's complaint this afternoon that Raoul spilled a cleaner all over their papers and photographs."

She flicked her hand. "Nonsense."

"Agreed. Ivan and Tad didn't believe it either. They suspect the couple took the cleaning fluid from a stateroom attendant's cart. Luckily for Raoul, my camera proved the two would stop at nothing to get a free cruise."

Sheila's mouth puckered in disgust but then shifted to a smile when Victor came by with their salads. Fresh mozzarella and parsley, drizzled with balsamic dressing, topped four perfectly sliced tomatoes. After a delicious first bite, she said, "Will this be enough to get poor Raoul off the hook? He won't get in trouble because of your camera, will he?"

"No. I assured them Raoul had nothing to do with it. His job is safe. And the couple won't be getting a free cruise anytime soon. In fact, quite the opposite. They've been banned from all future sailings with the cruise line."

"Phew, that's a relief. What awful, awful people." She twirled her empty wine glass. "I need something stronger. Where is that sour sommelier?"

Victor approached with their entrées and placed wonderfully aromatic lemon chicken, mashed potatoes, and asparagus in front of them.

"Thank you, darling," she said to him. "Could you ask Tina to stop by when you get a chance?"

The waiter eyed their wineless glasses. "Oh, I am so sorry. This is inexcusable."

"Please, don't worry. It's not your fault."

Victor scanned the massive dining room for Tina. "I don't see her, but you tell me what you would like, and I'll make sure she brings it to you."

They did so, and by the time Tina finally arrived with the two bottles, her hair bun as stiff as her walk, they were halfway through their meals. She poured white for Sheila and red for Shane, not even bothering to give them a sample to taste. Before the second bottle was even fully upright, she pivoted to leave.

"Wait a minute, miss." Sheila's tone was sharper than she'd intended.

Tina froze and then turned back around, her expression pinched. "Yes, madam?"

"What have we done to offend you? Please tell us. You've been brusque with us the entire time we've been here, and it seems to be getting worse."

The normally polished sommelier blinked anxiously, her posture rigid, her legs tense. "You have done nothing. I'm sorry you feel that way." Once again she started to leave, and once again Sheila called her back.

"You know something about our daughter, don't you? What do you know? Tell me." Sheila's pitch rose, and guests at nearby tables glanced in her direction.

The Indonesian woman stammered. "I...I don't...I have no idea what you're talking about. Please, I must go." The sommelier shifted back and forth on her feet, as if they were on fire.

"We saw you in the infirmary yesterday morning. Did you tell someone we were there? Are you the one who informed the red-haired man about us? What do you know about my daughter?"

Tina looked utterly befuddled. "Nothing, I promise. I..."

"Then why are you so rude to us? I hate to do it, I know how hard you all work, but I might have to speak to your supervisor."

"Rude? I...it's not you...it's just that I..." The sommelier's eyes widened, and her face froze in panic. Her legs pressed tightly together. "Oh no." She started to back away. "I must leave. I have..."

She turned around and started duck-walking, her legs stiff and her glutes squeezed beneath her pencil skirt. Sheila stared off at her incredulously. What was wrong with the woman?

But then, when the polished, perfectly pristine sommelier had made it only three feet, it hit Sheila. It hit both her brain and her nose. In fact, the odor was so sudden and awful that the guests around them recoiled in horror.

"Oh no," Tina squeaked. She stood for a moment, as if hoping no one had noticed, her face a twisted wreck. Then she resumed her duck-walking in that tight-legged waddle, a streak of brown running down her legs.

Shane stared in disbelief, his fork halfway to his mouth. "Did she just poo herself?" He blinked. "Well, what are the odds of that?"

Within seconds Sheila was on her feet. She shuffled past the unhelpful gawkers and hurried over to the poor woman. "Here, dear, come this way," she whispered, putting her arm around her. "The closest restroom is just there by the entrance."

She guided the mortified sommelier to the door, dozens of guests watching (and smelling) their passage. "Nothing to see here," Sheila said to them as they went. "Go back to your dinners, please. Didn't your mothers teach you the Golden Rule?"

When they reached the bathroom, Tina was in tears. "This is horrible," she sobbed. "What will my coworkers think? I've been sick all week, that is why I've been so quick with everyone. I saw the doctor yesterday and thought I was well enough to return to work, but tonight I...I..."

"Shh, shh, don't you worry about that. Let's get you cleaned up. I work in a medical office. Nothing I haven't seen before."

For the next fifteen minutes, Sheila deftly blocked off the restroom, asked the hostess to summon a new uniform, and reassured the sommelier it would all be fine.

Meanwhile, she chastised herself. All this time she had thought the young woman rude, never stopping to figure out what might be wrong. Now she understood why Tina had transformed from an initial blue aura of efficiency to a troubling haze of brown.

The poor dear had food poisoning. It was as simple as that. As simple as chocolate mousse gone bad.

25

A CANAL RIDE OF WONDER

To SHEILA, driving through the Belgian countryside was much like driving through the American countryside. Flat fields of grass and trees gave way to scattered businesses, which then gave way to crops and cows. On the coach's left side, a cluster of three-vaned wind turbines caught Shane's eyes. Sheila listened to his snippets about wind velocity and air density, but mostly she focused on the tour guide's stories. The woman stood adjacent to Sheila's first-row aisle seat, and though the microphone wasn't needed in such close proximity, at her age Sheila would always welcome an extra decibel or two. Shane had requested the window seat and was now making wind-power density calculations in his notebook.

Their main goal of the Ghent excursion was to go to St. Bavo's Cathedral and see the Ghent Altarpiece, where hopefully clues about their daughter would manifest. Before that happened though, they would drive into Ghent, located in the northern Flemish Region of Belgium, and take a canal ride. Despite her nervous energy, Sheila figured she would try to relax and enjoy the time. Though she hoped to live to be a hundred years old, she had enough of Shane's realism to know this would likely be her first and last trip to Belgium.

Their guide, Eva, had not recognized Shanna or Mr. Smelly from the pictures Sheila had shown her earlier. Currently, the woman held the clip-on microphone next to her mouth. "I am here to tell you Ghent is the best-known vegetarian city in the world, did you know that?" Her perfect English carried an elegant Dutch inflection. Gray, bobbed hair matched her fleece jacket, and her fit body belied her age, which must have been north of fifty, if not sixty. "And I am here to tell you there are over one hundred and fifty breweries in Belgium and over one thousand varieties of beer." As seemed to happen every time booze was mentioned, a rowdy cheer broke out on the bus. "But that number changes all the time, you know?"

"And lots of chocolates and waffles," a woman behind Sheila offered.

"Oh, yes, we have many tasty foods for you to try. Our waffles are heavier than what you know in your own countries, yes? You can have whatever you like on them: sugar, strawberries, banana, chocolate, cream."

Shane stopped his wind-farm talk at the mention of sweets. For a man with a flat, thirty-two-inch waist, he enjoyed his desserts.

"And if you need more, try our Belgian fries. You buy them for take-away, to snack on the go, you know? Lots of delicious sauces to dip them in."

It was barely an hour since Sheila had eaten breakfast, but her mouth was already watering.

"Ah, we are coming into Ghent now, you see?" Eva lowered her head from her upright position and looked through the windows along with the passengers. At first, if it wasn't for the foreign traffic signs, Sheila wouldn't know she was in a different country. Older homes lined each side of the road, some row houses, some stand-alones. Businesses came in waves. A few high-rise apartment buildings too. But as they drove on, crossing a canal and nearing the inner parts of the city, everything new became old. Hundreds and hundreds of years old.

"I am here to tell you," Eva said, "Ghent is the capital of East Flanders province. It is old and new mixed together and goes back to the six hundreds. Much of the old city center is car-free. Only delivery trucks and special cars come in, so we must walk from our drop-off point over to the canal boats. Yes? You can manage that?"

The tour guide's gaze went straight to Sheila and Shane. Well, that's a bit presumptuous, Sheila thought, but as she flexed her feet and felt the bones rebel, she supposed it was a fair question. She nodded to Eva. Nothing—no bone spur, joint inflammation, or stiff spine—would keep her from Ghent. Between her twenty minutes of morning yoga and a hearty bowl of granola, yogurt, and berries, she was ready to roll. Grateful that raincoats and umbrellas were not needed on this sunny and warm day, she patted her cardigan pocket. Her peanut bar was in its place. Yes, she was ready to go.

"You will see lots of bikes here," Eva continued, her tiny microphone still raised to her lips, making Sheila wonder why she didn't simply clip it to her fleece jacket. "But don't worry. The bike riders are not as crazy here as they are in Amsterdam. There you must be careful. They will take out a tourist, no problem."

With this, the passengers laughed, and Sheila nodded in agreement. Though she and Shane hadn't ventured far from their Amsterdam hotel, the little they had traveled nearly gave them panic attacks. Bikes zipping around everywhere, the riders paying no heed or mind to who might be in their paths.

"Also, I am here to tell you Dutch is the primary language in this part of Belgium. At a young age children learn French as well, and around twelve or so they start studying English. Some learn German too."

"I really must learn Spanish," Sheila whispered to Shane. "We're too monolingual in the United States."

"You've been saying that for forty years now."

"Yes, thank you, Mr. Helpful."

From the bus window, the streets grew older and narrower. The buildings changed as well, morphing into centuries-old brick and stone edifices, their facades and towering gables a feast for the eyes. According to Eva, the medieval buildings with Gothic architecture mingled with seventeenth-century Baroque and eighteenth-century neo-Classical design. Canals with beautiful bridges crisscrossed them all.

The bus came to a stop.

"This is as far as we can drive into the old city," Eva said. "We will stop to use the underground toilets, and then we will walk to our canal ride. The ride will be about an hour long, yes? And then you will have free time to explore our lovely city."

"And buy some chocolate," the same woman as before called out.

"And beer," a man countered.

When they stepped off the coach, the dark beiges and browns of ancient buildings encircled them. After descending to the promised subterranean bathroom, the women's line longer than a book-signing queue, Sheila climbed back up the stone steps and rejoined Shane. Taking in the scenery, he was intermittently jotting notes in his notebook. At their age, snapping photographs was of less interest. No sense taking in the sites behind a camera. Simply enjoying the moment while they still could was the best way to preserve their memories.

As they made their way back to Eva, her raised hand holding a sign bearing the *Celestials of the Seas* name and their group number (her "yellow lollipop" as she'd called it), Sheila blinked in surprise. A man she hadn't expected to see was chatting with Eva.

Officer Gorgeous.

She took Shane's arm and pointed. A gentle breeze lifted her hair beneath her sun hat, and the scent of a nearby bakery tempted her taste buds.

When they reached Niko, who was out of uniform and dressed in gray jeans and a polo shirt, she asked him, "What are you doing here?"

"If our free shift times right and there's an extra seat, we're allowed to tag along on excursions." His heart-stopping smile seemed to catch Eva's eye. With a goofy grin, the tour guide commented on his wonderful English.

"I didn't see you on the bus," Sheila said.

"I was all the way in back." His face sobered. "I know this stop is important to you. I thought I would come along to…support you."

Suspicion sprouted in her mind. "Did Officer Sourpuss send you?" She covered her mouth at her mistake, but not before Niko frowned.

"Who?"

"Officer Ivan, I mean. Did he send you?"

"Of course not." Niko bit back a smile. "Nice name for him, by the way."

"How did you know we'd be on this excursion?"

"I'm with security, Mrs. McShane. That's not difficult to find out."

"Hmm, I suppose not."

"But please, don't get your hopes up," he warned. "I know you think that wasn't your daughter on the Ghent footage, but—"

"I *know* it wasn't my daughter."

Niko bowed his head in acknowledgment. "Okay, then all the more reason to have someone from security nearby."

Sheila narrowed her eyes, still not convinced he wasn't sent as a spy. Yet his presence comforted her. After the Blarney Castle experience, if they ran into Hivey Red again, she wanted Officer Gorgeous by their side.

Though Shane remained quiet, taking in the buildings around them with their tall spires and stained windows, she could see similar suspicion on his face.

Twenty minutes later, after a pleasant, breezy walk over cobblestone streets and medieval bridges, canal water lapping the dank surfaces, Sheila and Shane were seated on comfortable chairs in the center of an open-top boat. Less fortunate passengers sat cheek-to-cheek on padded benches along the periphery. Being the most senior people on a trip had its advantages. The sun shined gloriously, and the temperature was cool enough to enjoy it. Even Sheila's foot bones held back their usual complaining.

Their large group required three canal boats. Eva rode along on Sheila and Shane's. Officer Gorgeous stayed with them too, and for the next hour the three of them absorbed the sights, scents, and sounds of Ghent.

Centuries-old buildings with pastel facades and elegant gables rose skyward. Aided by Eva's explanation of the different styles of gables, the passengers made a game of calling them out when sighted: "Neck. Bell. Step. Spout."

Water rippled along the boat's side, and ducks floated and bobbed in the wakes of a constant stream of canal traffic. Celebratory boats passed by as well, including one filled with a group of women from an apparent bachelorette party. They hooted and hollered and raised champagne bottles in the air. Everyone waved and greeted each other, the mood magical and bright.

Up above on the canal streets, bikes were a constant presence, their frames leaning against iron railings. The sight of them prompted Eva to say, "I am here to tell you hundreds of bicycles have been fished out of these waters." Also lining both sides of the canal were houseboats, many of which were vibrantly painted and decorated with flower boxes. Sheila wondered about the people who lived in them.

High above the boat passengers' heads, massive trees offered intermittent shade from the bright sun, their pendulous branches suspended over the water. From time to time, arched bridges required passage beneath them, some so narrow only single-file crossing was allowed.

Sheila's *oohs* and *ahhs* were too numerous to count. When the canal boat passed the Castle of the Counts, she squeezed Shane's arm in awe. According to Eva, the castle's first stone was placed as far back as the eleventh century. If she lived in Europe, Sheila would never tire of seeing such majestic structures. When the canal boat paused for picture-taking of the castle, she and Shane simply absorbed its magnificence.

Still, despite all the beauty and despite all the wonder, the farther they traveled down the canal, the darker Sheila's mood became. Maybe it was because the buildings themselves darkened, their bases blackened and stained by the water and their doors opening eerily onto the canal. One would need a boat to exit them.

Or maybe it was the increasing desolation of the area, the earlier boat traffic tapering off and the buildings becoming less aesthetically pleasing. Some even looked abandoned, their empty essence filling Sheila with a gloom she couldn't define. She longed to return to the city center and the wonder it inspired.

In the warm air, she shivered. As if magnets were separating her molecules, her body felt disjointed and jumbled. Was Shanna somewhere in this city? Was she being held against her will, forced to commit unethical acts of art fraud as Sheila had deduced?

Or was she simply deluding herself? Had she taken her fear and inability to accept Shanna's loss and turned it into something else, using the false guise of intuition to justify it?

And yet, she swore she could feel her daughter's presence, her spirit, her soul. Something in this city announced it. If only Sheila could find it.

A cloak of grief enveloped her, its weight so heavy she reached for Shane's hand to help carry its load. As always, he accepted it unconditionally. Perhaps he felt the weight of it too.

26

DIVINE INTERVENTION

THE INSIDE OF ST. Bavo's Cathedral was dark and cool and, despite the throngs of tourists, reasonably quiet. Within its aged stone walls and massive vaulted ceilings, the noise seemed to simply disperse. This muted din heightened Sheila's sense of gloom even more. Gone was the touristy lightness she had felt on the first part of the canal ride. In its place, fear and unrest.

Arched, stained-glass windows rich with religious symbolism soared to great heights, some reaching as high as the ceiling. In the upper nave of the high choir, a baroque-style altar dazzled with its accents of gold. Stone statues, marble columns, ornate woodwork, and beautiful paintings competed for the eye, the cathedral as much a museum as a place of worship.

As Sheila strolled the black- and white-tiled floor, Shane by her side and Niko not far behind, she only half-listened to Eva's hushed commentary. Was her apprehension stemming from her suspicion that something within these walls had led to Shanna's disappearance? Or was it because the church was their last hope to find Shanna, and Sheila was terrified of walking away empty-handed?

Small chambers and chapels lined the periphery of the cathedral, each depicting artwork or graves of religious figures. It was to one of these chambers their tour guide led them now. Inside, they would see a replica of *The Adoration of the Mystic Lamb* before viewing the actual polyptych in a separate room. The real paintings required an entrance ticket, which, as part of the excursion group, had already been provided to them.

As they waited their turn to enter the room with the replica, Sheila struggled to see inside it through all the tourists. A tall man hurried past their group, bumping into a woman and nearly toppling her over. His coat was zipped to the neck, his hat pulled low over his head, and his sunglasses still on his face. Normally such rudeness would bother Sheila, but she was too anxious to dwell on it. Besides, he had disappeared quickly into the crowd, and all that mattered was that he was too tall to be Hivey Red.

When they finally entered the chamber with the rest of their group, packed in like passengers on a rush-hour train, Sheila's heart rate sped up. Shane seemed tense as well, his pen gripped tightly in one hand, his notebook in the other. Officer Gorgeous stood nearby, giving Sheila a reassuring smile when she looked back at him. She remained uncertain whether his presence was truly to help or to ensure they didn't make trouble.

"So, I am here to show you the famous Ghent Altarpiece," Eva began, her voice hushed in the small room. "This is a replica of *The Adoration of the Mystic Lamb*. Perhaps you have heard of it? The altarpiece with the stolen panel?"

Affirmative murmurs riffled through the group. Someone flashed a photograph.

"Oh no, sir," Eva said. "There is no flash photography in the cathedral."

With a sardonic tone, Shane whispered, "Guess he missed the multiple signs posted all over."

Their guide continued. "As you can see, it is a series of panels. In this position, it is closed. In a moment, I will open it for you. Understand, this is only a replica to show you. The real thing, which you will soon see, is behind glass in a separate room." The bottom of the polyptych fell a foot below Eva's head. The top extended several more feet above her. Sheila had to look up to take it all in.

Wooden frames divided each individual painting. In a closed position, on both the left and right side, four paintings made up the top half and two the bottom. Robed religious figures filled most of them, a single figure per panel. Though Shane scribbled down the guide's description of each painting, Sheila's attention drifted from the commentary. She wondered about slipping away to ask the entrance staff if they recognized Shanna. She hadn't yet had the opportunity. She decided to wait for the time being, lest she miss something important.

Their guide opened the two boards, first the right and then the left. The same set of paintings they had seen when they researched the altarpiece in the Internet Café appeared. A total of twelve panels filled the open boards, each divided by rich wood framing. Vibrant robes of green, blue, and red cloaked the religious figures. The largest painting was in the lower central panel. It depicted several groups of worshipers in a meadow of trees and shrubs. In the middle of them, the Lamb of God lay on an alter encircled by fourteen angels. Blood gushed from a wound on the animal's chest and flowed into a golden chalice, which, according to Eva, represented Christ's sacrifice.

This wasn't the panel that interested Sheila though. Nor Shane, despite his frantic scribbling to catch every word the guide said. Sheila saw it in the crease of his forehead, the twitch of his lip, the hard set of his jaw every time his gaze drifted to the lower left panel. That painting was *The Just Judges*. The stolen panel that was never returned. The panel Sheila was convinced had something to do with their daughter's disappearance. In it, just as on the internet, Sheila saw several robed men on horseback with three castles in the background. It was the back half of the panel adjacent to it, which showed a similar scene.

Eva moved on to it now. As she described the history of the theft, which Sheila already knew from their research, Sheila exchanged a look with Shane, one that was part dread, part hope, and part helplessness. She looked back at Officer Gorgeous. He offered a sad smile and a shake of his head, which could have translated a number of ways, not the least of which was, "You're a couple of senile old fools."

She didn't care. As the tour group left the chamber and made their way down the nave of the cathedral toward the actual *Adoration of the Mystic Lamb* paintings, her spirit darkened even more, so much so that she could see her own emanating aura of fear. By the time the group reached the viewing room and started handing their tickets to the attendant, single file, for that was the best way to proceed through the narrow pathway that bordered the glass-enclosed paintings, Sheila's heart pounded more erratically than the poor sacrificial lamb's. She didn't need to see the original, didn't care about its details, which was why she was at the back of the line with Shane and Niko. She only wanted to ask the attendant if she had seen Shanna. So before she handed her ticket to the woman, she plucked out her phone and pulled up Shanna's picture.

She readied herself for a negative response. Millions of tourists passed through the cathedral's doors. How could the woman remember her daughter from two months before? It might not even be the same attendant. But Sheila held out hope that Shanna might be recognized, because she would have lingered a long time to study the polyptych. It was the piece she had most wanted to see.

If one needed divine intervention, the cathedral was evidently the place to be, because the attendant did remember Shanna. "Yes, I've seen your daughter." Her English had a Dutch inflection like Eva's. "And that man too."

Sheila cried out in gratitude and squeezed Shane's hand. She felt it tremble around her own. Niko expressed similar amazement.

"Oh yes, I remember her well. She was here for a long time viewing the panels."

"I'm not surprised," Sheila said, eager for the woman to continue and relieved the line in front of her was still moving slowly around the paintings. "She works as an art restorer."

"Yes, well, I was about to tell her it was time to move on, when a man—that man," the clerk pointed to Sheila's camera, though the screen had since gone dark, "budged through the line to reach her. The more he talked to her, the more upset she became. They were too far away for me to hear what was said, but at one point, he grabbed her arm and she shook him off. Like this." The woman jerked her arm forcefully in the air and frowned at the memory.

Sheila's mouth went dry. "What happened then?"

"I wondered if I should call someone. I was worried your daughter didn't want the man there. But before I could, they left."

The viewing line in front of them had thinned enough to allow more visitors into the room, but Sheila didn't budge. "Did he force her to leave with him? Did he hurt her? Did she look scared?" Her voice grew more panicked with each syllable, as if the event were happening now and not two months before. "Why didn't you call security?"

Shane put his arm around her. "Shh, it's okay. Let her finish."

The woman was stammering now. Though the line behind them was long, no one seemed irritated by the delay. On the contrary, they seemed to be listening to the exchange in hushed anticipation.

"I did, madam, I did. I called security as soon as they walked away. That's another reason I remember her so well. But your daughter and the man left the premises before our guard found them. The cathedral is very large."

"Did she look scared?" Sheila repeated, crushing her phone against her ribcage.

"Your daughter didn't look happy, and yes, a bit scared too." The attendant wiped a nervous hand over her forehead. "They were pressed together, almost in an embrace, and left quickly. That's all I know. I'm sorry."

The woman looked so distressed Sheila reached over and gave her a small hug. "I'm sorry. I didn't mean to pounce on you. It's not your fault. You've been very helpful." Sheila stepped back and blinked away tears. "You see, our daughter has been missing for two months, and I'm terrified that man took her."

AFTER LEARNING THE NEWS, Niko escorted Sheila and Shane to a nearby staircase that led to the crypts of the cathedral. "It's much less crowded down there, cooler too. You can collect yourself. I can see by your faces you think your daughter disappeared from here, but it's too early to say. Our camera shows her leaving the ship in Amsterdam."

Sheila didn't know who Niko was trying to convince more—them or himself—but they followed him to the basement, where it was indeed a relief to be free of the masses.

Still, the atmosphere was eerie, especially since the crypts went on for some distance. The stone walls with their low-arched ceilings and yellow hue made Sheila feel more trapped than collected. Medieval frescoes adorned many of the walls, and in normal times, she and Shane would have marveled at the centuries-old paintings and architecture.

Officer Gorgeous pointed to a bench. "Here, sit. I'll see if I can find some water for you."

She nodded as Niko took off to the left, deeper into a crypt, and turned a corner. A few tourists wandered by: a woman with a whining child hurrying back toward the stairs, a middle-aged couple strolling slowly to take in the frescoes, and the man Sheila had seen earlier with his hat pulled low and sunglasses on. Although she had thought little about him up in the nave, other than his rudeness in bumping into the woman from their group, she now realized his attire was all wrong for a warm day in the cathedral. She had been too distracted by the polyptych to reflect on it earlier.

He walked past them, down the same crypt Niko had just gone, and though his head was lowered and he didn't look at them, he somehow seemed familiar.

She pivoted toward Shane, nearly falling off the bench. "We need to find Niko. Something's not right."

Shane's head leaned against the ancient stone wall. With his drawn face and tense jaw, he looked pale, worn, and completely stressed out. "He'll be back soon." He licked his lips. "I could really use that water."

She scanned the crypt where Niko had disappeared. "I'm worried about him."

The few tourists had moved on, and Sheila and Shane were alone. Silence enveloped them like the tombs of the dead priests.

"I don't—"

A thump echoed off the low ceiling. It came from where Niko had ventured.

Sheila jumped. "What was that?" She sat ramrod straight, her entire body trembling.

Shane was fully upright now too. "I don't know. Probably just tourists." His strained expression suggested he believed otherwise.

They looked at each other and then off to the left, waiting for Niko to round the corner. He didn't.

On shaky legs, she stood. "Officer Niko?" she called out, softly at first but then louder. "Niko? Are you okay?"

She tiptoed a few steps to peer around the corner, Shane behind her. Niko was nowhere to be seen.

27

IN SEARCH OF THE YELLOW
LOLLIPOP

WANDERING alone in the underbelly of St. Bavo's Cathedral was not on Sheila and Shane's wish list. They had already had three run-ins with Hivey Red. They didn't relish another. So at the corner of the crypt where Niko had disappeared, Sheila tugged on Shane's blazer and said, "I don't dare go any farther."

"Me either. Let's find the rest of the group before they leave."

"But what about Niko? Where did he go? That noise sounded like someone falling."

"Niko is a big boy and a security guard to boot. He'll be fine." As if his words hadn't convinced even himself, Shane added, "But let's inform a cathedral rep on our way out just to be safe."

He took her hand and guided her back toward the same stairwell they had descended a short time before. With as pale as he looked, she worried she should be the one guiding him. "We need to get you some water." She tasted the dryness of her own mouth. "Me too."

When they reached the stairs, Shane stopped and checked his watch. Alarm flashed in his eyes. "Oh no. It's already past noon. Our group might be gone by now."

Sheila saw the fear in his thinly pressed lips and the stress in his furrowed brow. He was the timekeeper, the one who kept them in check, so his failure to watch the clock told her he was more anxious over the attendant's news about Shanna than he had let on. Hearing their daughter had been led away by Mr. Smelly, possibly with force, appeared to have left him as addled and shaken as her. Overexerted too, as evidenced by his heavy breathing up the stairs. She scolded herself for forgetting her water bottle. They had been under the hot sun for an hour on the canal ride.

Inside the main cathedral, the crowd had grown. Despite craning their necks and standing on tiptoes, Sheila and Shane couldn't find their group through the sea of tourists. No sign of Eva's yellow *Celestial of the Seas* lollipop anywhere. Sheila's anxiety mounted.

They spotted an employee, dressed darkly in a respectable skirt and sweater, a name badge on her lapel. With breathless speech Sheila explained to the woman about Niko, what they had heard, and their inability to find him. "He's probably fine," Sheila added, her hand against her chest, "but I think someone should check on things down there."

"No problem. I will send someone down."

"Thank you," Sheila said. "We have to go outside and look for our group. We were supposed to reconvene at noon for our next stop."

The employee told Sheila that was fine, and as she and Shane made their way to the cathedral's entrance to leave, she scanned the crowded aisles and pews for Niko or anyone else from their group she might recognize. She also looked for men with red hair, convinced Hivey Red would pop up any second.

When they finally stepped outside into the sunlight and cool breeze, she exhaled in relief, but it was short-lived. She didn't see anyone from their group or Eva's yellow lollipop.

Shane pointed off to the side, a sheen of sweat on his forehead. "There's a water vendor. I'll get us some. I'm drier than sandpaper. You keep looking for our group."

Sheila nodded, following him, her eyes scrutinizing the crowds for a recognizable face. The courtyard was thick with tourists, their throngs extending all the way across the street to the old buildings with ornamental gables that lined it.

"I don't see the yellow lollipop anywhere. What if they walked back to the bus already?" She tried to keep her voice controlled, but a high pitch of despair crept in. "We learned in Chester the coach won't wait long."

Shane purchased two bottles of water from a man behind a stand and handed her one. Together they guzzled like desert dwellers, slowly rotating in a circle to scan every area of the court-yard for Eva's lollipop.

"Shaney, look!" Water sprayed from Sheila's mouth. She pointed to a man in jeans and a T-shirt jogging toward them. "It's Officer Floppy Ears. Thank heavens, someone we know."

"What's he doing here?" Shane recapped his half-empty bottle and wiped his mouth, but he still looked pale and drawn.

When Tad reached them, he said, "There you two are. We've been looking all over for you."

"You have? I don't understand. Niko was the one on the excursion. How…" Sheila was too confused to continue. Maybe she needed a bit of her peanut bar. She was starting to feel shaky.

"I tagged along with another excursion group. Here, follow me." The officer's British lilt was chipper and upbeat as he started leading them away. "Niko's with me. He felt bad you got separated. Blames himself for you missing your coach, but we've got a ride all ready for you here."

Still blinking in bewilderment, she stared at the white van awaiting them at the curb. "I thought only special vehicles could drive into the old city."

Tad chuckled. "It is a special vehicle. See?" He pointed to the van as if that explained it. "You're not the first tourists to get left behind, and seeing as how you're our VIP guests, we didn't want to make you walk far."

Sheila paused at the curb. Something was off about Officer Floppy Ears. His purple sensitivity was still there, but a mustardy color of unease faded in and out. Maybe it was her own discomfort over the news about Shanna that blurred his hue. After all, rolling out a figurative red carpet for them made sense. After losing Shanna, the ship would suffer a PR nightmare if her parents got left behind in Ghent.

"Come on." Tad opened the van's side door. "We'll get you back to the ship in time for a nice lunch."

Lunch sounded wonderful. She was hungry and shaky. She broke off a piece of her peanut bar to munch on while Shane helped her into the vehicle. A partition separated the second seat of the van from the front, its sliding panel currently closed. Though she couldn't see the driver, she assumed it was Niko. It felt wonderful to sink back onto the cool leather seat, her tired and anxious body in need of a good rest.

Best of all, they had made progress. Armed with new information that Shanna had been led away by force by Mr. Smelly, Sheila would insist to Officer Sourpuss that he put them in touch with the Ghent authorities. She wouldn't let the ship set sail again until he did. She closed her eyes and took deep breaths. Yes, they had made progress. While she uncapped her bottle and took another sip of water, Tad closed the van door. Moments later the front passenger door slammed shut as well. Soon they drove away.

"I'm glad we found you, Niko." She spoke loudly so she'd be heard over the partition. "I was worried something happened to you."

No answer came from the front. Sheila and Shane exchanged glances.

"Officer Niko?" She tried again.

Still no response.

Shane reached for the panel and slid the partition open. Sheila leaned forward to talk to Officer Gorgeous.

But he wasn't there. Not in the driver's seat and not in the passenger's seat.

Her uncapped water bottle fell to the floor. Water splashed her feet.

A red-haired man with blotchy skin sat behind the wheel. "Surprise," he said and then laughed.

FROM GHENT TO NOWHERE

STILL SITTING up near the partition, her body not yet restrained by a seatbelt, Sheila sputtered, "It's Hivey Red!" She whipped her head back and forth between him and Officer Floppy Ears and then at Shane, who looked too bewildered to speak.

The Scottish man's face twitched. He looked down at his hive-marked and excoriated bare arms and, in doing so, almost drove the van up onto the curb.

"Watch it," Tad said. "We're not even supposed to be in this part of the city." Though his own skin wasn't rashy, he rubbed his forearms furiously as if it were.

"You know him?" Anger and betrayal twisted Sheila's face. "This...this horrible man?"

The young security officer gave her a fleeting look and turned away. "Hand me your phones, please." His voice quavered with contrition.

"How could you do this to us? *What* are you doing to us?"

Next to her in the backseat, Shane raked a hand over the side door to open it. No luck. He reached over to Sheila's door, but it too was locked.

Hivey Red snickered. "Ya won't be escaping from here, mate."

Shane rubbed a hand over his mouth, his gaze darting back and forth. His agitated gestures suggested he was either formulating a plan or simply trying to process the startling situation.

"Just give me your phones," Officer Floppy Ears repeated.

"I most certainly will not," Sheila protested. "What would your mother think of your duplicitous behavior, young man? You told me how close you two are."

Tad flinched. He stared out the passenger window at the medieval buildings beyond, his thigh bouncing up and down on the seat. "You just couldn't leave things alone, could you? Had to keep digging."

Sheila sensed he was out of his element. "You've been lying this whole—"

"Give him yer stupid phones," Hivey Red shouted. Everyone in the van jumped. "And don't even think of using it first." He looked in the rearview mirror at Shane, who Sheila now realized was powering on his phone to call for help. Could he turn it on, get it out of airplane mode, and activate his cellular data quickly enough? He hadn't used it for anything but a rare picture-snap since they had stepped foot on foreign land, the costs too prohibitive. "If you complete that call, you'll regret it." The hive-pocked man maneuvered the vehicle around a group of tourists crossing the narrow cobblestone road, and then leaned over and popped open the glove compartment. Next to an epinephrine auto-injector, which was an allergy drug Sheila recognized from her work in Dr. Shakir's office, lay an object that nearly stopped her heart.

A gun.

Hivey Red picked it up and waved it through the open partition.

Sheila shot back in her seat and pressed against Shane, the phone frozen in his hand. His face paled, and he passed his mobile through the partition to Tad.

"Give them yours," Shane said to Sheila.

"But—"

"Beetle Bug, give him your phone."

She fished it from her purse, shifted forward again so she could see them through the partition, and tossed it at Tad. It bounced off his floppy earlobe.

"Ay," he cried, rubbing the spot before retrieving the mobile from the floor mat. He powered both of them off and tossed them in the glove compartment.

"Take this." Hivey Red held the gun out to Tad.

The young guard looked at it like it was a poisonous frog. "I don't want it. That's not my job."

"Take the bloody thing." Hivey Red dumped it in Tad's lap, the van swerving as he did so. "You can give it to me when we get there."

Sheila still couldn't fathom the baby-faced security guard's role in this. How could she have read him so wrong? Other than his occasional mustardy color of unease, he had shimmered a purple glow of gentleness and awareness.

"Where are we going? Where is Officer Gorgeous?" Her tone was indignant but her face cautious.

Tad looked up from the gun. "Who?"

"Niko, Officer Gorgeous," she snapped. "You said he was in the van. Where is he?"

The young guard said nothing, but the worried glance he gave Hivey Red was not lost on her. The ginger-haired man simply laughed. "Hivey Red. Officer Gorgeous." He jerked a chewed-up thumbnail at Tad. "What's this one's name? Or don't he wanna know?"

Sheila snorted a rush of fear and anger from her nose. "Believe me, he doesn't want to know."

Shane decided otherwise. "Officer Floppy Ears," he growled through gritted teeth. "That's what she calls double-crossing idiots."

Tad's face fell. His hands flew to his ears, a flush creeping up to them.

Hivey Red chortled. "Guess me own name's not so bad now, huh?" He raced through a yellow light and rounded a corner so sharply Sheila fell into Shane.

"Good Lord. And here I thought your gun was dangerous." She

righted herself, slid back, and clicked her seatbelt into place. "Is Officer Sourpuss in on this too?"

Tad blinked through the partition at her. "Do you mean Ivan?" When she nodded, he looked stupidly pleased to have cracked her code, but his expression quickly sobered. "No, and he'll never know about it either."

Though Sheila had already deduced they wouldn't be returning to the ship, the finality of Tad's words made her realize they wouldn't be returning anywhere. At least not alive, where they would be free to flap their tongues. A shiver licked the base of her spine and spread to the rest of her body. She forced herself to remain calm, though it was proving futile. "What do you plan on doing with us? Where's our daughter?"

The men up front ignored her. Since Officer Floppy Ears was looking forward again, she couldn't see his whole face through the partition, but even in profile he seemed tense. Scared, even.

"You told me it would never get this far," he said. "You told me I only had to act as your eyes and ears." His timbre rose. "Now you've got me abducting old people? Giving me a gun?"

"Quit yer whining," the blotchy man said. "Did ya take care of *Officer Gorgeous?*" He drew out the nickname seductively in his Scottish accent.

"He never saw it coming. I got out before he came to."

Hivey Red squealed the van onto a paved road, the old part of the city disappearing behind them. "Ya didn't finish him off? What kind of a guard are you, for cryin' out loud?" Though Sheila couldn't see him from behind the partition, his anger was palpable.

Then the meaning of what they said dawned on her, and she inhaled sharply. She glared at Tad. "You were the man in the cathedral with the hat and sunglasses. I saw you in the nave and then again down in the crypts."

Tad ignored her and addressed Hivey Red. "You're a fancy fellow to talk. Least I'm not the one who got bested by old people." His floppy earlobes flashed red. "Four times already. All you had to do was scare them off. How hard is that? Bloody hell, you'll be lucky if Jordan doesn't use this thing on you." Tad raised the gun in the air, and though not aimed at them, Sheila and Shane jolted their heads back against their seats.

She replayed Tad's words. She had heard the name *Jordan* before, back when Hivey Red said it in the Blarney Castle dungeon. Was that Mr. Smelly? And once again she tried to recall their fourth encounter with Hivey Red. She remembered only three: the Edinburgh museum, when the fall down the stairs failed to stop them; the walk on Duke Street in Liverpool, when they escaped in a taxi; and the Blarney Castle dungeon, where Shane had turned the man's private parts into purple plums with his pointy umbrella.

Her eyes widened. She remembered now what she couldn't recollect before.

"You were at the airport in Boston," she said in disbelief. "I remember your red hair. Outside the men's bathroom when we rode past in the cart. You were all mottled and angry." Had he been trying to scare them away back then, only to be thwarted by the passengers-assistance vehicle summoned by the nice TSA agent?

Shane seemed surprised by her revelation. "You didn't tell me that."

"I just remembered it now." She scratched her palms with her fingernails and tried to make sense of it all. The water bottle sloshed around at her feet, most of its contents drained out. "Were you trying to stop us even then? How in the world did you know we were flying to Amsterdam for the cruise?" The higher her voice got, the more tightly she fisted her hands, her gnarled knuckles aching from the hyperflexion. All the confusion and fear made her dizzy.

"Enough with yer questions." Hivey Red turned left at a light. "Sheesh, you're worse than me father." To Tad, he said, "And for yer information, *Officer Floppy Ears*, these two old people ain't normal. That wrinkled old bloke walloped me balls so hard I barely made it out before I got caught. I thought maybe some chokin' in a cave would scare them off, but nope, they just kept at it." Incredulity laced his speech. "There's something not human about them, I tell you."

"It's called desperation, you terrible, terrible man." Sheila could barely speak through her anxiety and breathlessness. "Desperation to find our daughter. What have you done with her?"

Shane wrapped his arm around her. "Calm yourself," he whispered, not in a patronizing way but in a steadying one. "We can't help either ourselves or Shanna if we come apart."

Thank God for Shane. He was her calm when she was distraught. She was his peace when he was in turmoil. As long as they didn't self-combust at the same time, they would always be each other's rock. She squeezed the hand dangling from her shoulder and stared into his eyes for strength.

Outside the window, old buildings gave way to more modern architecture, though still aged by American standards. The van crossed over a bridge. When it did, the same macabre buildings she had seen earlier on the outskirts of the canal ride came into view. The desolateness of their black, water-stained bases heightened her dread, as if they served as a physical reminder of their departure from the comfort of humanity and safety. Soon the traffic and buildings thinned out. Despite Shane's calming presence, Sheila's shivering turned to visible trembling.

After what could have been minutes or hours since they'd left the cathedral, the van pulled into an abandoned lot of what appeared to be an equally abandoned building. About the size of a movie theater, its gray, industrial appearance was that of an old school. As for its landscape, gone were the lush greenery and pretty flower boxes of Ghent. In their place, dying trees, weedy fields, and isolation. A canal flowed nearby, and though a small, tethered boat dipped and bobbed in its water, no other craft sailed through. Debris littered the parking lot and the field around it.

Hivey Red stepped down from the driver's seat and held open the side door. "Get out," he commanded.

Not wanting to, but having no choice but to comply, Sheila unclasped her safety belt and peeled herself off the seat, the blouse underneath her cardigan sticking to her skin. With joints too stiff for an agile exit, she clutched her purse and awkwardly slid out of the side door, her slacks riding up. Her sun hat fell off in the process and landed on the water-soaked floor of the car. She was given no time to retrieve it.

Like Tad, Hivey Red was dressed in a T-shirt, but instead of jeans, he wore cargo pants, the pockets bulky with items Sheila didn't care to contemplate. When she stumbled a few steps on the ground, she nearly tripped over a hubcap near the van, its metal too rusted to reflect the sun.

With leaden feet, one shoe still soaked with her spilled water, she followed Tad toward the building. Shane shuffled beside her, his hand never leaving her body, his own hat still in place. Hivey Red trailed behind with the gun. She sensed Shane's own calm disappear —if it was ever really there to begin with. His features were strained, and his fingers trembled against her side.

They climbed the concrete steps of the building's entrance. Was this the end for them? Could they escape? No umbrellas this time. No weapon of any sort. Choking off a sob, she willed herself to remain composed.

Inside the foyer peeling walls, moldy baseboards, and a dank smell greeted them. The farther they traveled down the hallway, the fainter the musty smell became. A faint chemical odor took its place.

Several steps and two doors later, Hivey Red shoved them into an empty room. No furniture, no sunlight, no bathroom. Only a counter with a sink running along a wall and two windows, both boarded shut. He switched on the overhead lights. "Electricity, running water, all the comforts of home, eh?" He cackled like a witch. "Jordan owns this place, so no worries. No one be botherin' us here."

Aware of the hidden threat within his words, Sheila embraced Shane, their combined bodies a quivering mass. Tad looked about nervously, not making eye contact. Hivey Red scratched a new welt on his arm. Just as he was about to speak again, another man strutted into the room.

His identity was no surprise. Sheila had been expecting him.

LEAVE NO WITNESSES BEHIND

SHEILA PERFORMED a head-to-toe sweep of the man who had just positioned himself between Officer Floppy Ears and Hivey Red. The descriptions from the ship personnel and tour guides were apt. He looked like a middle-weight boxer, his nose slightly skewed, his face stubbled, and his dark hair lightly styled. Dressed in a tight crew-neck tee, chinos, and boat shoes, he had the comfortable air of a man in charge. Neither his red aura of confidence and narcissism nor his black aura of villainy were surprising. It was likely the latter that Victor had smelled.

Still clinging to Shane, her gaze shifted to Tad. "I *knew* it was Mr. Smelly who took our daughter, I just knew it."

Mr. Smelly did a double take. Looking wounded, his nose twitched, as if he were tempted to sniff himself, but he refrained.

Sheila continued lighting into Tad. "And you knew it too. Yet you made us look like senile old fools. How cruel of you." Her voice shook as much from fury as from fear. Tad stared at the unswept floor. He kicked the heel of one sneaker with the toe of the other.

"So," Mr. Smelly finally said, clapping his hands together and cutting short the scolding, "I get to meet the opponents who KO'd my goon." He nodded his head at Hivey Red, and his Australian inflection hummed with sarcasm. "I can see why you had so much trouble with them, mate. Tough-looking couple. Weigh all of about fifty kilos."

The hive-pocked man seemed about to protest but bit back his retort. His breathing was heavier than in the van, and his nose more congested. A cut bruised the bridge of it, compliments of Sheila's shoe two days before.

She loosened her grip on Shane and stepped forward. "Where is our daughter?"

Hivey Red smirked, as if trying to make up for the chiding from his boss. "What makes ya think we took her?"

Sheila's eyes narrowed in irritation. "Are you a moron?" Shane reached out and squeezed her arm, but her anger trumped her fear, and she continued. "Why would we be here otherwise?"

Mr. Smelly chuckled. He slapped Tad's back. "I like this one, don't you? She's feisty."

Officer Floppy Ears nodded, a hopeful expression on his face. "Yes, Jordan. They're a very nice couple."

Shane pulled Sheila back to him, his face pale with worry. "What my wife means is, the probability you would abduct us if you had nothing to do with our daughter's disappearance hovers around zero."

Seemingly confused by Shane's big words, Hivey Red rubbed his congested nose and sniffed. "Cheese on a pony, those chemicals be making my allergies worse. My breathin's all tight."

Though furious with the Scottish man, Sheila had to agree he was right. The chemical smell was prominent. It reminded her of something, but at the moment she was too discombobulated to place it.

A phone buzzed. Jordan, AKA Mr. Smelly, pulled his mobile from his back pocket and strolled to the corner of the dilapidated room. His chat was brief. He trekked back to them, and in a casual manner, as if simply discussing the weather, he jerked his thumb in Sheila and Shane's direction and said, "Take care of them. I'm on a schedule."

Tad's head shot up. "Wait, what? You told me it wouldn't come to this. Lewis was only supposed to scare them off."

Jordan positioned himself into a sparring stance and lightly punched Officer Floppy Ear's skinny arm. "Tad, Tad, Tad. Don't wet yourself. Lewis will do the dirty work. I need you with me for something else."

The security guard jabbered on. "But I'll still get caught up in it, and I can't get caught up in it. At best I'll lose my job. I already lied about a family emergency to get away from the ship. At worst I'll go to prison."

Hivey Red, AKA Lewis, closed one nostril with a finger and inhaled. A sharp whistle was his reward. "You got bigger problems than that." The Scottish man turned to Mr. Smelly. "He didn't finish the other guard off."

For the first time, Jordan's cheery attitude hardened. "You left a loose end?" He got up in Tad's face. "What if he comes looking for them?"

"He never even saw me coming, I promise." A fine spray of spittle flew from Tad's lips. "What did you think I would do to him? I'm not a killer! And how would it look if he went missing too?" Tad spluttered on, twisting his hair and rubbing his floppy earlobes. "You promised it wouldn't get this far. You said all I had to do was keep an eye on them and keep you posted of their whereabouts. I did that. It's not my fault they kept pushing. It's not my fault everything fell apart. I didn't know Niko would be there."

Clinging to each other, Sheila and Shane watched the exchange, their hearts hammering together.

"Told ya he was a whiner." Hivey Red switched to the other nostril. Its whistle was the same as the first.

Sheila opened her mouth to speak. Maybe they had a window of opportunity with Tad. "It's not too late for you, young man. If Officer Gorgeous is really okay, then you don't have anything to worry about."

"Officer Gorgeous?" Once again, Jordan looked wounded. "That's a sight better name than 'Mr. Smelly' now, isn't it?"

"Count yer blessins." Lewis rubbed his watery eyes. "I'm Hivey Red and he's Officer Floppy Ears."

Jordan blinked at Sheila. "You really are a nutter, aren't you?"

She ignored him. To Tad, she said, "You can still get out of this. I know you're not a bad man. You have a purple aura of gentleness and sensitivity. The mustard color is only because of your guilt over this whole thing."

Mr. Smelly burst out laughing. "Oh, your boy's a bad man, all right, purple or not." He tugged Tad's ear. "Officer Floppy here has been smuggling stolen art for us. Making a proper penny for himself too. Don't let that baby face fool you."

"But it's for my mum," Tad pleaded with Sheila, as if desperate to exonerate himself. "She'll lose her house. My dad died and—"

"Oh fer cryin' out loud, can we just get on with it, then?" Hivey Red coughed and scratched his irritated forearms. "I need to get away from these chemicals."

Sheila released Shane and stomped toward Jordan again. "So you *are* an art thief." She turned back to her husband. "We were right, Shaney, we were right. He's having our daughter do work for him. Where is she?" Her arthritic fingers seized Mr. Smelly's shirt. Tears of distress sprang to her eyes. "Where is our daughter?"

Jordan laughed, and although he brushed her off like a fly, his face showed admiration. "It's a shame to get rid of this one."

"You don't have a choice, boss. They know too much. Who would've thought a couple of oldie moldies could be so smart?" Hivey Red pulled the gun from his waistband. Sheila hadn't even seen him place it there. At the sight of it again, her confidence faltered.

Mr. Smelly's smile faded. He growled in frustration. "If you'd have just scared them off like you were supposed to, I wouldn't have had to meet them. Now they'll be stuck in my head."

Hivey Red shrugged. "Easier to get rid of everyone at once now, anyway."

"Where is our daughter?" Sheila implored.

"Oh right, like it's not going to look suspicious if they all disappear?" Tad said to Hivey Red.

"Don't be such an idiot," the blotchy man wheezed. "Easy enough to make it look like an accident for mum and dad. Two old people simply fell into a canal and died. Happens all the time."

Sheila doubted that was true, but she could barely focus on their words, so desperate was she to find Shanna. Seeing Shane's posture falter and his strength seem to dissolve, she shuffled back to his side. Her turn to prop him up. Their enormous relief at knowing Shanna was still alive—and maybe even in the same building—was eclipsed by the fear they might both end up in a canal before reuniting with her. The physical toll that realization took on Shane was obvious.

As if confirming their worst fears, Hivey Red added, "Gonna have to get rid of the daughter too, boss. At least as soon as she's done."

A moan escaped Shane's lips, and he sagged against Sheila. His hat toppled off. It took all her strength to hold him up.

Mr. Smelly swatted the air in obvious frustration. "That breaks my heart, it does. Look at the work she can do. She's fixing that painting up as good as new." He leered at the McShanes. "It's on you two, you know. If you hadn't kept pressing, we could've kept her around. She's valuable, that one."

"No, please." Shane's plea was feeble. "Just take me." His face blanched, and he sank down to his knees, Sheila no longer able to support him.

Sheila choked down a sob. "Just let us see her. Is she here? Is she in this building?" And then it hit her. The chemical smell. The same smell that came from Shanna's workspace at the museum in Boston when she cleaned her brushes. "Shaney, she's here. She's in this building." Like the old woman she was, it took great effort to join her husband on the floor, her knees resisting the motion. "Those chemicals are what she's using to repair the stolen panel."

Mr. Smelly had been saying something to Lewis, but when he heard what Sheila said, he cut himself off. "How do you know about that?" He spun around and grabbed the collar of Tad's polo shirt. "How does she know about the missing panel? Why didn't you tell me?"

Tad wobbled, the onslaught throwing him off balance.

"Between that text message and their asking around, they figured it out on their own. Honest. I had nothing to do with it."

Hivey Red sneezed. "I told you there's somethin' not human about these two, her with her color-seein', him with his fancy maths."

Jordan released Tad and groaned. "That stupid text message. I check her progress for one second and she manages to grab my burner and fire it off. Crazy woman." He paced the room and rubbed a hand over his mouth. "If word gets out we've got that painting, that it's back in circulation, the buyer will never go through with the deal. Too risky for him."

He halted and stared at the McShanes hugging each other on the floor. Sheila's gaze traveled back and forth between Jordan and the gun in Hivey Red's hand. She pondered escape, but it seemed ludicrous. At their age it was like being outnumbered a hundred to one.

Finally, Jordan sighed, his reluctance seemingly real. "Okay, Lewis, do it. And don't screw up this time. The only way to keep the news about the panel quiet is to silence them and their daughter."

"No," Tad cried out. "Don't hurt them."

Surprising everyone, Jordan smacked Tad in the face. Gone was the Aussie's earlier cheer and levity. In its place, the ferociousness of an ear-biting boxer in the ring. "You keep your mouth shut, you hear? You screwed up enough by leaving Niko free to flap his mouth. You better hope he—or anyone else these two might have told about the panel—thinks they're Looney Tunes, at least until Lewis can get to him. If not, your boss will be hearing about your extracurricular activities in the art world, and your mum will lose everything she owns, her life included. Got it?"

Tad rubbed his reddened cheek and nodded. Sheila saw his Adam's apple bob up and down.

Mr. Smelly turned back to Hivey Red. "Get it done, but keep it quiet and clean. Don't use your gun." He tossed a set of keys to Hivey Red. "And check on the daughter too." He turned and headed for the door, demanding Tad follow him. "I need you to come with me. There's a package we need to pick up."

"But…" Tad looked back at the McShanes, his face twisted in painful indecision.

"Help us," Sheila begged him. "Look at my husband. Look how pale he is. He needs a doctor."

Tad tugged at his earlobe. He flicked his temple. His color was so mustardy yellow Sheila could practically smell it.

"Come on," Jordan ordered. "Or Lewis will take care of you and your mum next."

Tad sputtered a little more and then lowered his head and left with Mr. Smelly. Their footsteps echoed down the hall. Shortly after, the front door of the abandoned building slammed shut.

Hivey Red pocketed the gun and turned to face his two captives. He cupped the crotch of his pants. "Me nutties are still buzzin', old man. Now it's yer turn." He waggled his bushy red eyebrows and laughed through his wheezing.

THE NECESSITY OF AIR

As MUCH AS Sheila feared for her life, she feared for Shane's more. Still seated on the dirty floor next to her with his legs extended at an awkward angle, he no longer embraced her. Instead he leaned against her, his hands pressed against the floor, as if trying to prop himself up. As she cradled him, his heartbeat throbbed against the sleeve of her cardigan.

All the while she watched Hivey Red, her own heart thumping, its blood flow rushing in her eardrums. The allergic man pulled something from a side pocket of his cargo pants and stepped toward them.

A clear plastic bag.

Quiet and clean, just as Mr. Smelly had ordered.

"Please, you don't need to do this. I know there's some good in you." Her attempt at dissuading him was feeble, she knew. The only thing inside Hivey Red was a dark, malevolent soul. "My husband needs help. Look how pale he is."

"I'm okay," Shane said through clenched teeth. "Just a little flutter in my chest." As Lewis drew closer, Shane pushed himself higher, his shoulder digging into Sheila. "Don't you dare hurt my wife."

"Ah, it's a little late for that, mate. Nowhere for the two of ya to run to now. No taxis and no umbrellas." He squatted and looked back and forth between them. Up close, Sheila could smell his sour sweat and see the confluence of welts on his arms, three on the right and a giant one on the left. He scratched it now. When the itch was calmed, he raised the bag. "Was gonna start with yer husband. Thought he would put up more of a fight than a little birdie like you." He sucked air through his teeth, displaying stained canines. "But yer man don't look so good. I'm thinkin' you should go first."

As Hivey Red duck-walked the last few inches toward her, she shrank back. Her instinct was to bolt and run, but she could no more move that quickly than she could leave her husband behind, even though Shane would want her to.

Lewis raised the bag. "Yer husband's so weak, the sight of ya sucking plastic might take care of him all by itself. Make my job easier. Be less fun though."

Shane managed to push himself up onto his knees. He shoved Lewis back, but his effort was anemic. The man laughed and reciprocated, knocking Shane to the floor.

The next thing Sheila knew, the bag was over her head, muffling her cry. She kicked the man's thighs and punched his arms, but she might as well have been fighting an oak tree. Panic consumed her. Though a few breaths of air remained in the bag, she seemed unable to catch them. Instead, she gasped and flailed. A cruel uncle popped into her mind. When she was young, he had held her head under the lake in the name of "fun." She had squeezed and scratched his arms, but he wouldn't let her up. When he finally released her, laughing, as if the game was mutually enjoyable, she coughed and sputtered and vowed never to speak to him again. It had been the most terrifying sensation of her life.

Until now.

She clawed at the bag, trying to rip it open. She scratched at Lewis's beefy hands. In her peripheral vision she saw Shane crawling forward. Hivey Red kicked him back with his heavy shoe.

I'm going to die. I'm going to die, and then my husband will die, and my daughter, and then...

A tiny voice fought through her panic. *Act*, it cried. *Do something.*

Her bulging eyes caught sight of the hives on Lewis's arms. A thought came to her, one that could only come from a higher power, no matter who might try to tell her otherwise. *Yes. Do it now!*

She stopped clawing his arms and instead jerked her hand frantically around the bottom of her cardigan. When she finally found the pocket, she pulled out her partially eaten peanut bar.

Blindly and with wildly shaking hands, she plucked the bar out of its plastic wrap. Thank God she had opened it earlier to eat part of it. With a spasmodic arm, she brought the bar up to Hivey Red's mouth and pressed it onto his lips.

Please, please be allergic to peanuts.

She mashed and pushed while he spit and sputtered. Her vision started to fade. Her arms grew weak. *Oh dear God, I'm going to die.*

"What the—" Hivey Red's grip on her loosened, and the plastic bag yawned a tiny opening. He knocked the bar out of her hand.

The laxity from his momentary surprise gave Shane a window. Crawling back toward Sheila, he managed to rise once again to his knees, something in his hand. While she gasped the tiny bit of air that had entered the bag, a red laser beam of light lit up Hivey Red's eye.

The man cried out. He released the plastic bag and fell back. When he did, Sheila ripped the bag off her head, and Shane snatched the bar from the floor. He buried it into the man's open mouth, far deeper than Sheila had been able to. Gasping and gulping in the fresh air, just as she had in the lake all those years earlier, she saw Shane's gadget pen rolling at her feet, its red laser beam spinning around the room.

Shane finished the job with the bar. He scooted back to Sheila, and together they watched Hivey Red pry crumbles from his mouth. "Is this...what have ya given me...oh sweet heaven, are these peanuts?" The shock on his face could not have been greater if Shane had just plucked nunchucks from his blazer and wielded them like a ninja.

Sheila was still sucking air, but her vision had normalized, and her jerking movements were back to a more stable trembling. She saw Hivey Red pull something from his pocket.

"Shaney," she cried hoarsely. "It's epinephrine." Of course the man would carry an auto-injector on his person, not just in his car. Why hadn't she thought of that? A man that allergic would go nowhere without one.

Like a broken bag of bones, she tottered toward him. To her relief Shane was already there, lying on his belly, as if he had no strength left to give. He wrestled the injector out of the weakening man's hand.

"No," Hivey Red wheezed through a narrowing windpipe. "Must...have...that." His lips were inflating like balloons. "I'll..." wheeze, wheeze, "die..." wheeze, wheeze, "without it..." wheeze wheeze.

Sheila was on her feet now. Barely. She reached out to help Shane up. He handed her the auto-injector, which she shoved in her cardigan pocket, unsure where her purse had gone. Before Shane grabbed her hand, he said, "The keys. We need the keys to get Shanna." His voice was a shadow of its former self.

Shane dug into Hivey Red's right front pocket. A set of keys materialized. In what seemed like delirium to Sheila, the allergic man was also fishing around his pockets. He looked awful, his lips like a puffer fish, his face blotchy and swollen, his breaths so wheezy and tight he would die any minute. Reactions to peanuts happened quickly, and vile man or not, she hated knowing his death was on her.

"Come on," Shane said, taking her proffered hand and pulling himself to his feet. He groaned and nearly fell, but adrenaline must have kicked in, because after a few unsteady steps, he took the lead and guided them out of the room. "It's time to get our daughter."

REUNITED

LIKE AWKWARD HATCHLINGS, Sheila and Shane hobbled down the hallway of the abandoned building in search of their daughter. Their clothes were dusty and rumpled, and their bodies stiff from wrestling on the floor with Hivey Red. Sheila struggled to block out his swollen and welt-laden face, hardly believing she had left him there to die. He almost smothered you to death, she reminded herself. It was self-defense. Besides, Shanna was her priority now.

"Follow the chemical smell," she told Shane, turning left at the end of the dark corridor. The opposite direction ended in an exit door a few feet away.

Every time they passed a room, they opened the door (if it was closed) and looked inside. None were locked and each was similar to the one they had just escaped: peeling paint, cracked tiles, boarded-up windows. Most had counters and sinks lining the wall and scuffed work tables in the center, though any semblance of order was long gone. The whole place had the appearance of an old schoolhouse, only without desks or chalkboards.

"Maybe she's not here." Shane's speech was winded, his tone fretful. His pallor had not improved. "Maybe we're wrong."

Sheila shook her head and rounded another corner. "She's here. Mr. Smelly told Hivey Red to check on her and tossed him the keys, so she's here." She slowed her steps, ignoring the shooting pain in both feet and the knot in her spine. She sniffed the air. "The smell. It's not as strong here. I should've turned left." She pivoted. Shane put up no argument and followed behind her. Her sense of smell had always been acute. When she reached the crossway, she headed in the opposite direction and sniffed again. "Yes, this is the right way."

As they advanced, she kept looking over her shoulder, so anxious she could barely breathe. It was as if that awful bag was still on her head. At the end of the hallway, another exit door cast a sliver of light from its base.

Shane grasped Sheila's shoulder. "Do you hear that?"

She paused and listened, her pattering heartbeat somewhere in her throat. A scraping noise was followed by running water. Her eyes lit up in hope. "I do. I hear it too. Is it Shanna?"

She started to call Shanna's name, but Shane stopped her with a squeeze. "What if it's not her?" he whispered.

Limping, he tugged Sheila down the hallway. The noise was coming from the last door on the left, just before the exit. When they reached it, Shane grabbed the knob with one hand and clutched the keys from Hivey Red's pocket with the other. They rattled like chains in his shaky grip. One after the other, he inserted the keys until one clicked. When he opened the door, Sheila nearly dropped to the floor.

Shanna. Inside the room was her beautiful Shanna.

Dressed in jeans and a smock that was covered in paint, their daughter stood at a sink against the far wall, scrubbing a metal basin. Her reddish-brown hair was tied loosely into a ponytail, and her feet wore unfamiliar loafers. Her back was to the door, and thin cords dangled from both ears and snaked into her pocket. Some type of music player, Sheila thought, which was probably why Shanna hadn't heard their commotion with Hivey Red. Either that or she was simply too far away.

Unable to articulate words, Sheila choked off a sob and fell against Shane. Equally leaning on her, Shane managed a small squeak.

After grabbing a dish towel, Shanna turned around and started drying the basin. When she saw them, it clattered to the floor.

"Mom? Dad?" Her wet fingers flew to her lips. "Are you really here? Am I imagining this?"

Sheila finally found both her words and her legs. "It's us. It's really us." She rushed to her daughter as best she could. Shanna ripped out the ear buds and embraced her so fiercely Sheila almost suffocated for the second time. But it was a beautiful suffocation. A suffocation she would happily relive a thousand times over.

Shanna hugged Shane just as intensely. Seeing her rational, often unexpressive husband weep in happiness started Sheila's waterworks too. She joined in their hug, and for several moments, mother, father, and daughter clung to each other in joy. Shanna spoke into Shane's shoulder, her lightly freckled face pressed against his blazer. "I never thought I'd see you again. How did you find me?" She reached out and touched Sheila's cheek. "I can't believe you're really here, Momma Girl."

Finally, Sheila pulled away. She wiped her eyes. Fear, adrenaline, and low blood sugar were taking their toll. She wasn't sure how much longer she could remain upright. Fainting again would help no one. "I need to rest a minute. Your father too. So much excite-ment." She sank down onto a chair near a work table, which held a collection of paints, varnishes, dry pigments, solvents, brushes, and other tools of Shanna's trade. "Officer Floppy Ears and Mr. Smelly left, so we're alone for now."

Shanna's forehead creased, her overgrown bangs grazing her eyelashes. "Who?"

"One of the security guards on our cruise ship has been helping Jordan."

At that name, Shanna's eyes narrowed. "And what about Lewis? Where is he? He's crazy. He'll—"

"Don't worry. He can't hurt us now." Sheila swallowed and left the allergic man's demise at that. She scanned the room. On an adjacent table lay a painting. Several lamps were propped up around it, in addition to the overhead lighting. As with the other rooms, the two windows were boarded up, but this one had a bathroom in one corner and a cot in the other. The tidily made bed tugged at Sheila's heart. Even in captivity Shanna was neat. Next to the cot were two plastic tubs containing clothes and scattered food items. When Sheila thought of her daughter living in that decrepit room for over six weeks, she wanted to throttle Mr. Smelly as badly as her peanut bar had throttled Hivey Red.

Her gaze returned to the painting on the table, its significance dawning on her. "Is that...?"

Shanna nodded. Sheila stood unsteadily, and the three walked over and stared down at *The Just Judges*, the stolen panel from *The Adoration of the Mystic Lamb* altarpiece. It was a perfect match to the online images and cathedral replica they had seen.

"So it's really true?" Sheila whispered. "This is the actual stolen painting?"

As if seeing it for the first time herself, awe softened Shanna's face. "It is. Initially, I couldn't believe it either, but it is."

"Why did Mr. Smelly—I mean, Jordan—need you? The painting looks fine."

"It does now. I'm almost done. But it had significant moisture and humidity damage from improper storage, especially at the base. See?" Shanna pointed to the bottom of the painting, where hooves of a white horse pranced on brownish-black soil. "The panel was warped and paint had flaked off. The black-market buyer wouldn't take it as is, so Jordan needed someone who could do the job right. Very few could. In fact, his own restorer messed it up, which is why he sought me. I could've been done by now, but I've been dragging my feet. For obvious reasons." Shanna flattened her lips into a thin line and looked at the ground. She shook her head, as if clearing a horrible image. Then she ripped off the smock and tossed it on the floor. She wore a plain white T-shirt underneath. "I don't know the whole story, but Jordan was all too eager to get me here. When I wouldn't come voluntarily, he abducted me."

"In St. Bavo's Cathedral, right?" Shane rubbed his daughter's back, as if not touching her might make her disappear again.

Shanna nodded. "He tracked me down and admitted to having the stolen panel. He insisted I restore it for him. When I threatened to go to the Ghent police instead, he stuck what felt like a gun in my side and said he had someone back in New Hampshire who'd kill you both if I resisted or called for help." Shanna's voice shook, and she blinked rapidly. "I wasn't about to call his bluff with those stakes, so I let him walk me out of the church. He made me change my clothes and got someone to pretend to be me to get back on the ship for the last night. A girlfriend maybe? I don't know, and I suppose I never will." Her jaw steeled. "But I do know I haven't seen freedom since. I tried to send you a text message, but that didn't go so well."

Shane squeezed Sheila's hand. "Your mother called everything right." He stumbled the tiniest bit.

"Dad, are you okay? You don't look too good."

She tried to help him onto the wooden chair Sheila had vacated, but he resisted. "No, we need to go."

His hand nearly toppled over a jug of what appeared to be solvent. Shanna grabbed it before it could fall off the table.

"Careful, Dad," she said, the jug still in her hand. "This'll—"

The door banged open, its knob striking the wall behind it. In the doorframe stood Hivey Red, his face still doughy and blotchy with hives, but not as swollen as before.

Sheila clutched Shane. "What…? How is it possible?"

Lewis lumbered toward them, one leg dragging behind the other, as if even his ambulation had been affected by the severe allergic reaction. When he opened his palm, Sheila's eyes widened at what was in it: a used epinephrine auto-injector. She squeezed her cardigan pocket. The one she had taken from him was still there.

"How did you get that?" Her voice was tight with disbelief.

"Ya think a man like me wouldn't have a backup?" He sneered in amusement. "Of course, it took me some time to recover in the state ya left me in." He scratched a welt on his face, then another on his arm. All humor drained from him. "Time's up. Forget the quiet and clean." He closed the distance between them and dug in a pocket by his knee. He pulled out a weapon. "This time, we're gonna do it the sure-fire way."

Dear God, Sheila thought. We took the auto-injector and left the gun, thinking the man dead.

He aimed it at Sheila's head.

A NOT-SO-GREAT ESCAPE

IF IT WAS HER TIME, so be it. She had lived a good life. But Sheila refused to let Hivey Red hurt her daughter.

With the brave thoughts at odds with her trembling limbs and galloping heart, she stared into Lewis's eyes. "You can have me, but let my daughter go. Please. I know there's a good man somewhere inside of you."

He snorted and added another scratch to his already red-streaked forearms. "Good, bad, it's not about that. It's about my paycheck." His sausage finger settled firmly on the gun's trigger.

Shane grunted and stepped in front of Sheila. Shanna was off to Sheila's side, and she heard rather than saw her daughter creep up behind her, the solvent jug skimming Sheila's lower back.

"I'll deal with you next." Lewis waved the gun higher, presumably at Shanna's head, who stood a few inches taller than Sheila. "I'll make you quit dallyin' around on that paintin', believe you me." He aimed the gun back at Sheila.

Shanna cried out, "Run, Mom and Dad!" She pushed them aside and swung the arm holding the solvent jug up in an arc. Sheila, still stumbling from the shove, watched in slow motion as the plastic bottle of solvent splashed its contents into Hivey Red's face.

The shriek that followed would have shattered the windows were they not boarded up. "My eyes, my eyes," Hivey Red cried. The gun clunked to the floor. His blotchy hands flew to his now closed eyelids and rubbed, while his feet stomped the floor in a maniacal dance. "My eyes," he shrieked again.

Shane reached down and grabbed the gun. He placed one hand on his thigh to push himself up again, and when he did, he looked about to faint. His pallor had worsened, and sweat dripped off his nose and chin.

"Let's go." Shanna grabbed both their arms and hissed at Hivey Red. "If you don't want to go blind, you better rinse your eyes in that sink for a good five minutes."

The three of them fled the makeshift art room as quickly as their weakest member would allow, which at that moment happened to be Shane. His left hand held the gun, and his right, the building's keys. When he tried to lock the door, he was too shaky to do it. He passed the keys to Shanna. She hurriedly trapped Lewis inside.

Rubbing his chest, Shane wheezed out an order. "Go to the front exit. Run to that boat we saw. I doubt Lewis can get through that boarded-up window, but in case he does, we'd risk running into him by the side exit."

"There's no getting out of those windows, Dad. Don't you think I've tried?" As they started off, Shanna's tone shifted from pragmatic to distressed. "Oh no. I should have taken the panel with me. It's priceless."

"The police will find it." Sheila hobbled down the hallway toward the front entrance. "Let's just get out of here."

"Turn right," Shane said.

Shanna did so, taking the lead. "Hurry. Five minutes won't buy us much time."

"Will he really go blind?" Sheila huffed behind her daughter, nothing but grays and shadows in the neglected hallway.

"Who knows? But I figured he'd take time to flush his eyes, so I made something up."

"This way to the front." Shane pointed to a right turn in the hallway, reversing the direction they had initially come in search of

Shanna. As always, Sheila thanked the heavens for his sense of direction. She added a prayer for his well-being too. He'd never had heart problems, but his ongoing pallor and sweating in the abandoned building, not to mention his weakness, worried her tremendously.

When they reached the main entrance, Shanna flung open the heavy door.

A *thwunk*, followed by a yelp of pain, stopped them in the doorframe.

There, at the top of the cement steps, stood Mr. Smelly, surprise widening his boxer's face. At his side, leaning against the metal railing, was Officer Floppy Ears, his nose cupped in his hands. Blood gushed between his fingers. "I think it's bwoken," he moaned, his voice thick with blood.

Oh dear, Sheila thought stupidly. His nose will now be as big as his earlobes.

Mr. Smelly stepped forward, but when he saw the gun in Shane's shaking hand mere inches away, he backed up. To Tad, he said, "Quit crying like a toddler and grab the gun."

Shane transferred the weapon to his right hand. When he raised it, his arm shook so much Sheila feared any one of them could be shot. "We're leaving." He put his free hand on Sheila's back, and with a gentle nudge, indicated she should head down the stairs. He nodded toward Shanna to do the same.

"Maybe you should give me the gun," their daughter said uncertainly.

"Just help your mother get into the van." Shane's breath was choppy, his voice weak, and his face a glistening mask of misery. "Give me the car keys," he said to Mr. Smelly.

Shanna led her mother down the steps, but once they were in the parking lot, about eight feet away from Shane and a few feet from the van, she stopped. "Get in, Mom. I'm not leaving Dad up there."

They both looked toward Shane. Descending backwards, he had made it down to the last of the concrete steps. The gun quivered like jello on a roller coaster, but he still managed to aim it at the two men at the top of the staircase. Tad cradled his injured nose with one hand.

"Toss me the keys," Shane repeated. "I won't ask again."

"The keys?" Mr. Smelly laughed and took one step forward. "You're in no shape to drive."

Shane ordered him to stop.

Jordan dangled the van keys in his hand. "You want the keys, old fellow? Here they are." He turned and threw them into the weedy field at the side of the building.

Sheila saw Shane's profile deflate. He wiped sweat from his eyes, and when he took a step backward toward them, he faltered. Still, somehow, her methodical, rational husband kept his cool. "Shanna, take your mother to the boat over in the canal."

"Not without you." Shanna started to say something else, but Mr. Smelly cut her off, his face clearing all traces of humor.

"Enough, old man. Give Tad the gun. You don't even look like you know how to use it. With as bad as you're shaking you'll only shoot yourself."

"I was in the service," Shane said. "I know how to use it just fine."

"Yeah? Well, that was a hundred years ago." To Tad, who by now looked like a murder victim with all the blood on his face and hands, Jordan said, "For the last time, go down and get that gun."

Officer Floppy Ears stared at Shane and his unsteady arm. His expression suggested retrieving the gun was the last thing he wanted to do. He turned back to Jordan and shook his head. In his congested, blood-clogged voice, he said, "Nope. I'm done. I won't be a part of this anymore."

"Good boy, Tad," Sheila called out from the parking lot. "Good boy."

"Get to the boat, Sheila." Shane sounded exasperated, and the fact he had enough energy to be frustrated with her was a relief.

She and Shanna started for the boat.

"Careful, Mom." Shanna pointed out the rusty hubcap Sheila had seen earlier. "Don't trip on that. Keep heading toward the boat. I'm going to help Dad. He's too weak."

"Oh for crying out loud," Mr. Smelly said behind them, displaying his own exasperation. "I'll take the gun myself. He's not going to shoot me. I doubt he can even see me."

Sheila turned back around. Jordan started down the stairs toward Shane. Tad went back to leaning against the railing on the top step.

"Stop," Shane croaked. His strain was so obvious Sheila gave up going to the boat. She couldn't leave him there.

Shanna reached him. "Give me the gun, Dad."

Jordan descended another step.

The gun exploded.

Tad screamed. Mr. Smelly jumped in fear. When he realized he hadn't been shot, he laughed and said, "Told you, old man, you're too—"

"Me, you idiot, he shot *me!*" Officer Floppy Ears was screaming and blubbering and holding his leg. A dark circle blossomed on the side of his jeans halfway down his thigh. "Bloody hell," he stammered at Shane. "Who exactly were you aiming at?"

Shane looked stunned. He lowered the gun.

Mr. Smelly seized the opportunity and lunged toward Shane. When he did, Sheila instinctively scurried forward and grabbed the hubcap lying near the van. With a strength she didn't know she possessed, she charged toward Jordan and heaved the rusty metal high in the air. When he grabbed the gun from Shane, she whacked the Australian in the head so hard he stumbled. She whacked him again. And again. In the face and on the head.

He fell to the ground. The gun flew from his hands and landed in the weeds with the keys. Looking stunned, he held his head and blinked at Sheila.

"Hurry." Shanna grabbed her parents by the arms. The three half-ran, half-stumbled to the canal's edge, about a hundred feet from them. When they reached it, they slid down its grassy embankment toward the tethered boat.

Shanna helped Shane in first. The commanding calm he had displayed earlier was gone, but whether from his deteriorating physical condition or his shooting Tad, Sheila wasn't sure.

"Easy, easy, Dad. Don't fall in. I have no idea how deep this is." Shanna glanced over her shoulder. "Hurry, Jordan's looking in the weeds for the gun. Tad's on the stairs, bleeding. He's calling someone."

By the time Sheila got her gnarled body into the tiny boat, which, like the tender rides in Edinburgh, required an act of gymnastics to achieve, she saw Mr. Smelly huffing toward them. His hands were empty, implying he hadn't found the gun, and fury bathed his face.

With urgency, Shanna started untying the rope that anchored the boat to a wooden pole on the embankment. Shane took a seat on the middle of three small benches. The only space to move within the boat was a couple feet in front of and behind the seats.

When Shanna finished untying the rope, she climbed into the boat and stood behind Shane. Jordan slid down the embankment and was nearly at their side. Shanna grabbed an oar and pushed the boat away from the thin shore.

Mr. Smelly leaned over and grabbed the edge of the boat. His upper body skimmed the water, while his lower dug into the embankment. His face, already reddened from the blows of the hubcap, deepened to an almost purplish hue as he strained. With both hands he tried to pull the boat back against Shanna's oaring. Through gritted teeth, he seethed, "Lewis is right. You two aren't human."

SPLASHING AROUND

INSIDE THE SMALL WOODEN BOAT, Sheila and Shane hovered together on the middle bench. Shanna stood straddled over the one near the stern. Despite her frantic rowing, she got nowhere, Mr. Smelly's clutch on the boat too secure. With a grunt, he managed to pull the boat back up to the embankment. When he did, Sheila tightened her arm around Shane, who was now slumped over and grimacing. She feared terribly for his life.

Moments later Jordan climbed into the small space between the bow and the front bench. The craft wobbled and rolled, so much so that he had to touch down on the edge to avoid falling. Once the boat smoothed out, he planted his feet.

Before Sheila could think what to do next, Jordan plucked her up from the bench, spun her around, and pressed her spine against his chest. Her bones cracked, and her knee pulled from the sudden movement, but that pain paled in comparison to having his arm encircling her neck like a noose.

To Shanna, Mr. Smelly said, "I still need you. If you don't climb out of this boat right now, I'll snap your mother's neck."

"Don't do it." Sheila's voice squeaked, for that was all she could manage in the headlock. She stared at her moaning husband. The fact he hadn't stood up to help her told her his own demise was not far away.

"Now," Jordan ordered Shanna.

Shanna remained frozen near the stern, the oar clutched in her hand, her expression suggesting she was uncertain how to proceed. Was the man bluffing? Sheila wondered. Would he really do the dirty work himself? Her ears picked up a noise in the distance. She strained to hear it over her pounding fear.

Were those…were those sirens?

They must have been, because Shanna said, "You might as well give up now, Jordan. Looks like your little stooge called the police."

"Sirens happen every minute around here." Despite Mr. Smelly's bravado, Sheila felt him stiffen behind her, and although she couldn't see his face, she imagined he was wondering if Tad really had called the police.

"Please," she squeaked again, straining to speak against Jordan's hold. "My husband needs help—"

Running footsteps and a man's sharp command startled them all. "Let her go. Now."

Mr. Smelly pivoted toward the voice, jerking Sheila with him. Shanna seized the moment. She swung the oar in a smooth, rapid arc and thumped Jordan in the head. In his already precarious position, he lost his balance and wobbled in the small space of the bow. When he did, Sheila slipped through his grasp and shoved him. He flailed his arms and stared at her in disbelief. One last kick with her orthotic shoe sent him sailing over the edge. He splashed into the water.

"Are you okay, are you okay?" It was the same voice that had ordered Jordan to release her. The man attached to it jumped into the water and hurried toward them.

When Sheila saw who it was, she almost toppled over the side of the boat in happiness. "It's Officer Gorgeous!" She clambered over the first bench and sat next to Shane on the middle one. She wrapped her arms around him. "It's going to be okay, Shaney. It's going to be okay." She blinked back tears of relief.

Shanna looked up in confusion at Niko. Her attention went right back to Jordan in the water, her oar at the ready should he attempt to climb back in.

More footsteps stomped toward the embankment. This time it was two policemen. They demanded Mr. Smelly get out of the water. When Jordan started swimming away, they looked at each other and hesitated. Though clearly not enthusiastic about going in after him, they sighed and grunted and then slid into the water to catch their escapee.

Niko was still in the water next to the boat. He pulled it back to the embankment, from where it had drifted a few feet during the commotion.

"It's Officer Gorgeous," Sheila repeated to Shanna. "He's from Croatia, just like that man on the ER show."

Once Niko re-tethered the boat to the wooden pole, he helped Sheila out. Her exit was gentler than her entrance had been, and for that her throbbing knee and spine were grateful.

"Hurry, please. My Shaney needs help. How in the world did you find us?" She melted into Niko's arms and let him set her gently on the grassy field next to the canal. She couldn't stop babbling in relief. "Are you okay? Did Tad hurt you? He's in on this, you know."

Niko helped Shanna out next. "Tad might be a good security guard," he said, "but he's a terrible criminal. I wasn't knocked out for long in the cathedral." He rubbed his head, as if reexperiencing Tad's blow. "After I came to, I looked all over for you, both inside and out. I couldn't find you, but I spotted Tad getting into a van right before it drove off. There was no mistaking his ears." He guided Shanna down next to Sheila. "I assumed you were inside the vehicle, and one call from Ivan to Tad's mother confirmed he lied about needing to leave the ship for a couple days. There was no family emergency as he'd claimed. So we put things together. I'm sure my presence at the cathedral was quite the surprise for him."

"Ivan is Officer Sourpuss," Sheila clarified for Shanna. "He's the head security guard."

"Yes, well, Tad's mother used her tracking app to find Tad's phone for us. That's how I knew you were here. We called the local police too."

"She follows her son's whereabouts?" Sheila asked, but Niko had already returned to the boat for Shane. She supposed that made sense. Officer Floppy Ears had claimed he was only smuggling art to help his mother financially. He was so young, the woman probably worried about her baby in all those different seaports. Being able to track his whereabouts on her phone probably calmed her. "I always knew he was a momma's boy," she mused to no one in particular.

When Niko helped Shane onto the field, she wrapped her arms around her husband. "It's going to be okay now." Looking at him, she prayed that was true. One arm was stiff against his chest. The other was pressed into the ground. Though his face was tight, he gave a slight nod and a half smile.

More sirens wailed. Moments later an ambulance pulled into the parking lot. Two paramedics jumped out and ran to Officer Floppy Ears, who was still seated on the concrete steps and clutching his leg. Sheila figured if it was Officer Gorgeous who had called the police, it must have been Tad who called the ambulance. For himself, no doubt.

As quickly as her limbs would allow it, she rose from the grassy field. She shouted and waved her arms. "Here, over here. My husband needs help. I think he's having a heart attack."

By now, the policemen had caught Mr. Smelly. The three water-logged bodies climbed out of the water and up the embankment, where the Australian man was soon handcuffed. One of the EMTs jogged toward them.

Before the police could lead Jordan away, Sheila called out to them. "He has the stolen panel from the Mystic Lamb altarpiece in the building. You must get that too." The two cops stared at her. One started to smirk.

"No, really, he does. That's why he took my daughter. So she could restore it. And be careful, because his partner is locked in the room with it." She leaned down and got the keys from Shane. She gave them to Niko, who tossed them to one of the police officers.

The two policemen exchanged a look that said, "This woman is bonkers." But then one nodded and said, "Yes, of course, we will secure the building."

Sheila shrugged. They would believe her soon enough.

Next to her, the dripping-wet Officer Gorgeous rubbed his chin and caught his breath. He looked at the trio of McShanes. To Shanna, he said, "You are the missing daughter, I assume?"

"I am."

Niko grinned. "You have very tough parents, do you know that?"

Before Shanna could answer, Shane slumped over onto the grass. His eyes were glassy and vacant, and his aura the whiteness of death.

FILLING IN THE MISSING PIECES

WITH THE SUN making its afternoon descent over the abandoned building and grassy field, a paramedic who smelled of cigarette smoke rushed to Shane's side. Though Shane was awake and alert, he mumbled unintelligibly. Holding his head in her lap, Sheila stroked his hair and cooed soothing words. To the EMT, she said, "I worry he's had a heart attack. Please help him." As always, she was grateful so many Europeans spoke English. She couldn't imagine tackling the difficult events of the past twelve days through a language barrier.

The EMT whistled over to his colleague and shouted something in Dutch. Over near the building's entrance, his partner, a sturdy woman Sheila had first mistaken for a man, was tending to Officer Floppy Ears. Upon her partner's call, Sheila saw the woman assess Tad's injury, press something white against his wound, and place his hand over it. Then she shouted back in Dutch to her colleague and wheeled the gurney toward Shane. The young security guard plopped back onto the concrete step. Even from a distance, Sheila could tell his expression was pitiful. But he looked okay, and she suspected a little delay in his care might teach him an important lesson about getting caught up with smelly criminals.

At some point, she didn't know when, another police car had arrived, and two female officers joined the male one to whom Sheila had given the building keys. He had just exited the front door with Hivey Red in handcuffs. The officer spoke animatedly to the arriving cops. Though Sheila couldn't understand the Dutch words, she suspected he was sharing the incredible discovery of *The Just Judges* painting.

She watched as one of the policewomen cuffed Tad to the handrail of the steps. Despite the young man's transgressions, Sheila didn't want him to bleed to death on the stairs. "What about him?" she asked the paramedic.

"He is all right. My partner said the bullet barely tore the flesh. It's not deep. She called for another ambulance."

When his colleague reached them with the gurney, a tiny pigtail curling out from the back of her cap, the two hoisted a grimacing Shane up onto the gurney and rushed him toward the ambulance. At least her husband had found the strength to tell Sheila he would be all right. She prayed that would indeed be the case.

Sheila, Shanna, and Officer Gorgeous followed behind, the latter wrapping his arm around Sheila to guide her through the weedy grass toward the parking lot. Although desperately worried about Shane, she took the opportunity to press into Niko's strong frame and inhale his masculine scent. It would be a waste not to.

By the time they reached the ambulance, Shane was already inside. A fluid bag hung from a pole and dripped through a tube into a vein in the crook of his elbow. Sticky EKG leads dotted his bare chest, the gray hair around them spindly and tufted. One of the police cars had already left, apparently with both Mr. Smelly and Hivey Red inside, because neither was visible, nor were the female cops. The male officer who had exited the building with Hivey Red a few minutes before was now lingering near Tad and speaking excitedly into his phone. Canal water still dripped from his uniform. Sheila suspected the fourth cop was still inside the building, guarding the stolen painting.

Inside the ambulance, the male paramedic smiled. "Your

husband's heart rhythm is too fast, but it's otherwise normal. His oxygen level is good."

"Oh, thank God." Sheila put a hand to her own heart. With the other she wrapped an arm around Shanna. She wanted to go to Shane's side, but there was no room inside the vehicle. The best she could do was lean into the open door and stroke his ankle. "We're right here, Shaney. You're going to be okay."

"Did he have a heart attack?" Shanna asked. Though her daughter's calm demeanor might fool others, Sheila heard the trill in her voice.

"They'll run tests in the hospital." The pigtailed EMT adjusted Shane's IV fluid rate. In excellent English, she added, "He's very dehydrated though. Maybe his problems come from too much stress and too little water."

The EMTs asked about Shane's medical history and whether he took any medications, had heart disease, or suffered any other health problems.

"He's the healthiest eighty-four-year-old man you'll ever meet," Shanna said. "Right, Momma Girl?"

Shanna's nickname of *Momma Girl* blanketed Sheila in a peaceful warmth. She squeezed her daughter tightly, never wanting to let go, and confirmed to the paramedics that Shane was healthy.

"Is he a smoker?" the female EMT asked.

"I'm right here, you know, you can ask me." Hearing Shane's testy reply buoyed Sheila further. "And no, I don't smoke," he added. "Never have."

Sheila glanced at the male EMT who smelled of tobacco but decided to hold her advice. After all, he was saving her husband's life.

As the paramedic listened to Shane's chest with his stethoscope, Shane waved an arm at Sheila and said, "Go learn what you can from Tad before they take him away."

Since he seemed to be stabilizing, Sheila nodded and ambled over to Officer Gorgeous and Officer Floppy Ears on the stairwell. The cop watching Tad was a few feet away, still talking on his phone. Sheila heard Niko say, "But why? Why would you get caught up with these guys?"

Drying blood stiffened Tad's jeans. Fortunately for him, the gauze he pressed against the wound with his free hand was less saturated than his pants. Shanna's door smash had left its mark too, his nose swollen and elongated like a walnut. More dried blood caked his face. Other than that, he seemed okay. If one didn't count the despair on his face and the handcuff on his wrist.

"Jordan offered me money I couldn't refuse. I did it for my mum, I swear." Tad stared at Niko with beseeching eyes, as if willing him to understand. "All I had to do was store a few paintings on the ship. Help him get them to other countries without notice."

"How did you get them on?" Niko's arms were crossed and his stance rigid.

"I carried them on board wrapped up, said they were prints from the museum for Mum. I had to help her, you get that, don't you, mate? She's lost everything." Tad's whine lowered the pleasantness of his British accent by a good forty degrees. Or maybe it was the swollen and clotted nose.

"But how could you want to hurt these good people?" Niko's arm went out to Sheila. She took the opportunity to clutch it.

Tad shot up on the step, his gauze falling to the ground. The swift movement caused him to cry out in pain, probably both from the bullet wound and the torque on his handcuffed arm. When he recovered, he said, "I didn't know it would end up that way, you have to believe me. Lewis was supposed to scare them off, but he failed." He shifted his imploring gaze to Sheila. "Jordan just asked me to keep an eye on you. Let Lewis know what you were up to, make sure you weren't getting too close to figuring things out, cut Jordan out of any security footage, that sort of thing—"

"So he *was* caught on camera? And you erased it?" Sheila was so shocked by Tad's admission she released Niko's arm.

"A couple times in the dining room with Shanna, that's all. I was in charge of going through the ship's security footage when we were looking for your daughter. Jordan said he couldn't risk being seen with her."

Sheila lurched toward Tad, her cheeks burning with anger and betrayal. "But he tried to kill us," she said. He flinched as if she would strike him. Perhaps she would have if Niko hadn't pulled her back.

Officer Floppy Ears grew even more contrite. "I didn't know, I didn't know, I promise. Lewis couldn't get on the ship—he wasn't a passenger—so I informed him of your excursions. That's all. Honest, honest, honest." With each *honest*, Tad thumped his uninjured thigh, despite the discomfort the motion clearly caused his injured one. Sheila swore his earlobes jiggled too.

Even amid the blood she could see the earnestness of his purple aura, but she was still confused. "Why was Hivey Red at the airport in Boston?"

"Jordan wanted him to make you miss the cruise so you wouldn't come snooping around. Thought he could scare you out of coming. But Lewis said he couldn't get to you through all the airport personnel."

Thank God for Agent Dickman, Sheila thought. Without him and the cart he summoned for them, they might not have made it to Amsterdam at all. And then they would never have found their daughter. "But how did Jordan even know we were coming?"

Shamefaced, Tad flicked a small pebble from the concrete step. "From me. After calling the cruise line and our ship so many times to ask about your daughter, you said you'd come find her yourself. As a security officer, I check the passenger logs."

Shanna appeared at her mother's side. "Dad's doing okay. They're going to take him to the hospital now. They said we can drive there with Niko and meet them in the emergency room."

"Of course, of course," Officer Gorgeous assured them.

Sheila turned back to the departing ambulance. "Wait, shouldn't I ride with him? What if something happens?" She started to trot over, but Shanna stopped her.

"He's okay, Mom, really. He told me to tell you to continue finding out what you can from Tad before the police take him away. You won't get a chance after that."

Sheila rubbed her neck, still sore from Jordan's hold. "Always thinking logically, your father. Such a dear man. And we *have* learned a lot, haven't we, Niko?" Sheila sidled up to the handsome Croatian and leaned against him for support. It would be a waste not to.

"Yes we have, and our superior officer will be interested in learning it too." Niko glared at Tad and shook his head in disbelief.

Another thought occurred to Sheila. She frowned. "How did Mr. Smelly know Shanna would be on that cruise? And before you say it was a coincidence, my husband will have the statistics and probabilities to prove otherwise."

Tad slumped back on the steps, his handcuffed wrist suspended at an odd angle from the handrail. He looked about to cry.

As nice as Niko felt against her, Sheila decided she was too tired to remain upright. With Shanna's help, she sank down next to Officer Floppy Ears, the concrete step hard on her bony behind. She reached into her cardigan and pulled out a tissue. When she began wiping crusted blood from Tad's face, he melted into her touch. "There, there, you'll be all right. You're very young. Lots of time to make better choices." A tear plopped down his cheek.

Shanna rolled her eyes, seemingly not quite as touched by the young security guard's mournful display. "Jordan got me here on my own naiveté," she said, her tone bitter. "He told me so himself. Remember how I kept getting those fliers from Dreamline Cruises about their British Isles tour? The ones that came to my work address at the museum?"

"Of course, dear. Your father and I would burn every one of those brochures if we could."

"After several of them I figured, why not? Why not see art from this part of the world? And with my boss insisting I finally take a vacation, I played right into Jordan's hands."

Officer Gorgeous patted her shoulder. "Don't be so hard on yourself. You couldn't have known."

Sheila raised an eyebrow at the exchange. There was more than reassuring platitudes in Niko's eyes.

Her businesslike daughter seemed not to notice. "It's my own dumb fault. I should've wondered why I suddenly started getting their brochures. Jordan was the one who put my name and address into the Dreamline Cruises website to receive information, and once they start sending those things, they never stop."

"Well, that's certainly true." Sheila thought of the endless fliers for New England cruises she and Shane had received over the years.

"Ugh." Shanna smacked her forehead. "I was so stupid. He knew about my experience with restoration and my area of expertise, and I fell right into his sick plan. Once he knew I was in, he booked a ticket for himself."

"Sweetie, don't blame yourself. If you hadn't taken the trip, Mr. Smelly would have found some other way to get to you."

"It's true." Officer Floppy Ears sniffled, his nasal congestion growing more pronounced from his crying. When he leaned deeper into Sheila's embrace, she realized how badly the poor boy needed his mother. "When his own restorer wasn't up to the job, he was determined to get you. He tried it the easy way first with the fliers and couldn't believe it actually worked." He must have seen the shame deepen on Shanna's face, because he added, "Oh, sorry."

A vehicle lumbered into the parking lot. All four looked in its direction. It was another ambulance but without the bells and whistles.

"See?" Sheila gave Tad's shoulders a squeeze and then tugged one of his earlobes. "Your injury is minor. They didn't even have to come speeding in."

As another set of EMTs came with a gurney for Tad, the cop pocketed his phone and wandered over to uncuff him. With excitement, he said to Sheila, "You were correct, madam, you were correct. That may very well be the missing panel. My partner is guarding it inside."

Told you, Sheila thought with a smile. She extended her arms up to Officer Gorgeous. "Come. Let's follow behind my husband and tell him what we've learned when we get there." To Shanna, she added, "Then, after he's released, let's get back home to New Hampshire where we belong."

Niko helped lift Sheila off the stairs. As he escorted her back to his car, she leaned against his sturdy chest and patted his pectorals.

It would be a waste not to.

35

GOING HOME

To Sheila, the Amsterdam airport was a confusing tangle of numbered check-in counters and the many escalators needed to reach them. If not for Shanna's guidance, she would have been a mouse in a maze who simply gave up. Even Shane, with all his navigational wisdom, seemed bested by the design.

After they finally checked in for their return flight to Boston, the three of them waited on a row of plastic seats near the counter. Wheelchair assistance was coming for Shane, which, of course, he didn't want.

An assortment of travelers from all over the world hurried by. Some carried single bags. Others dragged more luggage than a fashion model. Perhaps they *were* fashion models. This wasn't Sherry, New Hampshire, after all. A few toted service dogs and several more toted children, many of whom were dressed in matching T-shirts, as if their parents worried they would lose them in the crowd. The rush of bodies, the cacophony of human voices, and the fuzzy overhead announcements lulled Sheila into a relaxed fugue.

"I don't need a wheelchair," Shane grumbled for the fifth time. "I'm perfectly capable of walking to the gate."

"I know you are, dear, but the doctor said you need to take it easy."

"It wasn't even a heart attack. My EKG, stress test, and enzymes were normal, and my pain went away in the ambulance. That lowers the probability of an MI to a minuscule amount. Any study's p-value and confidence interval would back me up."

Shanna put her arm around her father. "Maybe so, but the doctor said you probably had angina, brought on by all the stress, which means you didn't get enough blood to your heart. Make sure you follow up with the cardiologist in New Hampshire like she told you to. I'll drag you there myself if I have to."

Shane waved her off. "Only back with us a couple days, and you're already telling me what to do." But he grinned, grabbed her free hand, and squeezed it.

Sheila closed her eyes and smiled at their banter. She was so anxious to get home she could practically see the flowers in Shane's garden and smell the coffee cake in her kitchen. Every time she looked at Shanna, she wanted to touch her to make sure she was really there.

They had done it. They had actually done it. *As it turns out, two old people can do a lot,* she thought to herself. Of course, she had been determined they would find their daughter, but determination wasn't always the same as success. And yet there Shanna was, their smart, introverted, practical daughter, ready to get back to her life and make up for the days that were stolen.

Shane's hospital observation in Ghent had made them miss their original return flight to Boston. They stayed another two days in the Belgian city to answer the authorities' questions and give Shane a rest. This morning, Dreamline Cruises had sent a private vehicle to their Ghent hotel to transport them to Amsterdam for their flight home, along with reimbursement for all three cruise fares and an impressive collection of coupons and free offerings for future cruise travel. In fact, Dreamline Cruises had gone out of their way to assist them "in any way we can." Sheila happily took their offerings, her lips curling into the teensiest smug smile, all while assuring them she wasn't the litigious sort. She did, however, take satisfaction in knowing her family had ended up with free cruises when the awful, messy couple who tortured Raoul had not.

She was sad not to have had the opportunity to say goodbye to their stateroom attendant. Raoul had been lovely. Same with their waiters, Victor and Renny, and even Tina, the sommelier who had suffered such an unfortunate public accident compliments of spoiled mousse. When Sheila had returned to the dining room that evening after helping the woman clean herself up, Renny had confessed his romantic pursuit was none other than Tina herself. The fact he still desired the woman after her poo-tastrophe illustrated his pure, golden heart. She hoped the two worked out together. He would calm her efficient but brusque nature, and she would teach him the valuable lesson that women were more than the sum of their parts. Sometimes odd unions were good unions, and Sheila was happy to have assisted in theirs.

At least she had written goodbye letters to all the crew members. She sent those, along with generous tips, back with the driver who had delivered their belongings from the ship. Even her normally frugal husband hadn't raised an eyebrow when she told him how much she was giving the staff. "They work so hard and don't see their families for months," she had said to him, licking the envelopes to seal up the tips. "It's the least we tourists can do."

She had even spoken to Officer Sourpuss. He had personally called her at the Ghent hotel and apologized for his resistant behavior. "It was ego, nothing more. I am not man who likes to be wrong."

She had responded, "No one with a red aura ever does, dear."

He then surprised her by chuckling. A moment later he added, "Am very glad daughter is safe. Truly."

With that, she accepted his apology and dropped the *Sourpuss* from his name. He simply became *Officer Ivan*.

Sheila smiled at a new thought: Tina and Renny were not the only ones with romantic sparks. During Shane's hospitalization, Shanna and Officer Gorgeous had become quite friendly. Officer

Ivan had allowed the Croatian security guard to remain in Ghent to assist the McShanes in their dealings with the authorities. Despite their eight-year age difference, Niko and Shanna made plans to meet in Amsterdam a few months down the road when Niko was between contracts. He had promised to show Shanna the Amsterdam artwork she didn't get a chance to see, given her abduction. He was wise to choose that angle, because those were probably the only words that would convince her serious daughter to meet up with him.

Although Sheila was fearful about Shanna leaving the country again so soon, at least she would be in good hands with a security guard. Plus, as Shanna had told her, "If I don't bite the bullet again now, I'll never dare travel again."

Such a pragmatist her daughter was, just like her father. Though in the past Sheila had wondered about Shanna's taste in men, this one gave her no qualms.

"Momma Girl, you're smiling that weird smile again. What's on your mind?"

"Oh, nothing." Before Shanna could press, Sheila said, "I wonder how Officer Floppy Ears is doing. That poor young man. Getting caught up in something so terrible."

"People make their own choices, Beetle Bug."

"I just hope he gets a light sentence. He'll never do well in prison with those fleshy ears."

"I don't think the two are statistically correlated." Shane reached inside his blazer, fished around a bit, and then sighed, probably remembering he had lost his gadget pen in the abandoned building (which they had later learned was an old art school Jordan had purchased some years ago for his nefarious deeds). Shanna had already promised to buy him a new pen. Fortunately, Sheila's purse had been rescued by one of the police officers.

"Can you believe Mr. Smelly had the missing panel in Ghent all along?" Sheila glanced at Shane's watch, hoping they wouldn't miss preboarding.

"Maybe he thought it would be too risky to move it." Shane

leaned forward and scanned the large waiting area. "Where is that wheelchair? We'd be at the gate by now if I'd walked."

Sheila turned to Shanna. "Did Niko tell you where the painting was hiding?"

"No, the police didn't tell him much from Jordan's interrogation. Only that the painting had been in Ghent all along, and that when Jordan had acquired it, he found a buyer for it on the black market. The transaction was supposed to go down right away, but then Jordan discovered the moisture damage. That much I knew from him." She removed her arm from Shane's shoulder and raised both palms to the ceiling. "Enter idiot art restorer, Shanna McShane." She kicked at the tiled floor with her ballet flat. "I still can't believe I fell for his trick with the brochures. Am I really that gullible?"

"It's not your fault. At least his plan of seducing you didn't work. The lure of a missing painting is not enough to make my honorable daughter cross over to the dark side."

"A lot of good my ethics did. He abducted me. Tried to woo me first by joining me on the cruise, hoping I'd be so enchanted by him and his illicit art collection that I'd come willingly. Less dicey than snatching me from a public place, I suppose. But when I didn't, he abducted me anyway. That's not exactly a win." Shanna stared off at a man in a religious robe. "Back in Dublin, and even before then, he'd hinted about having 'secret' artwork that I 'just had to see.' I didn't believe his boasts and just wanted to be rid of him. Guess that didn't work out too well."

"You're always too hard on yourself, sweetie. Mr. Smelly is a bad man. Bad men do bad things. Maybe he got others to do his dirty work, like Hivey Red and poor Tad, but he's still a stinker. You couldn't have stopped him. At least he didn't hurt you." Sheila shuddered. "Even on video I could smell his bad aura."

Shane and Shanna exchanged looks.

"I see those smirks," Sheila said, taking no offense. They might not understand her gift, but neither did they pooh-pooh it when it served them well.

Shanna tucked her long hair behind her ear. "Niko told me

Lewis may have been behind a murder of an art dealer in Scotland. Up until now, it's been unsolved."

"Oh how awful. He deserves whatever's coming to him." Sheila smoothed the collar of her blouse. "Although I have to admit, I'm relieved my peanut bar didn't finish him off. I would hate to have a man's death on my conscious."

Shane patted her thigh.

"Niko also told me the police found other stolen artwork in Jordan's possession." Shanna made a sour face. "Stealing treasured art for your own profit is the lowest of the low."

Sheila suspected murder was lower, but she kept the thought to herself. "The whole experience was awful. So awful and frightening." She swallowed a walnut-sized lump in her throat and reached over for Shanna's hand. "But you're here now."

"I'm here now."

For the next few minutes, mother, father, and daughter said nothing. Just held each other's hands and pondered their good fortune.

A woman in an airport uniform broke their silence. "Are you the man who needs the wheelchair?"

Shane's cheeks flamed, and his jaw twitched, but he allowed the woman to help him into the chair. Shanna and Sheila collected their carry-ons and followed the employee through a series of hallways and elevators until they reached the security area. Thanks to Shane's wheelchair, they bypassed the long line and jumped right to the front of the queue.

"Well, isn't this lovely," Sheila said. "Maybe we need to try this wheelchair thing more often."

They loaded their bags onto the x-ray belt. As Sheila stepped through the scanner, the agent stopped the conveyor belt, narrowed his eyes, and scrutinized her bag's contents. He then handed the tote to his partner. The second agent opened the bag and blinked. He pulled out bottle after bottle. Toiletries. Juice. Water. A sparkly pink can of Foxy Glossy. Most everything over three ounces.

The Dutch agent looked up at Sheila and blinked some more. He waved her over.

She fluffed her wispy hair, patted the peanut bar in her cardigan pocket, and stepped up to the young man. "Hello, sugarplum, is there a problem?"

THE END

AUTHOR'S NOTE

This novel was inspired by a British Isles Cruise I took my mother and stepfather on in August 2017. (Fortunately, there were no abductions, but key cards did frequently go missing!) My stepfather was of Welsh and English ancestry and always wanted to visit the area. Sadly, he passed away less than five months after our return. We miss him dearly, but I'm grateful I was able to experience the trip with him. We had a wonderful time.

Although drawn from a number of cruises I've taken over the years, *The Celestial of the Seas* ship and its crew are entirely fictional. Though the ports and cities are real, and I drew from the humorous experiences we shared in them, all references to tour guides, museum employees, and bus services stem from my imagination. On the other hand, The Ghent Altarpiece, also known as the *Adoration of the Mystic Lamb*, is indeed a real collection of paintings, from which a panel remains missing to this day.

ACKNOWLEDGMENTS

A big, heartfelt thank you to my mother and late stepfather for going on the British Isles cruise with me, not only for their joy, humor, and wonderful companionship, but also for making the trip rife with literary possibilities. Thank you also to my oldest son who accompanied us to Europe and kept us grounded in humility, as college students often do. My sincere gratitude extends to my keen-eyed editor, Kevin Brennan, and my invaluable beta reader, Kate Johnston. Also to Alec, Cheryl, and Mike for your early reads and insights. Furthermore, I wish to thank my wonderful and supportive online community. Your social media shares, comments, and kindness prove the internet can be a sweet and wonderful place.

Finally, as always, I want to thank you, the reader, for giving me your time in a world that's already too scarce of it. Without you, writing wouldn't be nearly as much fun.